*W*hat the critics are saying...

ॐ

5 *Angels* "Emjai Colbert has a great writing style that draws you into the story and makes you not want to put down the book." ~ *Fallen Angel Reviews*

5 *Cupids* "I really, really enjoyed this book. The writing is superb, the plot is interesting, and the characters are so realistic that you forget that this is a fictional story." ~ *Cupid's Library Reviews*

If Tomorrow Never Comes

EMJAI COLBERT

Cerridwen Press

A Cerridwen Press Publication

www.cerridwenpress.com

If Tomorrow Never Comes

ISBN #141995413X
ALL RIGHTS RESERVED.
If Tomorrow Never Comes Copyright © 2005 Emjai Colbert
Edited by Mary Dawson.
Cover art by Syneca.

Electronic book Publication August 2005
Trade paperback Publication September 2006

Excerpt from *Meant to Be* Copyright © Denise Agnew, 2006

Excerpt from *Passion's Blood* Copyright © Cherif Fortin & Lynn
Sanders, 1998

Cerridwen Press is an imprint of Ellora's Cave Publishing, Inc.®

About the Author

80

Emjai Colbert, pronounced simply as two initials and a French pretension in the same vein as cousins Steven and Claudette (no relation...really), didn't graduate college though she did go for several years. She studied history mostly (but Pirate 101 wasn't offered), with stops in early childhood education (where she discovered a dislike for any rug rats she didn't give birth to and left quickly) and business (she didn't want to wear one of those silly power suits). She wanted very much to study theater and fencing but didn't have the time or guts but hey, she's still young so maybe one day...

Emjai loves her children, her husband, books, music, and crime dramas in that order. However Emjai does not love to write. No matter how much she wishes this weren't true, she can't escape the fact that she is possessed by people other than herself who demand that she sit with a keyboard on her lap for hours on end and peck out their story. Needless to say, Emjai is constantly on the lookout for new ways to not write. Frequently eBay and Spider Solitaire are the main conspirators.

Emjai makes her home along the steamy Alabama Gulf Coast. She has three children, two dogs and a cat who loves bubble baths (as long as he isn't in the bubble bath). She has had many jobs from pizza delivery (where she was last hit on by an ugly transvestite) to seamstress (she possesses the secret to how those crew neck T-shirts get their crew neck). When she grows up she wants to be a pirate queen...move over Anne Bonney. Wait, Emjai has no current plans to ever grow up...Anne Bonney is safe for now.

Emjai welcomes comments from readers. You can find her website and email address on her author bio page at www.ellorascave.com.

IF TOMORROW NEVER COMES

☙

Dedication

❧

To my husband and my children.
Thank you for supporting me in fulfilling this dream.

Chapter One

ஒ

Turning her back against the sultry storm-fed wind, Tara Jenkins grabbed the signpost and rocked it back and forth with all her might. Finally, the heavy sign came free of the ground and toppled onto an overgrown azalea bush. The "sold" banner that covered the realtor's name made Tara's heart soar.

After all the years of planning and hard work, she finally had her dream house. With a small shout of triumph, Tara took a step away from the fallen sign to study her new home, which even in the pre-storm gloom was beautiful to her romantic heart.

Built in the 1880s the two-story Victorian complete with turret was far from new but it was hers and that was all that mattered.

Just then, a jagged bolt of lightning sliced through the nearly black sky revealing the brutal injustice the grand old house endured with patient grace. Someone in its rental past had painted it purple. And not a pretty shade of purple either, but a sick, ugly shade that reminded Tara of a neon eggplant. Maybe alone the purple wouldn't have stood out so badly if that same renter hadn't slathered the beautiful gingerbread trim that decorated the two porches a garish neon green.

As she stood admiring her beautiful, ugly house, headlights swept the yard. A late model silver truck pulled into the drive next door, briefly illuminating the horrible colors once again. Tara smiled proudly despite the disgrace for she knew that the painters would arrive first thing in the morning to begin stripping away the offensive colors. With any luck, that god-awful purple and green would be history by the end of the month.

Next door, the owner of the silver truck slammed the door. Tara glanced over with a ready smile to greet her new neighbor. But as the man came around the truck, a blast of hot storm-fed wind slammed her in the face. She stood breathless for a moment while he walked down the drive to his mailbox, the light from an overhead street lamp illuminating him in all his glory.

Tall, at least six foot, he had shoulders broader than the neat blue oxford shirt could hide. The top button of his shirt gaped open; the tie pulled loose, leading Tara to assume the man was uncomfortable in the business noose. A pair of gray pleated pants hugged narrow hips and, feeling as if she were studying a prime stud at auction, Tara forced her eyes to take a more northward journey, which was a mistake too.

His face was exquisite with eyes as dark as sin nestled under a pair of arched brows. A narrow nose and full lips completed the rugged face. Short dark brown hair that wanted to curl a bit at the neck completed the package. Indeed, this particular neighbor damn near came close to male model in sheer hunkiness.

"Hi, I'm your new neighbor." Somehow Tara managed to say when super-stud looked up from his mailbox.

Unlike his mouth, his eyes, when they met hers, didn't smile. For an instant, Tara thought she could detect a trace of sadness hidden within those obsidian depths. "Oh, hey, I didn't see you standing there," he said in a voice that had to be the male equivalent to harp-song. His deep melodious accent was very Southern but not so thick that she needed a translator. His words caressed her much like the sultry autumn wind that swirled around her, warm and velvety, creating erotic images of hot sex and cold mint juleps.

Wow. Tara pulled off her gloves and prayed that the water company had made it out that day as scheduled to turn on the water. After that last thought she was going to need a very cold shower.

"So you bought the purple dinosaur? I'd wondered if that old house would ever sell," he of the velvet voice said as he pulled a stack of letters and catalogs from his mailbox. He then crossed over the low azalea hedge that separated their lawns, his right hand extended.

"Yep, I bought the old girl but by the end of the month y'all will have to find her a new name." Tara swept her hand out to indicate the entire neighborhood before she took his hand. She gasped as she felt her hand disappear inside his large rough hand, a hand that was so at odds with the way he dressed, the hand of a workingman. "I'm Tara Jenkins." Tara felt her face flush as the thought of hot sex and cold mint juleps suddenly lost the mint julep part.

"Nice to meet you, Tara Jenkins. I'm Brent Chambliss," he said, his voice catching on her name. "Glad to hear you're painting. For a while there I was afraid the place would stay empty and purple indefinitely." Letting go of her hand, he shoved his now free hand into his pocket. "Well, gotta run. If you need anything at all don't hesitate to ask."

"I won't. And nice meeting you too, Brent Chambliss," she said as the man lifted the hand holding his mail in a mock salute as he hopped the hedge. The gold of his wedding band gleaming in the dim light of the streetlamp caught her eye. And in that instant hot sex turned into cold mint juleps—alone—on her purple and green front porch.

Chapter Two

ഗ്ര

Brent let himself into the modest bungalow he had carefully restored the first year of his marriage and dropped the mail onto the little foyer table just inside the door.

The green light on his answering machine blinked furiously, demanding his immediate attention. He ignored it as he stripped off his tie on his way to his bedroom, to change into a pair of worn jeans and an Auburn War Eagles T-shirt.

Barefoot, he walked back to the living room to face the barrage of messages waiting on his machine. His mother had called three times that afternoon. She was worried about him. She wanted to know if he was eating right, sleeping well, yada, yada. The same questions she'd asked at least once a week for the last three years now. A couple more messages were from friends wanting to get together that night for a game of basketball at the park. Too late for that, he thought. Besides he doubted even they would risk a game if the storm that was brewing chose to let loose. The last message was from Jamie Hutchinson, his business partner.

Brent picked up the telephone and dialed the office. "Yeah, Hutch, what's so important you couldn't wait twenty minutes for me to get home?" He raked a hand through his short hair. He hated his hair and should never have given in to his mother's nagging and gotten it cut.

"Did you take a look at those contracts I left on your desk?" Brent pictured Hutch rifling through the clutter on his long-lost desk and couldn't help smiling. Hutch tended to get frantic over the smallest details. Hutch was the backbone of the company, logical, anal and comfortable in a suit and tie. Whereas Brent would rather be out on one of the job sites caked with dirt and pouring sweat, not that he was able to do that very much these days. But they worked well together.

"Relax, Hutch, I have them. I wanted to look them over tonight." Brent looked around for his briefcase while he assured Hutch. It was then he realized that he had left it along with his jacket in the truck.

"Okay, good." Hutch sounded relieved. "Mrs. Miller called after you left. She decided she definitely wants the bay window in the breakfast nook and the island work area in the kitchen. Can you handle that?"

"No problem. I already added them to the plans. Sometimes I can just tell, you know."

"Good, good, then let's get that contract signed in the morning and get a crew over there first thing Monday. I've got the permits all in order and the Millers are checking into The Grand Hotel down on the bay for a week. After that they will make other arrangements for the duration."

"The Grand." Brent whistled, "Nice place. Me and Kelly honeymo…" Caught off guard Brent stopped, ruthlessly squashing the memory of his wife before he was dragged back into the gaping chasm he'd fallen into that first year after her death.

"The Millers will be here at eleven so there's no need for you to get here any earlier. Sleep in, go for a run, whatever floats your boat." Hutch went on, patently ignoring Brent's slip of the tongue as he did every time Brent forgot and wandered down that road.

"I might just do that," Brent said after thinking on it for a second. He felt odd lately, restless somehow, and work had lost its charm now that he could no longer get out to one of the construction sites.

"It will do you good, buddy. Well, got to go, see you in the morning."

"Whatever you say." Shrugging off the melancholy that threatened to engulf him, Brent hit the disconnect button then punched in his mother's number.

Twenty minutes later he walked out the front door and into a blast of wind so hot he thought he'd melt on the spot. Thunder rumbled overhead and lightning flashed close by but so far, the much-needed rain remained elusive. He was just about to retrieve his briefcase from his truck when he heard a crash of a different kind, followed by a muffled curse, coming from the old Victorian next door.

The lights were on but he couldn't see any sign of life next door. Brent tucked his keys into his pocket and jumped the hedge of ancient azaleas that marked the property line between the houses. Before he was even aware of what he was doing, he found himself standing on the walkway in front of the old place.

On the porch, his new neighbor was struggling with a bed frame that looked as if it weighed more than the two of them combined. The mattress and box spring lay on the porch beside three overturned cardboard boxes. Deciding this was the source of the crash Brent took a step up onto the porch and into the light. "Need some help?"

His voice startled her and she jumped dropping the heavy iron headboard, just missing her toes. "Sorry. I didn't mean to scare you. I heard a crash and came to make sure you were all right."

"You didn't. Scare me, I mean. This thing weighs a ton. Help would be great." His new neighbor looked him over as if she were trying to decide if she could trust him or not. "This is the last of my stuff and I'd really like to get it inside before it rains."

She smiled at him and Brent let go of the breath he didn't know he'd been holding. "Why didn't you hire someone to at least move the heavy stuff?"

"I did," she laughed, "but their idea of getting me moved was to leave everything here on the porch for me to deal with.

Next time I'll know better than to hire someone whose ad reads, '>From porch to porch we move anything'."

"The nerve of some people," Brent commiserated although he wouldn't be laughing. He'd be on the phone raising hell with whoever had the guts to answer.

Somehow, they managed to get the whole bed inside and up the stairs. Brent stayed to set up the frame without asking.

"You don't have very much furniture," Brent commented on the way back down. He hadn't meant to but the nearly empty house preyed on his curiosity. "Did you just leave a convent or something?"

Tara shrugged, her eyes sparkling with amusement. "Something like that. No seriously, I've just never accumulated much more than my grandmother's bed frame. Besides, I'd like to redo the entire house. Furniture would just get in the way," she replied taking him on a tour of the old house. "The downstairs is fine but I'd like to enlarge the kitchen. Add a downstairs bathroom. Redo the entire second floor making the bedrooms larger and maybe make the attic into a third floor office area."

"That's a pretty big job." Brent took mental notes in each room. Renovating older homes was his passion, the reason he'd gotten into construction in the first place. He could picture the place after a complete makeover without changing any of the historic charm in the process.

In all, the house was in great repair except for the kitchen. It was a disaster area, proof of a rental past and Tara was right in wanting to do a complete makeover. He walked to a window overlooking the backyard. She had enough room to add on if she wanted to go larger. The upstairs wouldn't be a problem. He could knock out a couple of walls without destroying the integrity of the house.

"Yes, I know, but this old house deserves the best. Nobody builds houses like this anymore and if I let her fall apart I'll be no better than the people I bought her from." Brent heard the passion in her voice. He knew she was serious and not just dreaming like so many women her age with the fantasy of living in something out of *Gone With the Wind*.

"Well, when you are ready, I know a good contractor who specializes in restoration." He wasn't above self-advertising. Not if it got him out of the mini-mall glut on the west side of the city and into what he'd much rather be doing. "And I won't cheat you out of your hard-earned money."

"You?" She gave him another critical once-over. "I took you to be…I don't know, a banker, or a dentist. Not a contractor."

"Yeah, that's me. But lately I've been stuck in the office more than I like. If I'd only known when I went into business for myself I'd have to give up doing the actual construction I'd never have agreed." Brent didn't bother to keep the dissatisfaction out of his voice. "A dentist? You really though I was a dentist?"

"Maybe for a second." He caught the twinge of red as it crawled up her neck to her cheeks and couldn't help wondering what else she'd thought about him to make her go all rosy like that. "Okay, Mr. Brent Chambliss, I'll certainly keep you in mind when I am ready to get serious."

"Absolutely." Brent nodded. Getting serious was certainly something he could handle. She had the most amazing lips. "Ah, umm, yes, come by my office and I'll show you my portfolio. And check out the competition too. That way you'll know what a find I am."

"I'm sure you are an excellent find." She smiled those glorious lips of hers all pink and… Bet she could kiss like a pro with those lips.

"I'll give you my business card next time I see you and you can call when you're ready. Hope you like living in the old purple dinosaur. Good night." Panic surged in his gut. Kelly was walking down the aisle one second, the next she was pointing an accusing finger at him. Three years worth of panic coursed through him. He yanked on the door handle and stepped out onto the porch. Only then did he feel completely calm and clearheaded, all thoughts of kissing Tara Jenkins completely gone. "Good night, Tara Jenkins. You make sure you lock all those windows and doors and keep those painters in line," he said in parting then quickly made his escape back to his lonely house, full of dead memories. It took him a few minutes to remember that his briefcase was still in the truck.

Chapter Three

ಖ

"Was it something I said?" Tara uttered to the empty front porch as she watched her new neighbor cross over the azalea hedge.

Gorgeous but flighty, she decided once he rounded the corner of his house without looking back. But what did she expect, he probably had the little wife fixing him his supper while he was over here helping her. Tara snorted. Okay, so he was a complete jerk and he was married...end of fantasy.

So why did she feel so humiliated by his sudden retreat? Tara ducked inside shutting the door behind her. There was much to be done that night. No sense wasting valuable time mooning over a man she couldn't have. Boxes to unpack or at least hide in one of her many closets. Her stomach rumbled interrupting her ruminations, reminding her she still had supper to deal with. Supper that would have to be take-out as she had nothing in the house that passed for food.

She whirled around the house like a dervish straightening here, stashing there until she was exhausted and positively starving. She entertained the notion of going out for supper but the storm still brewing outside put an end to that idea. There was nothing for it; she would have to order in. What would the Chambliss' have for supper, Tara wondered, thinking of a huge meal cooked up by the little woman while...?

Stop it, Tara, that's an order.

Later that evening exhausted but well-fed on takeout from Ming's Wings and Things, Tara stood at the sink in her very own kitchen. On the counter beside her were several boxes of dishes and cookware to be washed and stored away in the very old very ugly cupboards. Several plates soaked in the soapy water in the sink, while she took her time washing only one, running the cloth over the stone circlet until the pattern threatened to fade clear away. Her attention was caught elsewhere.

"He had nice feet," she said to her reflection in the darkened window that looked out over her backyard, the sound of her own voice startling her in the silent house. "What am I doing? He's married for pity's sake." Tara turned her disgust into action, finishing the few dishes and cleaning up the sink and counter to keep her mind from wondering about the married man next door.

There was a lot to do before she went to bed that night and unwelcome crushes weren't helping. Lots to do, she yawned; it felt like days had passed since she'd met the movers at her brother's house, where she'd been staying, instead of just that morning.

Lots to do, she yawned again, but not tonight, tomorrow would be soon enough to unpack and settle in. Tara decided that sleep sounded like a better idea than putting away dishes. At least her bed was set up in the master bedroom. All she had to do was put her new sheets on it and crawl in. And as if the weather were agreeing with her, the electricity sputtered and went out leaving Tara in the dark.

"That's just great." Tara felt her way to the refrigerator where she'd stashed her candles that afternoon.

"If there are any ghosts in here, I warn you my uncle is an exorcist." The verbal warning no matter how false calmed her growing panic. She ran her hand along the top of the icebox for the long fireplace lighter she'd put there when she'd unpacked the candles.

She had candleholders in all shapes and sizes. Unfortunately, they were still packed away. So she grabbed the glass she'd just washed, placed the long taper into it and lit it. Outside the wind howled and the rain that had threatened all evening finally let loose.

19

Shielding the candle with her hand, she carefully climbed the back stairs to her bedroom. Making the bed and showering took very little time but she felt more awake than before, restless even. The house was big and old and strange. And she was alone, in the dark.

"Just remember what Mama used to say… 'There is nothing to be found in the dark that isn't there in the light' so go to sleep." She blew the candle out and set the glass on the tiny bedside table. There was nothing left to do but listen to the noises the old house made. Identifying every sound that she could, soon her fear passed and she was able to drift off to sleep.

* * * * *

The bride wore a white cotton halter dress that looked wonderful on her petite figure. Her veil was simple tulle with a wreath of spring flowers holding it onto her head, her long red hair curling loosely down her back. The groom wore a black suit, his dark shoulder-length hair blowing lightly in the breeze. They stood hand in hand at the altar, which was perfectly located in a meticulously manicured garden that surrounded a small lake. Only about twenty people were in attendance but all the chairs were full.

Tara sat rigidly in the back row wondering what she was doing there. She didn't know either of these people, yet here she was and in a T-shirt and jeans no less. She felt so out of place but she couldn't motivate herself to leave…not just yet.

"I've done him wrong, you know," the bride said from the seat beside her and Tara, never taking her eyes off the couple up front, nodded. "He doesn't know what I've done and I can't tell him."

"Why ever not? He looks like an understanding man and seems to care for you so very much," Tara replied as the veil fluttered into her face. With impatient hands, she pushed the material away without looking at the woman sitting next to her.

"Precisely the reason, -he cares too much. It would kill him," she said, her voice steeped in sorrow on what should be her happiest day. "That's why you've got to do it for me."

"Me? Why me? I don't know him. I don't even know you for that matter." Tara struggled to keep her voice down so as not to disturb the ceremony.

"You're the one. I'm sure of it. But be warned, Tara Jenkins. He'll hate you for it in the beginning."

"If you think I'm going to go up to some perfect stranger and tell him his new wife has done him wrong, you're crazy. Find someone else." Tara felt trapped. How could she tell this man the woman he was marrying wasn't what he thought her to be? For that matter, why was she still sitting here considering it? "Besides I'm not sure I want to know your dirty little secret if it's going to hurt him."

"You will, in time. Of that I'm certain," the bride said and Tara looked over for the first time ready to argue her out of her crazy notions only to find herself alone.

The smell of flowers lingered in the room as Tara awoke. It was a dream, just a dream. So why did she smell magnolias in the middle of October?

* * * * *

Brent reached over to shut off the alarm but no matter how many times he hit the button it kept making noise. He looked up at the red numbers and cursed. It was seven o'clock on Saturday morning, his one morning to sleep late in weeks. So what the hell was all that noise? He flung the comforter off and strode to the window. Inserting one finger into the slats of the mini-blinds, he tugged them open just enough to peer out without attracting attention.

It was Tara Jenkins' painters. Damn. He'd forgotten all about them. And why did they have to set up their damned scaffolding on the side closest to him? Why not the other side? Old man Williams was nearly deaf and wouldn't notice the noise. He yawned and ran his free hand through his hair in the age-old habit of his. May as well get up, go into the office early, hand over the paperwork for the Miller house and spend the rest of the day on a roof somewhere.

He was just about to let the blinds go when his new neighbor came out from behind the house carrying a large thermos and two coffee cups. Brent forgot all about going in to work early, choosing instead just to watch her walk.

With the crisp early morning sunlight shining on her, he was able to take in details he'd missed last night. Such as that mass of golden brown hair that curled to just below her shoulders, hair that she was constantly pushing back from her face in the breeze. And that body! She was far from petite, tall and curvy and oh so womanly. Dressed in body-hugging jeans and a short-sleeve sweater that stopped just at the waistband, Tara was lush in all the right places.

Her laughter as she talked with the painters carried through the glass and Brent felt the tingle of need race through his system. What was it that she found so funny? What would it take to have her laugh just for him instead of those two bozos?

What was he doing standing here like a Peeping Tom spying on the sexy new neighbor? Had all sense of decency suddenly left his head with the blood that raced to another location? But he didn't let the slats fall shut, as he should have. Tara turned as if sensing his eyes on her and pushed her hair back... He couldn't, for the life of him, let go then. She was so close he could see every freckle on her pert nose, the arch of golden brows over pretty, clear green eyes. Her face was naked, another surprise. He didn't know too many women who'd dare venture out without full battle paint on. She was so fresh, so...

He let the blinds fall back into place with a metallic snap. He *had* lost his mind.

He had to get out there, had to see her before he left, he had to hear her laugh at least once and know it was because she'd found him charming and witty. He had to... He caught sight of the photo of him and Kelly and Betsy sitting on the dresser and the hot blood racing through his veins turned to ice water.

He remembered that day, in the hospital, all too clearly. Kelly in the wheelchair, Betsy in her arms with him pushing his little family. They were going home and things were going to get better. And it did for a while; Betsy had brought them close again.

He had to get into the office. He had to forget about Tara Jenkins and her nice round bottom and pretty laughter. He had to be out of his mind.

Chapter Four

ೞ

The unrelenting sound of the sanding and scraping going on outside was driving Tara nuts. She set her coffee cup down on the kitchen counter with a thud. "For pity's sake, they've only been at it for an hour."

Sam and Paul, her painters, could be trusted not to rob her blind if she left them alone to make all the noise they wanted. She had grown up with them, after all, lived through their constantly torturing her. Besides, she could always kill her brother Tommy for recommending them if they did. They were his best friends not hers.

There were better things to do than sit around her kitchen on a nice cool Saturday with moving boxes staring at her. There was the mall and maybe she did need a chair for the living room at the very least. Oh, and while she was at it, a small table for the kitchen. Yes, that would be the best thing to do, go buy a few pieces of basic furniture to tide her over until after the remodeling. So with that decided Tara grabbed her purse and headed for the front door.

Outside, she had to yank on Sam's pant leg to get his attention. She didn't want the whole neighborhood knowing she'd left the back door open in case they needed to use the bathroom or something. Neither did she want to come back and find them gone and that same door unlocked. Sam and Paul could be trusted. They had to be or heads would roll, her bother's head in particular. Satisfied that she was doing the right thing she started for the driveway. Just as she was crossing the lawn, she caught sight of her neighbor out of the corner of her eye. "Good morning, Brent Chambliss," she shouted so that he could hear her over the noise of the sander that was rapidly eating its way through the purple paint job.

With his hand on the door handle of his truck Brent looked up in time to see Tara wave. Damn, she was even sexier up close. Heat prickled at the back of his neck. He closed his eyes hoping that the lust that seemed to infuse his brain at the very sight of her this morning would go away. The heat intensified until he reached a hand back to rub at the discomfort. "Hey, I see the painters got here bright and early," he said hoping she wouldn't see the lust in his eyes or worse, the embarrassment due to that lust. Despite his preoccupation with his current embarrassing situation, he yawned. He didn't mean to but late nights and early mornings had never been his thing.

"Did they wake you?" Tara gasped. "I'm so sorry. It never occurred to me that you might sleep on that side of the house when I suggested Sam and Paul start there."

"Don't worry about it. I had to get up anyway. Have to go into the office and then out to one of the job sites. There is no rest for the boss it seems." Brent felt the lust he nursed intensify as he watched her worry about him. Her pretty pixie face went pale and rosy all at the same time, her green eyes widened with alarm. She brought her hands to her mouth in a gesture of despair, causing her breasts to rise higher and fuller between her arms. Oh yes, it was lust, pure and simple. Lust like none he could remember ever experiencing before in his life. This wasn't good, not good at all. He squeezed the back of his neck hoping to inflict enough pain to take his mind off things he shouldn't be thinking about, things like her naked, in his bed, with his hands doing the lifting of those lush breasts.

"That reminds me, you promised me a business card." Tara wondered if he had a headache, the way he was holding the back of his neck. "Are you alright? You look flushed."

"What? Oh yeah, I'm fine. Had a bad night that's all." Brent dropped his hand. Great she could see it, damned lust. Maybe she would think he was coming down with something at the very least. Something other than a serious case of brain fever.

"Are you sure? You look a little pale now. Maybe you're catching a bug of some kind." This time she crossed the hedge, gliding gracefully around the front of his truck.

"I'm fine, really." Brent panicked the second she reached out her slim lightly tanned hand with its long fingers and pretty pink nails. He knew where she was going with that hand and didn't like it one bit. Yes he did, he wanted her hands on him if only for a second.

He felt the shock clear to his toes when she placed her cool palm on his forehead and then his cheek. Nerve endings that he hadn't used in several years suddenly sprang to life and the very breeze did things to him that sent shivers through his body. He was thinking about pouncing on her right here in the drive and she was taking his temperature. It wasn't right. It just wasn't right.

"You're not hot," Tara said as she stepped away from him, her hand tingling and her heart racing. She felt the blush start at the base of her throat where it usually did and slowly work its way up. She *was* hot, hot and bothered and—get a grip, girl. Oh but he felt so good. She wanted to touch him again and keep touching until she found all those touchable parts of him. But she couldn't, he was married. She shouldn't have touched him in the first place. He was still a stranger and she'd overstepped the bounds of propriety. Didn't you learn in kindergarten to keep your hands to yourself? Now you know why.

"No, I'm not." *Yes, hell I am*, Brent opened the truck door and reached into the center console. "Here's that card I promised," he held out the ivory-colored business card to Tara. His hand trembled but he controlled it—he had to get away. Had to get far away from the shameful need she caused in him. Her fingers brushed his as she accepted the card and Brent felt as if he were going to go up in flames.

"Thanks," Tara murmured as she grasped the card and pulled her hand away. Electricity tingled all the way to her shoulder and she wanted desperately to rub it away. She wanted to grab his hand and hold on tight, letting the tingling continue throughout the rest of her body. "Well, see ya."

"Yeah, later." Brent climbed into his truck and slammed the door. He could still smell the light perfume she wore, could still feel her soft hand on his cheek. He started the engine and waved as he backed out of the drive without checking to make sure the street was clear. Maybe he should put the house up for sale. Move out to the west side of the city, nearer work. The sudden blare of a car horn warned him of how stupid he was behaving over a pretty face and a nice set of boobs. He slammed on the brakes and watched as one of his neighbors from down the street sped by, his finger up in salute. Yeah, yeah that was just what he'd been thinking himself.

After the near accident, Tara crossed back over to her side of the hedge and onto her truck, a pretty, small pickup the color of a new penny. For a moment she stood beside the door trying to remember why she was going out in the first place, when she suddenly wanted nothing more than to crawl into a nice hot bath and get her thoughts under control. The noise coming from the side of the house reminded her of her reasons. A bath in that cacophony wasn't even a slight possibility. So she followed her plan and climbed inside the truck.

Tara had grown up in West Mobile but she had always loved the historic district where she now lived. Years had passed since she'd gone away and the city had changed tremendously. Straight out of high school, she had followed a friend to New York and with one of those bizarre twists of fate she became a model. Now she was retired and the lure of her hometown brought her back. No, that wasn't true. Her mother's failing health brought her back home in the early summer. It was then that she decided to retire before she either burned out or grew too old.

Her brother Tommy had cared for their mother for a couple of years now but she was getting worse with each passing day. Her mind was gone, and after the stroke in June, it was impossible to ignore the signs anymore. They put her in a home.

But despite the tears Tara had cried, it was the right thing to do, as she needed constant care. The type of care that Tommy couldn't give anymore and care that Tara couldn't give at all.

Guilt smacked her flat in the face and Tara pulled into the right-hand lane and turned onto I-65 instead of into the mall parking lot. She'd spend the morning with her mother no matter how much it hurt to have the old woman look through her as if she'd never met her before, much less given birth to her. But first she'd stop at a florist and pick up a bouquet of daisies with hopes that the sight of her mother's favorite flowers would draw her into the present and she would actually know Tara's name.

* * * * *

Brent stood on the flat roof of the convenience store his small company was building. He was hot and thirsty. He was also filthy. Damn, it felt good to be doing something useful instead of sitting in an air-conditioned office.

His beeper went off just then and Brent cursed when he read Hutch's 911 message. Hutch always knew when he was enjoying himself, Brent grumbled, but he cleaned up his work area anyway and climbed down to the ground. The Millers had been dealt with earlier that morning, so what was so all-fired important that Hutch needed to call him in from the site? He caught sight of Mac Johnson, his top foreman, and stopped to let him know that he was leaving and possibly wouldn't be back that day.

"You're not gonna go into the office with all that dirt on ya, are you?" Mac joked. "Hutch will surely have a heart attack if you scare away a new client."

"Can't be helped, Mac. Dirt and dust are part of the job and the sooner Hutch gets over it, the better off this company will be. See ya Monday morning," Brent said even as he tried to wipe the worst of the dirt away before he climbed into the truck. He peeled out of the future parking lot, spraying dirt in his wake.

At the office, Brent stopped off in the tiny kitchen area and grabbed a bottle of water from the fridge before heading in to see what Hutch wanted. Petty revenge he knew but still it felt good.

"Okay Hutch, what's up? I thought we were through with paperwork for today," he called as he neared the door to Hutch's office. Two sets of eyes greeted him when he walked in. The blue pair he'd known since college. The other pair, green. The same green eyes that kept crawling into his memory as he'd nailed shingles that morning. The same green eyes that were attached to his sexy new neighbor and Brent felt as if he were suddenly back up on that roof all hot and sweaty. Damn, why hadn't he bothered to wash up better?

"Brent, this is Tara Jenkins," Hutch said in that formal way he had as he gave Brent a disapproving look for his lack of cleanliness. "She wants to hire us to remodel her house."

"We've met. In fact, Tara just moved in next door to me. I gave her our card just this morning," Brent said refusing to let Hutch's disapproval bother him. "Good afternoon, Tara. I didn't expect you quite so soon."

"Hello, Brent Chambliss. I was out driving around looking at furniture and decided there wouldn't be a better time to get started on the renovation we discussed last night. And since you assured me you were the best, I thought I'd start with you and work my way down." Tara grinned as Brent rubbed a grimy hand through grimy hair. It had been a long time since she'd actually seen a real workingman complete with the sweat and dirt of his profession. If anything, it made the man even more attractive what with all those real work muscles bulging from beneath his T-shirt sleeve.

"Brent, man, I don't know what you were thinking of but don't you remember the Miller contract from just this morning? We put our last available men on that project. We can't possibly take on another project until Christmas when that convenience store is finished."

"Listen, Hutch, it's not that big a job. We should be able to squeeze it in," Brent said mulling over what Hutch said. "Well, Tara what did you have in mind exactly? Are you planning to apply for the historical registry?"

"I don't know what that would involve but I wasn't planning to change the outside of the house. The kitchen is plenty big just old and ugly. I'd like to have the inside of the attic finished and change the second floor around as we talked about last night. Add a bathroom on each floor. The floors and walls seem sound enough but I don't know about the windows and I'd like to change the existing furnace and air-conditioner." Tara scowled now as Brent's business partner Hutch groaned. "I can go elsewhere." He groaned again and Tara reluctantly snatched her eyes away from her neighbor just in time to see the man slump dispiritedly in his chair.

"See that Hutch, you're letting money walk right out that door. I'd wondered how you would react when this day came." Brent grinned and turned to Tara. "He's okay. He's just seeing dollar signs float around that he can't grab onto. Come on, let's go to my office and discuss this. At least get something down on paper and an estimate so that you can compare."

Tara glanced back at Hutch who was banging his head on his desk blotter. She got up quickly and followed Brent down the hall to a smaller more cluttered office. Blueprints scattered the desk along with papers, magazines and photos. Tara sat in one of the two narrow chairs in front of his desk and waited for him to finish unearthing his own. A 5x7 photo of him and a red-haired beauty quickly snagged her attention. And for some reason, she couldn't escape the feeling that she'd seen the woman before. "Is that your wife?" Tara asked once Brent had cleared his chair and was again facing her. "She is beautiful. I'll have to stop by and meet her soon."

Before the words were out of her mouth he darted out a hand and turned the photo over. Tara stared dumbfounded at the man. His eyes were bright with distress at the innocent remark. "She's dead." He stashed the picture frame into a desk drawer without looking at it.

"I'm sorry. I didn't know," Tara said. He's not married. He's not married! Oh for the shame of it all, what a thought. But he's not married!

"It's okay. Now about that remodel?" Brent felt all the joy wash from him. He'd forgotten about that picture, which just went to show how long it had been since he'd paid any attention to his surroundings.

"Really, if you don't have the manpower to fit me in, I can go to someone else."

"No, Tara, stay. I want to do the work. I can do it by myself if you're not in a super-hurry. The whole reason I went into construction in the first place was to restore old houses. I haven't been able to do that in a while. Not with this building boom." Brent put the ghost of his dead wife out of his mind and concentrated on work. Although he had lived right next door to Tara's house for nearly ten years, he'd never set foot inside until last night. And frankly, he wanted to be the one to tear it apart and put it back together as something completely different.

"I'm not in an all-fired hurry. I really did not intend to start this soon but after talking with you last night, I feel as if it's as good a time as any. Your partner showed me some photos of your work. They were all of new buildings but I am impressed enough to give you a try. That is, if you can start on the kitchen. We'll deal with the rest later on."

Brent stood and went to the row of metal file cabinets and pulled a large leather-bound book from one. "Here, look at these," he said opening what Tara discovered to be a scrapbook of sorts and laying it on the desk in front of her. She flipped pages filled with photos of several different old houses with both before and after images, sometimes of just single rooms, other times whole houses.

Emjai Colbert

"You did these?" The attention to detail and the quality of work that showed in the photos was awe-inspiring to say the least.

He shrugged. "Some of them in my spare time back when I was younger and punching a time clock. The two houses in the back of the album I did three years ago. Then Hutch and I decided to pool our talent and give our employer a run for his money and well—there hasn't been any time since. So, you see why I'd like to take on your project?"

"What about the other jobs?" Hutch interrupted from the doorway. "Are you just going to abandon me to concentrate on your little hobby?"

"Hutch, you sound like a jealous girlfriend," Brent said lifting a hand to stop Hutch from finishing his complaint. "We have good men working for us. Especially our foremen, so I'm not really needed at any of the job sites except in an emergency. And no matter how much you try to drag me into it, the office is still your domain. I'm going to do this for Tara, Hutch, and if I'm needed here you only have to beep me and I'll come running." Brent held his breath as he waited for Hutch to think it over. "So, how about it?"

"You'll put this business first and drop everything if something comes up?" Hutch asked and Brent nodded. "Oh all right."

"Tara?" Brent felt a renewed sense of purpose but he didn't dare hold his breath. After all, Tara could still say no.

"Let's talk numbers. What's this going to cost me?" Tara sat back in the chair with a smile for both men as they both put their special skills to work. An hour later they came up with a working plan for the remodel and a budget that wouldn't cost her an arm or a leg. And best of all, she would have the sexy *single* Brent underfoot for several weeks. What could be better?

Chapter Five

Tara sat in the oversized leather armchair she'd picked up for song at a furniture clearance sale on her way home the night before. One of every home décor magazine she could find littered the floor around her chair. In her lap were several ripped-out pages. Brent was coming over after lunch to measure the kitchen and do whatever it was he needed to do before he actually got started on ripping out the old Fifties-style cabinets. And she wanted to have something to show him that resembled what she had in mind.

Two weeks on the kitchen is how long he'd promised her, depending on the condition of the walls, floors and plumbing. Even shorter if she helped. She could do that. She'd done a little bit of everything in her life so why not construction work? After all, she had two whole months to kill before she started school in January.

The doorbell rang, its spastic buzz startling her. She hadn't heard it since she'd moved in and naturally assumed it wasn't working. In a sense it wasn't, if the buzz, gurgle, chirp was the best sound it could manage. Dropping the magazine she was leafing through onto the floor with the others, Tara crawled out of the chair to go answer the door.

Peeking through the narrow gap that the chain allowed she saw Brent standing there with a screwdriver trying to get the doorbell casing open. "You're early, I'm not dressed yet," Her pulse raced at the sight of him concentrating on the task. He was single. It was okay to let the crush have free rein until it wore itself out.

"That's okay, I can entertain myself for a while. Leave the door unlocked," he said without looking up and Tara closed the door softly although her vanity screamed that she slam it. He didn't even look to see how undressed she might be. That he wasn't the slightest bit interested in her stung.

True, she didn't really want him to see her in her fuzzy bunny slippers and old chenille robe but he could have at least looked. She undid the chain lock and left the deadbolts open before going upstairs to change. The crush was starting to wear off faster than she had anticipated.

"Damn," Brent breathed out when the door closed. He hadn't looked. He just couldn't. Now all he had to do was keep the caveman in him from busting down the door and following her inside to see exactly what she *was* wearing.

Though he ached with all his being to know, he concentrated on the old metal doorbell case that refused to open. The doorbell sounded exactly like a sick penguin. At least that's what he told himself to keep from rushing inside.

He uncovered the screws holding the little box onto the wall and pulled it apart. One set of wires was frayed and barely making the connection, just as he'd thought. He stripped the casing off the frayed wiring and spliced it back together, hooking the two wires together and taping them off. The whole process took less than five minutes. Five very short minutes that were not long enough to tame the wild caveman that raged inside him.

Upstairs, Tara heard the doorbell again as she pulled a long-sleeved T-shirt over her head. This time the chime was pure and loud. He'd fixed it. Just like that he'd fixed the spastic doorbell and would be inside at any moment. Her heart raced as she tucked her shirt into her jeans. Putting on a pair of socks and her favorite tennis shoes, she pulled her hair into a ponytail before heading back downstairs to help.

Tara stopped on the landing and leaned against the banister, her heart hammering in her chest at the sight of the man standing in her foyer. He was dressed in blue jean shorts, a white T-shirt advertising a local radio station and a pair of work boots with white socks peeking out above the leather at his ankles. Around his waist, he wore a honey-colored leather tool belt. He looked like a beefcake hunk fresh off the cover of a romance novel. She put a stop to the fantasy and hurried down the stairs before he caught her mooning over him.

"Good morning," she said again once she hit the bottom step. "I thought you said noon. I'm sorry if I've kept you waiting."

"I hope this is not a problem. Something came up this afternoon, so it was either now or tomorrow. I fixed your doorbell while I waited." Duh, what a stupid thing to say, Brent groaned inwardly. The mere sight of her gently rounded hips in those jeans made him want to carry her right back up those stairs and toss her on that huge bed of hers. *Whoa, caveman, settle down.*

"Can I get you some breakfast?" Tara asked and Brent shook his head no. "Coffee?"

"I think I can stand another cup before I get started," Brent replied and followed Tara out to the kitchen. "So have you done any thinking about what you want to do in the kitchen?"

He meant *besides* jump his bones on the cracked tile floor, right? Tara poured a cup of black coffee from her little coffeemaker. "I have an inkling but I'm not really sure how to explain it to you. That's why all those kitchen magazines are scattered on the floor. I was hoping I could find something similar."

"Did you?" He spooned sugar into his coffee, losing count as her voice wove him into her spell.

"Not really, but I keep coming back to a light pink stone floor and cabinets the color of your tool belt with a darker pink, maybe something a little closer to red for the countertop. I don't know, something with a southwestern feel. I really can't explain it." Tara worried that she sounded wishy-washy to him.

"Mexican tile on the floor. We'll rip this paneling and wallpaper out and put in new drywall where it is needed. The paint should be tan or maybe a little darker. I can get you a discount on granite for the counter if that's how you'd like to go and they probably have something in a red or salmon color to match what you want. Can I make a suggestion, though?" Brent walked from one end of the kitchen to the other mentally taking notes.

"You're the expert."

"Why don't we take out part of this wall," he swung open the kitchen door and stepped into the adjacent dining room. "It will open up the area and you can tie the two rooms together. It won't hurt your chances of registering the house with the historic society and you'll have what the decorators call 'flow' all the way to the front of the house."

"I see what you're saying but draw me a picture if you would, please, before I make up my mind." Tara scowled at him, wondering if he were trying to gouge her after he'd promised her he wouldn't cheat her.

"I'll do that while I'm at the office." Just being this close to her made him tingle and he didn't like it. Of course, her standing there, looking at him as if she were about to have him for her for breakfast didn't help any. "Where's the access door to your crawlspace?"

"I'm not sure, somewhere out back, probably under the porch somewhere." Tara replied, wondering why he needed to go under the house.

"I'm going to check your pipes, see what sort of shape they're in before we start ripping out cabinets. And check for any damage to the floors that might not be evident under that vinyl. Then I want to look at your air-conditioning ducts," Brent pulled out his heavy-duty flashlight and checked its battery strength.

"Well, if that's what needs to be done, then let's do it." Tara set down her cup and led the way outside. They took separate ends of the house to look for anything that resembled a little doorway in the lattice that concealed the underside of the house.

Tara found it but a hydrangea plant had grown so close to it that it was impossible to open.

"Okay," Brent sighed in frustration. "I can take off a panel of this lattice if you don't mind. If I damage it I'll replace it at my cost."

"If that's the only way then its fine by me," Tara agreed not wanting to rip out the shrub if she didn't have to. "Is there anything I can help you do?"

"No, I'm just looking right now." Brent dropped to his knees to look for the smallest panel. He was tense and edgy and it was all her fault for having such a nice butt, damn it. There was no way in hell he wanted to turn around down there and have her rear end be so temptingly close.

"All right then, I'll be inside, just yell if you need me for anything," she said and Brent wanted to howl. He needed her all right. He needed her naked and sweaty and writhing underneath him. This couldn't go on. He hadn't been exactly celibate these last three years but he wasn't a hound dog either. So why was it that sex had become the only thing he could think about? And why was it that this woman, this virtual stranger now played the most explicit role in those thoughts? He clenched his teeth, determined to get his mind to stay focused on work. With that thought he sighed and shined his light under the house where there was no room for lusty thoughts of the curvy Miss Jenkins.

* * * * *

"We've been all over this, Marty. I'm retired and I have no intention of doing another job," Tara said into the phone as she paced from the kitchen to the living room and back. Marty was desperate and Tara could hear it in her voice. But then, Marty was always desperate.

"Listen, Tara, we need you for this shoot. Come on baby… Sweetheart, do this for me just this one time," she wheedled and Tara felt herself start to cave.

"No, Marty, I'm not coming to New York and that's final. I'm starting a new life here. The life I should have started ten years ago when I got out of high school." Tara refused to give in to the whine in Marty's voice.

"You don't have to sweet-cheeks. We're coming to you," Marty said triumphantly.

"What!" Tara shouted into the telephone. Marty was making it hard to resist.

"Yep, one of those department stores down there wants a huge evening wear spread ready for the Mardi Gras season. I can't remember which one off the top of my head."

"Gaillard's?"

"That's the one. I have three girls on this shoot already. They need three more, all plus-size. Please, Tara, I need you." Marty whined. It was her way of making a person feel guilty for wanting a life outside the business.

"And you say they are coming here? Who's the photographer?"

"Willie James."

"He's good. Is the agency handling everything then?"

"So far. But I have one major problem. I was going to use Todd in this shoot but he's off with his latest *amour* and I can't find him. I'd hoped to have a man or two in there to spice things up."

Tara stopped pacing and sat on the floor just inside the kitchen. She didn't want to be such a wuss, she really didn't, but she felt her resolve slipping away as Marty talked. Besides, the money would come in handy now that she'd spent most of her savings on the house. Just then, she heard a muffled curse as the back door was thrown open and Brent stomped in. He tossed his shirt onto the countertop and turned on the water to wet a paper towel. He had a scrape across his chest that Tara noticed when he turned slightly and it was beginning to bleed.

"Okay, you talked me into it. And Marty I'll bring a friend to fill that opening. Where and when?" Tara said barely above a whisper. Her mouth had gone dry the second Brent walked in. Just the sight of all that golden flesh was enough to make a woman mute for life. Tara pressed the disconnect button after Marty gave her the details.

"What happened?" she asked when Brent turned to face her, the angry scrape turning purple before her eyes.

"There are low joists under the kitchen floor. I got stuck. It was my own stupid fault," Brent said angrily. If he'd been paying attention to what he was doing and not fantasizing about her, he wouldn't have tried to shimmy under that last joist. Hell, he was lucky he'd gotten out with just a scratch. He could still be under there and Tara would have had to call someone to come and rescue him.

"It's bleeding," Tara grabbed a clean dishtowel from the drawer and offered it to him but he just tossed the wet paper towel into the trash and held his arms out away from his sides.

"I know. It stings like a son of a bi—" he sucked in air between his teeth making a hissing sound when Tara pressed the cloth to his chest.

"Hush, you big baby. Let's get this bleeding stopped. I think I've got something in the first aid kit that will cover it," Tara babbled. Being this close to the man who'd occupied her every waking thought these past couple of days was unnerving—exciting—unnerving. "Here, you hold this." She took his hand and brought it up intending for him to take the cloth while she went in search of her first aid kit.

She felt his heart beat beneath her hand. Its steady rhythm began to race when she caught his hand and Tara looked up into his eyes, her hand somehow becoming trapped in his instead.

"I like the way you're holding it just fine," Brent said his voice low and velvety. Seductive. Tara found herself lost in the prettiest pair of brown eyes she'd ever seen.

"Oh," she said, proof that her mind had chosen that particular moment to take a vacation.

Desire ran rampant through his body and Brent was helpless to stop it. He didn't want to stop it he realized when her eyes met his. He wanted her hands on his chest, on his bare skin, more than he could ever remember wanting any other woman to touch him before. She smelled of soap and laundry detergent and sunshine. He lowered his head, brushing his cheek against her forehead. God, he wanted her more than he'd ever wanted his wife.

His wife. Kelly. He stepped away from Tara. The towel fell to the floor between them and he turned away in shame. Kelly, he'd forgotten about her. He'd forgotten that he'd pledged to love and honor her all the days of his life, forgotten when he'd never forgotten before.

"I have to go. I'll call you tomorrow and let you know when the permits will be ready," he said without looking at her, for fear that he might fall back under her spell.

"Okay. Uh, sure," Tara said awkwardly. *What just happened here?*

He'd almost kissed her. She was sure of it. And she had wanted him to so very badly, as if her very life depended on it somehow. Instead he retreated and she could only watch in confusion as he strode out the back door without another word. His shirt lay on the counter where he'd left it and Tara couldn't resist the urge to pick it up. She brought it up to her chest and hugged it close. It smelled of sweat and aftershave just like the man. She would take it back to him tomorrow, she decided as she caught a glimpse of white in her peripheral vision. Tara turned her head certain that there was someone standing there. But she was alone. Completely alone, she sniffed, wondering why she smelled magnolias at this time of year.

Chapter Six

ඍ

The blade glinted in the setting sunlight. With a deft twist of her wrist, she plunged in deep, meeting little resistance. She lifted her head wiping guts across her forehead as she sought to remove hair and sweat from her face and to examine her work. She couldn't help but to smile back at the face staring up at her.

She'd stopped at a charity pumpkin patch on her way home from visiting her mother that afternoon and picked up ten pumpkins. *Ten* whole pumpkins—she couldn't get over it. In New York she and her roommates only had room for two in their cramped apartment. Now she had two big front porches. Maybe ten wouldn't be enough after all.

The largest, roundest pumpkin specimen she'd ever seen currently rested between her feet on the step, half of a huge smiling grin already emerging from the orange canvas. Tara pulled out the little saw and angled it to start the other half of the toothy grin. God, how she loved this time of year.

Halloween was only a week away and she was waiting on pins and needles. She already had bags of candy and toys in her kitchen ready to give away. Decorations by the bagful were waiting to be put up after Sam and Pete finished painting the front of the house. And of course she was just dying to exhibit her new friends on her big front porch.

The sun was just beginning to sink behind the oaks that lined the street to the west when she finished the first jack-o'-lantern, just in time, too. Tara noticed a silver truck coming slowly down the street.

Brent was home.

She leaned back against the square porch column at the top of the steps and let her mind wander back to that almost kiss from the day before. She felt her body tingle a little when she remembered the feel of his skin, the beating of his heart and the feel of his breath on her face. Stop it…stop it right now. It is not as if you've never been kissed before.

"You're home early," she shouted out once he was out of the truck.

Brent slammed the door, his gaze drawn to the woman sitting in the growing dark on her front porch steps, the carcass of a giant pumpkin resting between her feet. His heart began to thump the beat to "Wipe Out", his body coming to life at the mere sight of her.

He crossed the knee-high azalea hedge and was halfway across the lawn before he realized his intent. He was drawn to her, like a fly to a bug zapper. And he wondered if in the end his guts were going to be splattered all around the neighborhood like that poor helpless fly. Just like after Kelly's death… He stopped the thought of Kelly cooling his impetuous behavior.

"Yeah, I guess I am," he answered without going into detail. He didn't have to explain his comings and goings to her. At least that's what he told himself when in fact he didn't have a clue as to why he'd knocked off early. There was work to be done both in the office and on each of the four job sites but he'd come home. He must be mad. "You carving a jack-o'-lantern there?" *Duh, Einstein, can you get any more stupid?*

"Halloween is next week and it's been such a long time since I've done this." Tara turned the gourd around for him to see the grinning face she had managed to coax out of the pumpkin. "I love these little kits they sell now, not being a very artistic carver myself."

"Nice," Brent smiled, feeling the tension that seemed to always be with him melt away with the light conversation. Just pumpkins, no pressure, no arguing about the long hours he spent at work, no money issues. He liked talking with Tara Jenkins, liked it a lot. "Um, Tara, Hutch will have the permits ready by Thursday if everything goes smoothly and I thought I'd get to work that night if it's all right with you?"

"No problem. Just let me know for sure when and I'll be here."

"And there will be a dumpster delivered either Thursday or Friday for the debris. It's going to take up your whole driveway. Sorry, can't be helped. So if you don't want to park in the street you're welcome to use my driveway."

"You don't mind?"

"Not since I'm the one who's going to be ripping your house apart. Now if it were some other contractor then I'd be mighty put out," Brent said, feeling relief wash over him when she didn't get bent out of shape about such a trivial matter like Kelly would have.

"How about a kitchen? Are you willing to share yours with me too since mine won't be usable for a couple of weeks?" She meant it as a joke. But he turned white and instead of laughingly refusing her as she had expected he turned on his heel and took off over the hedge without another word.

"Hey, Brent." Tara called after him. She dropped the little saw and picked up a towel to wipe her hands off. "I was kidding," she shouted as he rounded the corner of his house and disappeared before she could cross her lawn.

"Sometimes I swear if you put that boy's brain in a bumblebee it would fly backwards." Tara stopped just short of the hedge and turned toward the sound of the unfamiliar voice. An old black woman leaning on a heavy wooden cane stood on the cracked sidewalk.

"Pardon me?" Tara said when the woman merely studied her.

"That boy, Brent, I've known him since he was in diapers, honey. And let me tell you, sometimes he's not too smart. It seems now would be one of those times." The wizened old face lit up with a smile. "Oh, don't worry, honey, the good Mr. Chambliss has all the working parts going on upstairs. Just sometimes he pulls down the blinders and refuses to see things for what they are. He's hurting that boy is. Give him time and he'll come around." With that, the little woman crossed the street, leaving Tara at a loss for words. "Come over sometime, honey, and we'll have a cup of tea," the woman shouted in a strong clear voice as she climbed the steps of a small, one-story Victorian situated evenly between her and Brent's houses on the opposite side of the street.

"I'll do that and my name is Tara."

"I know, Tara Jenkins. Tomorrow at three." And the little woman disappeared inside before Tara had a chance to say, "Yes ma'am."

* * * * *

Another storm came up after dark, this time with less thunder and lightning and more rain. The electricity stayed on this time too. But the sound of the wind howling outside and the rain pelting the roof unnerved Tara and she decided to lock herself in her room with a mystery novel she'd been dying to read all day. Living alone in such a big house had seemed like a good idea. especially after ten years of apartment living, but on nights like this one, she couldn't remember exactly why. Yawning, she lay the book down on the bedside table and turned off the lamp. The old house made the same familiar noises she'd grown used to in just the three short nights she'd lived there and as the storm raged on outside, Tara drifted to sleep safe in her grandmother's old bed.

* * * * *

Bright sunlight warmed Tara's face and she leaned back on the park bench as she watched a red-haired woman push an adorable little red-haired baby girl in one of the infant swings. The baby's delighted giggles drifting on the spring air made Tara long for a child of her own.

"She's the spitting image of her father, except with my hair." A voice said from her right side but Tara didn't turn. She recognized the voice and didn't feel the need.

"She's beautiful. Brent must be so proud," Tara said as her fantasy of a child of her own burst into a million tiny fragments.

"He was for a long time. He loved her more than he ever loved me. But she wasn't enough...just wasn't enough to make our problems go away."

Tara watched as the baby's chubby arms reached out for the dark-haired man snapping photos nearby. "Dada dada." She squealed in delighted babble and Tara felt her heart sink in her chest.

"Have you made a decision yet?" The red-haired woman asked drawing her attention away from the small family. But the sun blinded her when she sought out the owner of the voice.

"About what?"

"He has to know, Tara. He has to know the truth if he is ever to be happy. I can't tell him. I'm not allowed. If you care anything for him, you have to do it. You have to set him free for me."

"It's not my place!" Tara protested. She didn't want to be the one to break the man's heart after he'd been through so much.

"Decide soon, Tara, before it's too late." The sun went behind a cloud and Tara found herself gazing off toward the lake... She was completely alone. Even the family had deserted her to feed the ducks.

Chapter Seven

⁊⊙

At six the next morning, Tara crossed the hedge and squished through Brent's soggy front yard to the porch. Stalling for time, she closed her umbrella and shook the rain off it, while she gathered her courage to ring the bell.

He was up. She'd made sure of that before coming over. A light at the back of the house and one on the side had come on thirty minutes before. She gave up on the third ring. He must be in the shower or ignoring her after yesterday. Disappointed, she turned to leave when the door opened. She smiled nervously at the man standing in the dark entryway, dressed in nothing but a pair of pajama bottoms.

"Tara?" He looked from her to the light rain beyond, then back to her. She had awakened him after all, if his mussed hair and sleep-groggy eyes were any indication.

"I'm sorry if I woke you… I'll come back later." Tara bit her bottom lip She was nervous. Too nervous for her own good. Maybe she should just forget this silly notion and go but she had promised Marty she'd bring a friend along. A friend she didn't have the courage to ask outright. Sneaky and underhanded wasn't exactly her forte but she'd try anything once.

"I'm up. What's wrong?" Brent asked running a hand through his spiky hair. He was just about to get into the shower when he heard the doorbell. He wasn't going to answer it but he'd had a feeling that it was Tara. He'd noticed her normally sunny face was troubled when he'd studied her from the peephole.

"No-nothing," she stammered in her nervousness. "I mean, my truck won't start and I have to be down at Bellingrath Gardens by seven. I was wondering if you could drop me off on your way in to work. I know it's out of the way and I'll pay you for the gas." A lie by omission was still a lie, wasn't it?

"Let me get dressed and I'll take a look at it." Brent glanced over to her truck to find its hood up.

"The battery is shot, if that rotten egg smell is any indication. I knew it was dying but I've put off replacing it... I shouldn't have bothered you. I'll go call a cab." What was one more lie?

"It's not a problem, really. I'll be happy to drive you down. Come in. Have you had breakfast?" He stepped back, opening the door for Tara.

"No. I'm too nervous to eat right now. I usually get like this before a shoot," Tara explained as she followed him inside, out of the dreary rain. She wasn't lying this time. Well, not completely anyway. She did get sick before she had to step in front of the camera sometimes but this wasn't one of those times.

"A shoot? Don't tell me you're an international assassin sent here to take out the mayor," Brent teased and was rewarded with a slight smile that actually threatened to reach her eyes.

"You bet. Double-O-Zilch, that's me." Tara let him tease her. It felt good. "No, I'm a model and up until Sunday a retired one at that. However, there is always a shortage of plus-size models and I let my agent talk me into one last shoot. But only because it is here instead of New York or Atlanta." She knew she was babbling but she was nervous and helpless to prevent it. Tricking Brent into posing for the Mardi Gras spread was a stupid idea but she didn't think he would come along willingly if she asked.

"A model? Who'd a thunk? And here I had you pegged for—I don't know—a kindergarten teacher," Brent said, happy to turn the tables on her finally. Although, a kindergarten teacher was far removed from what he really thought. In his mind she was closer to a dominatrix than anything else, but with sweet eyes. He felt himself shiver as the sexual fantasy he'd awakened to that morning came back full force when she brushed past him in his little foyer, her elbow grazing his bare belly with whisper softness. He shivered again, forcing his mind to contain the fantasy before he embarrassed himself by throwing her on the couch and pouncing on her.

"Touché." Tara remembered saying something similar the night they met. Her elbow tingled from the slight contact with his skin and she felt a rush of molten lava wash through her that she was desperate to subdue.

"Sure you wouldn't like some coffee at least?" Brent offered as he closed the door and followed her into the living room.

"No, thanks, I'm wired enough right now. Pretty house-did you do the work yourself or did you buy it this way?" She admired the beautiful woodwork that dominated the room, from the crown molding at the ceiling to the honey-colored fireplace mantel.

"Believe it or not, I rescued the house from demolition. She had been condemned and it took me three years to restore her working on weekends and evenings." He never would have believed himself capable of such delicate work back then. But the little house was his crowning achievement, born of blood, sweat and even a few tears when his wife had begged him to come home to their little apartment more often. Pride was quickly replaced with shame. Well maybe if he had gone home a little more often, his marriage wouldn't have fallen apart and his wife would still be alive.

Tara walked to the mantel and ran her hands over the glossy finish, the little niggling doubt about Brent's abilities suddenly gone if this was the outcome of his work. A gold frame on the mantel caught her attention. In the photo, an adorable red-haired toddler dressed in a blue sailor dress and red sailor hat played on the swings at the park.

The hair at the back of Tara's neck suddenly stood on end and goose bumps crawled down her spine. She'd seen this child before—last night—in one of those odd dreams she'd been having lately.

"Her name was Betsy. She was three when her mother took her away and they never came back."

Tara spun around at the sound of his broken voice. It was so obvious he was hurting. Not only had he lost his wife, but his daughter as well. Her heart broke for him and she wanted to cross the room and wrap her arms around him, tell him time mended all wounds. But she couldn't. He was after all, still a stranger.

"I'm sorry," she said simply and walked away from the little angel on the mantel.

"It was three years ago. You'd think I'd be over it by now." Brent scrubbed his face with his hands continuing the motion through his hair to shake off the grief before it could get him in a stranglehold.

He saw the pity in her eyes. He didn't want pity from this woman. He wanted... He wanted what? A warm, willing body to climb into, someone to take away the grief. He'd had that several times that first year and not one of those women had helped. So what did he want from Tara Jenkins? His skin prickled with fear when the feeling of forever came over him. "Uh, listen, I need to get a shower before I'm fit to go anywhere. Would you mind waiting about fifteen minutes?"

"No problem, I have a ton of last minute things to do before I'm ready to go. So I'll just run home and...do them." She needed to get away before he got into that shower. She absolutely did not want to be caught in the same house with Brent once he was all naked and wet. Plus it bothered her that she couldn't find any grief for his dead wife, the wife who had wronged him so badly. Her skin prickled again. She didn't know anything about his wife. How could she assume she had wronged him? Dreams, she'd been dreaming such oddly detailed dreams lately. "And I've got a few things I need to take with me, so I'll just go."

"Tara," Brent followed her to the door, stopping at the foyer table. "Here, take my keys.

The long skinny one is for the truck door, in case I'm not ready when you're ready to go." He tossed her the heavy key chain, which she deftly caught, a protest forming on her lips. "Oh, and Tara, you can use my kitchen as often as you'd like."

Chapter Eight

ಬಎ

Built in 1935, Bellingrath Gardens was the crown jewel in Mobile's string of gems, a diamond amongst rhinestones. The house, once featured on *America's Castles*, was opened to the public in 1956. The gardens were exquisite, the house divine, so why did Tara feel as if she were going to her execution as they drove through the service gates and up to the back of the house?

It was still dreary out although the rain had stopped. Tara hoped the sun would come out as the weatherman had promised or the shoot would be gloomy and tiresome.

"It's about time," Marty Stuart yanked open the truck door before Brent could come to a full stop. "We've been here for an hour already and those people at the front gate want us out by ten."

"Sorry, Marty. My car wouldn't start this morning and traffic on Government was a nightmare." Tara explained while Marty dragged her from the truck and started in the direction of a small rental tent that resembled the kind used at funerals.

"Wait, I need my bags and my makeup," Tara snatched her arm out of her agent's strong grip. "And there's someone I want you to meet," she whispered furiously casting quick glances to her neighbor who was just climbing out of the truck. She rubbed her arm where Marty's hand had been as Marty followed her gaze.

"He's gorgeous, Tara, sweetie. Wherever did you dig him up?" Marty's voice was fairly dripping with sugar as she gave Brent the once-over and then a twice-over from head to toe stopping at all those wonderful highlights in between.

"He's my neighbor. And Marty, he doesn't know a thing about this so don't implicate me. I feel bad enough tricking him into driving me out... Will you please stop looking at him as if you just got kicked off the cast of *Survivor* after three days of rats for dinner?" Tara whispered again hoping Marty would stop drooling.

"Where do you want me to set these bags?" Brent asked when he did catch up to them. He had her professional makeup case in one hand and the small suitcase she'd brought along just in case he decided to drop her at the front entrance and drive away.

"Well, hello there, sweet-cheeks," Marty said, her voice gone all Kathleen–Turner-husky. "Tara was just telling me what a wonderful neighbor you are to drive her all the way out here on such short notice." Tara relaxed a little, grateful that Marty had understood her warning after all.

"And Tara, darling, if I had known this place was so far out in the sticks I would have stuck to the original plan and gone to New Orleans. But we are so short-handed on this shoot and I do love you best, so you owe me one. Come along, kiddies, time to get into makeup." Marty flew into her whirlwind routine without giving Brent a chance to escape before she had him safely harnessed in one of her makeup chairs.

Tara took her heavy makeup case from Brent and shrugged her shoulder pathetically. "The things I put up with to earn a living." She reached for the other bag. "It's early still. Would you like to stay and watch for a while? Marty won't mind."

Brent took his eyes off the tall, mannish-looking woman who seemed to have boundless energy as she sprinted across the parking lot. Tara had seemed nervous and out of sorts since she'd knocked on his door and as she chewed on her lower lip. Brent decided to stay and lend her a little moral support.

"Sure, why not. I can call Hutch in an hour or so and let him know I'm going to be late." Brent agreed.

Thirty minutes later he wished someone had shot him before the words left his mouth.

* * * * *

"No cold feet, now, Bliss baby," the whirlwind Marty said shoving a three-page document in front of his face. "It's just for one shoot. And believe me, sweetums, the pay is real good."

"I don't need the money," Brent tried again to get out of this unexpected and unwelcome predicament. He didn't want to fill in for their missing male model. Nor did he want to put on one of those tuxedos they had on the rack behind him. And he damned sure didn't want to wear makeup.

"Darling, what planet are you from? Everyone needs more money," Marty said and Brent wondered which branch of the reptile family she hatched from when Tara walked into his little screened-off cubicle in the tent.

"Marty hasn't figured out yet Brent that some people can get along fine without being filthy, stinking rich," Tara said as she lugged the heavy makeup case to the vanity and collapsed into the director's chair next to Brent's.

"Blasphemy, pure and simple blasphemy," Marty tsked and whirled out of the room.

"Is she always like that?" Brent asked when they were alone and he felt comfortable again.

"You should have seen her before she switched to decaf."

"You're kidding right?"

"I wish I were," Tara popped open the makeup case and fiddled with the contents. "Listen, Brent, I have to apologize for all this. It's my fault you're here." She couldn't live with the guilt after tricking him into coming with her.

"It's all right, Tara. It's not like you had any idea they'd try to draft me." Brent watched her fidget with the little pots of makeup. He hadn't known her long but in the short time since they first met, he had never seen her look so forlorn.

"Yes, I did." Tara turned to the mirror. She couldn't meet his eyes but she had to tell him now while he was still free to walk away. "I knew they needed a male model Sunday when I spoke to Marty. And, well, just look at you... Plus-size models need men who are physically large so that we don't look like big she-hulks and there just aren't as many male models out there that fit that description. Tall enough, yes, but none broad enough. Anyway, I tricked you into bringing me down so that you could— I'm sorry Brent. I really am." Tara spoke rapidly without looking his way once.

"There was no truck problem, then?"

"I took the distributor cap off and hid it under the floor mat," Tara admitted shaking her head unable to look him in the eye. "You don't have to go through with this; I'll run interference while you sneak out. I'll make it up to you later."

"You think I'm pretty enough to be a model?"

"You're one hundred percent beefcake."

Brent chuckled softly, Tara looked into the mirror at his reflection. She smiled weakly as she met his twinkling eyes. "You're not angry then?"

"Yes, hell I'm angry. Pissed would cover it more accurately but I'll get over it." Brent tugged at his shirt. If he was going to do this, best to get it over with before he chickened out. Besides, Tara Jenkins thought he was a slice of beefcake. What could be better than that?

"You're staying?"

"Unbelievable as it may sound, yes I'm staying. Now which one of those monkey suits back there do you think this big body of mine will fit into?"

* * * * *

An hour later Brent stood in the blazing hot Alabama sun in a black jacket and makeup. He was hotter than he could ever remember being in his life and more miserable. "Bliss baby, face a little more to your left and lift your head a scosh," the photographer shouted. And if he heard that name one more time he was going to scream, Brent decided as he turned left and lifted his head a fraction of an inch. Bliss, indeed.

"Not too much longer now," Tara said as she placed her hand on his shoulder and faced the camera, while Brent stood facing away, one elbow on the wrought iron railing at the entrance to the Bellingrath home, the other hand in his jacket pocket.

"That's what you said ten minutes ago," he replied as irritably as possible but his irritation didn't last long after she touched him. Dressed in a barely-there black dress made of a filmy fabric that clung to her body like he imagined a harem garment would, Tara was very difficult to stay angry with. The thin black straps held up the skimpy bodice, which was covered with gold flowers and showed way too much cleavage for his sun-parched mind to deal with right then. A breeze picked up then and fluttered the delicate wisps of hair that framed her face and caused her black skirt to swirl around them. He watched her work, very much aware that he was merely a prop for her to play off. He longed to take her in his arms and swing her around until her lips were close to his. He yearned to caress her bare back.

"Perfect. That's what I wanted, Bliss Baby. Now turn toward her, take her in your arms and gently lean her back like you're going to kiss her."

Who was it that said be careful what you wish for? Brent wondered as he followed the photographer's orders, leaning her back until his face was only a fraction of an inch away from hers, as if he intended to kiss her. As their eyes met, her lips spread wide in a smile and he began to sweat ferociously. "It's going to rain again," she said unexpectedly, setting him a little more at ease.

"Wish it would. It's hot as blue blazes in this monkey suit," Brent tried to remember he wasn't supposed to do anything but *look* as if he was going to kiss her. This was pure hell on earth.

"Perfect. Hold that pose for-just-a–min-ute. There. Thanks Tara and Bliss. Thanks everyone." Brent heard the photographer shout over the blood pulsing past his ears.

"We're done," Tara whispered just as the rain began. "You can let me go now." But she didn't make a move to push him away. Instead she seemed content to stand there gazing into his eyes as if the world around them had ceased to exist. Her flimsy black dress was getting soaked but none of the others seemed to notice, as they were all racing to the tent. Brent straightened bringing Tara with him, her lips still so close he could feel her breath on his face. His hand skimmed her bare back and he felt her shiver.

"Cold?" he asked, unable to break the spell that held him.

"Wet," Tara said her hand still on his back as if she were unaware on some level that her flimsy black dress was soaked and clinging to her breasts, to her hips. Her nipples hardened as his gaze caressed them, his mouth suddenly dry.

"Tara, Bliss Baby. Come on before you ruin those clothes," Marty's husky shout intruded, breaking the spell, and Tara sprung from his arms like an arrow from a bow and raced on to the tent in her three-inch heels, while Brent, his body humming with desire stood for a moment watching her retreat. He couldn't go on like this. This wanting her was killing him. And just as suddenly as it had begun, the rain stopped.

* * * * *

Later, Tara and Brent sat at a table in Mobile's famous Mintzel's Oyster House. Marty and the pushy photographer were on their way back to New York along with two of the four other models. The remaining two shared their table and occupied Brent's attention until he excused himself to go to the men's room.

"Umm, girl where have you been hiding *him* all this time?" Coco asked with a delighted shiver as she watched him walk away.

"I just met him last week, Coco. For Pete's sake, he's my neighbor." Tara forced away the irrational ball of jealousy that formed in the pit of her stomach the very first time Coco had laid her pretty hand on Brent's arm.

"What do they put in the water down here to grow 'em so big and pretty? And that name, honey, I could die a happy woman right now."

"Coco, you are without a doubt the only women I've ever met who lives in a constant state of heat," Shannon Summers said from the other side of the table. Her pink lips spread in a wide grin as if this were an old conversation, which Tara knew it was. She'd only lived with them for most of the last ten years putting up with their bickering without much trouble. But today she couldn't stand it, they were driving her stark raving. Especially Coco.

"If God hadn't intended for me to look he wouldn't have put such a fine ass on that man." Coco let the insult pass without notice as Brent disappeared from sight. She turned in her seat to face both her current and former roommate. "Do you think he's gay?"

Tara choked on her water.

"If you'd seen him when he was with Tara this morning, you wouldn't have asked that question. I thought it couldn't get any hotter down here but when they did that little dip there at the end I thought all the warnings about global warming were about to come true." Shannon casually sipped her own water and grinned at Tara as if she alone knew the fate of the world.

Coco turned wide curious eyes on her and Tara fidgeted in her seat. "I have no idea what you're talking about. We were discussing the rain."

"Umm-hmm, talking about it so much you missed the fact that if was actually raining. That black dress is ruined by the way," Coco piped in raising one eyebrow at her friend. Tara turned pink. "Just what went on after I left?"

"Let's just say he was looking at her as if he were starving and she just happened to be a nice big juicy steak," Shannon supplied and Tara's blush darkened.

"Oh, tell me more," Coco beamed, her lust for the man forgotten in the face of fresh gossip.

"Shh, here he comes," Shannon said trying to wipe the grin off her face and hush Coco up at the same time. She'd known better than to say anything in front of Coco but Tara was her friend and she had a gut feeling Tara had already snagged the interest of the incredibly delectable Bliss. She also had a feeling Coco was dangerously close to treading on sacred territory.

"So, have you ladies decided what to order?" Brent sat between Tara and Coco, missing the quick glances the three women cast across the table.

"Why oysters, Bliss honey. Nice, raw, ooey, gooey oysters," Coco purred. "Interested in finding out if they really are an aphrodisiac?"

"Coco!" Shannon hissed. "Down girl."

"Actually to be quite honest I never could stomach the things, not even fried. So I think I'll pass this time Coco, sorry." Brent picked up his water glass to hide his growing discomfort. Whoever thought having a table full of beautiful women at their beck and call was heaven could certainly take his place he decided as the waitress finally arrived.

"What can I get you folks to drink?" she asked pulling a pen out of her apron pocket without looking at the group.

"Four beers and all the oysters you have," Coco piped in before anyone else had a chance.

"Charlotte Jackson, if you don't rein it in, girl, I'm gonna have to call your mama," Shannon said. Coco was out of control and she knew it was over Tara's neighbor. Coco wanted him and he didn't notice she was alive. Coco shot her a dirty look for using her real name and acted as if she had done nothing wrong.

"Actually, I'd like a crab salad and a glass of sweet tea," Tara folded her menu, handing it back to the waitress.

"That sounds good but make mine unsweetened tea. I still have a career to worry about." Shannon gave over her menu as well.

"Make it three and leave the tea sweet." Brent said following suit.

"Bliss, honey, won't you at least join me in a beer?" Coco pouted demurely as she wondered what she was doing wrong. By now, the man should be on the floor at her feet, salivating.

"I can't, Coco. I'm an alcoholic," Brent announced and Coco shut up. Tara could only stare as if she had discovered a terrible secret. The hair at the back of her neck stood on end. Secrets and Brent, what was there about a secret and Brent that seemed so familiar? Brent met her eyes the old sadness she'd come to expect to find there was back. And she knew without a doubt that his drinking had something to do with the deaths of his wife and daughter.

She viciously squashed the thoughts. There was no way this man would have caused their deaths, she was sure of it. So what was it about him and his announcement that bothered her so much?

"Still want those drinks and oysters, Miss?" the waitress asked Coco, who sank into her seat away from Brent, her eyes moody and unhappy. And Tara's heart went out to her friend.

"Just one beer, a dozen oysters and a salad will be fine, thanks." Coco said more subdued now. Tara and Shannon exchanged curious glances.

After lunch, Coco and Shannon took a cab back to their hotel. Shannon had agreed to drive out to Tara's later in the evening for supper and girl talk. Coco refused claiming a headache. "See you later," Tara said just as the taxi pulled away and Shannon waved out the open window.

"Come on Tara I'll take you home and help you replace that distributor cap," Brent said from behind her as she stood on the sidewalk watching her friends disappear into lunch-hour traffic.

"That's not necessary. I can do it myself," Tara turned to him now that they were alone. All the guilt she'd felt for dragging him into her life returning and she wanted to make amends.

"Really? What do you know about radiators? Mine seems to be running hot all of a sudden." Brent said and Tara, completely missing the double entendre, felt rather than saw his mocking grin.

"Maybe you have some blockage. Take it in to the dealer and get them to flush the radiator." It was just like a man to assume that she didn't know her way around under the hood just because she was a woman.

"Um, Tara? What's the deal here? I didn't mean to imply that you didn't know anything about cars and after dealing with your she-cat friend during lunch I expected a little more than to have my head bitten off."

"Oh..." She turned a bright shade of red. "I'm sorry, Brent— I— This day isn't going exactly as I'd hoped. Coco is behaving erratically and you drop a bomb on me in there and then treat me like a girly-girl... I just don't know...Sorry I snapped. Sorry for dragging you into my world. Sorry. Just sorry."

"Dropped what bomb? What are you talking about?"

"The alcoholism- I didn't need to know that. I wanted..." Tara gasped and started walking toward the parking lot where they'd left his truck. She didn't know what she wanted. A knight in shining armor? Talk about the girly thing! Had she already put him on that pedestal? Is that why she was so angry with him for being...what? Flawed? Human?

"Wait. Just wait a damn minute, Tara." Brent called out. She heard the anger in his voice. Anger she deserved for judging him. He caught her arm and turned her to face him. Sparks were dancing in his eyes. Eyes that were as dark as sin in the first place now burned with anger. "Where do you get off judging me? Yeah, I had a problem. I liked beer a little too much. It destroyed my marriage, drove my wife away. And after...after...I let it take control, let it become the only thing in my life. I lost my job. I nearly lost my house, my truck. I lost my self-respect and I realized that I was as much to blame for their deaths as that other drunk was. The one who actually climbed behind the wheel that night. The one who hit my wife and baby. And I couldn't be like that man. I couldn't become another pathetic excuse for a human being just because I have a weakness for drink. I got help, Tara, and I've been sober for two years now."

"I'm sorry. So sorry," Tara whispered, a single tear trickling down her cheek.

"Aw, damn it, don't do that. I won't have you feeling sorry for me. I won't have it, Tara, do you hear me?" Brent shook her arm, wanting to shake away her pity.

"I wasn't," she protested. "Let go of me. I'm sorry for judging you, for thinking the worst of you but you won't let me apologize for anything. It might hurt your pride, your manhood, to have some woman pity you. Well, I'm sorry, Brent Chambliss. I don't pity you. I feel for you, I understand your loss, but I don't pity you. In fact, what I do feel for you is rapidly changing direction as we speak. I… Just let me go." Tara snatched her arm away and started back down the sidewalk in the direction they had come.

"God damn… Tara!" He was doing it again, just like before, getting too close and putting up barriers. Just like with Kelly, he didn't want anyone to care for him. And he did everything he could to drive them away, why hadn't he learned *that* lesson when he learned how to live without the booze? "Tara, wait. Where are you going?"

"Home," she called out without turning without stopping.

"The truck is the other way." Brent shouted in exasperation. He didn't have time for this, he really didn't.

"I know. I prefer to walk, thank you."

"Come on, Kelly, get in the truck. Let me take you home."

Tara stopped then and turned to face him her eyes wide with shock, her face noticeably pale. "You called me Kelly."

Brent felt all the blood drain from his face and the sidewalk began to spin beneath his feet. "I didn't."

"Yes, you did. I'm not Kelly. I'm not... Goodbye Brent Chambliss." Tara turned. She felt the tears stinging her eyes. Oh for Pete's sake, she wasn't going to cry. One tear fell then another. Tara ran down the busy sidewalk back to the restaurant. In the bathroom, she locked herself into a stall until the tears stopped. She felt so foolish so stupid. He'd called her Kelly. Kelly... Oh God, how had things gotten so out of hand that it mattered what the man called her?

It didn't, nothing mattered but her new house, her new life. She wouldn't let it. No more modeling. She would eat what she wanted and get as fat as a house, it didn't matter. In January, she was going to start college, as she should have ten years ago. She was going to be that kindergarten teacher Brent had accused her of being that morning. It was her plan, her dream and that was all that mattered. And no haunted man, no matter how much she wanted him, was going to get in the way of that dream.

When the tears were over, Tara scrubbed her face with cold water from the faucet and went back into the restaurant. She didn't expect Brent to be there waiting for her but the fact that he wasn't hurt.

"Hey, are you all right?" The waitress from lunch came up beside her. "You and your boyfriend have a fight?"

"He wasn't my boyfriend."

"Whatever. But if you ask me, for those kind of tears, he'd better be a heck of a lot more than just a friend." The waitress said and walked off leaving Tara to stew in misery.

At the bar Tara ordered a soda to go and called for a cab, which she waited for at the door. She had to go see her mother, she had to fix her truck and she had an invitation to have tea across the street with a little old lady she'd only met once. Tara didn't want to do any of those things; she wanted to go home and crawl into bed with a tub of Rocky Road ice cream and just stay there until January. The cab pulled up in the No Parking zone in front of the restaurant and Tara rushed out giving the driver directions for the nursing home where her mother currently resided instead of to her home. Which, at that very moment, was way too close to a certain creep for her taste.

Chapter Nine

ะດ

Pain throbbed through Brent's temples matching the rhythm of the hammer in his hand. The Millers' kitchen was lying in shambles all around him, with debris strung from the back of the house to the front driveway, all because two crewmembers were down with the flu. Which ordinarily wouldn't bother him but since the stupid argument with Tara that morning, he just did not want to be there.

Stupid, stupid, stupid, his hammer sang as he nailed up new framing for the bay window. The beeper went off. Brent threw the hammer onto the floor to check the message. Hutch again and this time with a 411 emergency, requesting information. At least he wouldn't have to haul butt back to the office but still the time it would take to return the page was irritating. Brent went to the Millers' wall phone in the hallway and punched in the number for the office. "What!" he growled when Hutch answered.

"Hey man, don't bite my head off," Hutch replied smoothly and Brent could swear he heard the man grinning. "Nothing major, I just thought you'd like to know that the permits for Tara's house are all ready to go and you can start over there whenever the urge strikes."

"Great." More Tara. As if she weren't already on his mind every waking moment of every day...and night. "How about that dumpster? When will you have it delivered out to her house?"

"First thing tomorrow. Everything on this end is handled...so I'll let you get back to work," Hutch hung up leaving Brent holding a dead phone. His headache worsened and he wanted to crawl into a hole and take a nap.

Tomorrow, he would start the renovation on Tara's kitchen. Oh God what was he going to do...? Nail more framing that was what he was going to do. After he took a half dozen aspirin.

The sun had finally overcome the rain but it was as if Brent had just noticed when he went out to his truck for the pain reliever. His headache dulled a bit as he looked into the deep blue sky that always came with autumn. He wondered when the cooler weather would come to stay. In the truck, he noticed the two bags thrown into the backseat and sighed.

Tara Jenkins was like a bad penny. She just kept turning up and frankly he was beginning to resent it. Almost as much as he looked forward to it, he sighed again.

Okay, so he now had three reasons to stop by her house that night, the third, being to go over the final drafts of the kitchen before he started ripping things out. He sighed a third time. Fate it seemed had stepped in with a not-so-gentle nudge. So who was he to argue? He popped two aspirin into his mouth and swallowed. Who was he to go against fate? Tara Jenkins had better be alone, that was all he had to say about it.

Brent groaned and tossed the bottle back into the glove box. Fate be damned. Tara Jenkins had better have an army of family and friends around her if she knew what was good for her. And Lord help her if she was wearing that slinky black dress... There was only so much torture a man could stand.

* * * * *

Maybelle Lewis affectionately called Miss Belle by her friends and Memaw by her family went all-out for tea. Small sandwiches, the crusts trimmed away, were stacked on a platter that Tara suspected to be older than her and her own mother combined. Little jam-filled cookies arranged delicately on a matching platter followed. Tea was served in fine china cups so dainty that Tara feared dropping hers more than she had ever feared anything in her life. Belle was the last member of her family that still followed the old ways and high tea was a tradition in her family passed down from the days when the first Lewis had come to America.

"This is delicious chicken salad, Miss Belle. You'll have to give me the recipe." Tara said truthfully, as the sandwich dissolved in her mouth like ambrosia.

"Honey, I will be taking that recipe to the grave with me," Miss Belle said as she sipped her tea and sized up the young woman across from her. Tall, sturdy and smart, she'd taken a wrong turn in life but that would soon be remedied, Belle decided. Just where this young woman fit into her fine young man's life Belle couldn't determine. But then Brent had always been hard to read. Even as a child, his only passion seemed to be in restoring old houses. People, as far as she could tell, had never touched him deep enough to snag his interest. Maybe that was about to change, she thought as she smiled at the young woman. "Maybe we can work out something later. Lord knows not one of those granddaughters of mine deserves such a treasure."

"I'm sure your granddaughters are all fine, upstanding women, Miss Belle. With a grandma like you around to keep 'em in line." Tara smiled and took another chicken salad sandwich.

"Don't sass me young lady or I *will* take that recipe on to heaven." Belle returned her smile. Tara Jenkins it seemed was more astute than Belle had given her credit for.

"Well, I guess that's as it should be. Just you make sure God knows that he won't be getting the recipe either when he asks or I'll be very put out," Tara said over her tea cup. Miss Belle laughed. It was a throaty coarse sound that vibrated through the dining room of the old house.

"You, child, are a terror. I bet you gave your poor mama gray hairs on top of her gray hair."

"Yes ma'am I did, I admit it." Tara's good humor faded as she remembered the frail listless woman she'd just left and her heart broke. Sometimes she wondered if maybe she'd been too much of a trial and was responsible for what her mother had become. "She was forty when I was born and my dad died a few years later. She had to spend her golden years worrying about a teenager. Not that I was a troublemaker or anything. Just that...well, you know how teenagers are. Then I went to New York and decided to stay. So I guess most of her gray hair is my fault."

"Child, it ain't your fault. Old age affects us all differently. Look at me. I'm eighty-nine. I might not be this sprightly when I get old so I'm enjoying myself while I can." Belle said. She didn't need to ask the details of Mrs. Jenkins' health. The pain in the young woman's eyes said it all.

"Thanks Miss Belle. I guess I'm feeling a little sorry for myself today," Tara said with a grin.

"Trouble between you and Mr. Smarty-pants then?" Belle said thinking back to the boy's childhood when he used to sass her every chance he got. "I noticed you left with him this morning and came back in a cab."

"Why, Miss Belle? Are you one of those people who spends their days spying on their neighbors?"

"That's Mr. Williams next door to you. I just happened to be out watering my gardenias."

Tara smiled again at the woman's spirit. Watering her gardenias in the middle of a downpour, now that was pluck. She wolfed down the rest of her second sandwich and sampled the cookies, mentally tabulating calories as she ate. So much for her plan to get fat, she sighed when she stopped at only two cookies. "We had words this afternoon. Brent called me Kelly." Tara shrugged away the hurt that still lingered. "I'm assuming Kelly was his wife?"

"Some wife that one was," Miss Belle snorted but didn't elaborate. "It was a slip that's all honey. That boy just won't let her go. The baby I understand but not her, not that Kelly. She ran off and killed them both and he is just wallowing in guilt over it."

"I know. I've seen it but…I'm not his wife. I'm not anything to him. Why would he call me by her name?"

"Maybe Mr. Brent Chambliss thinks of you as more than just a neighbor, Tara Jenkins. And just maybe it was his way of pulling himself back down into the muck. He'll get over it or he'll implode. There's not much anyone can do for him at this point." It was Miss Belle's turn to sigh. "But I have always hoped someone stronger than him would come along and set him on his ear. Being pretty doesn't hurt either. You remember that, Tara Jenkins. Now go on home, I need to get a little beauty sleep before my great-grandbabies get home from their after-school activities."

"Oh?" Tara said, surprised by the abrupt dismissal and she stood, taking her dishes to the sink as she went.

"Leave those dishes, missy, and go see to your truck. I'm sure you want to get that part you hid back in before dark."

"But – Thanks for the tea Miss Belle and the sympathetic ear." Tara set her dishes on the table and let the old woman shoo her toward the door.

"Welcome child, come back tomorrow same time. This lonely old woman needs all the company she can get," Miss Belle said just before she closed the door in Tara's face. And all the gossip too, she thought to herself as she chuckled. Tara was just the sort of woman to shake her boy Brent out of his guilt tree she was sure of it. Now she needed to call Gloria and let her know what their boy was in for.

* * * * *

The bright orange autumn sun was just beginning to set when Tara dropped the hood of her little truck and wiped her dirty hands on a rag. She'd checked all her fluids while she was under there and decided that her oil was a little low. Tomorrow she would take it in to have it changed and a new filter put in but the truck was still in great shape for its age.

A horn sounded in her driveway and Tara jumped dropping the rag onto the concrete. A yellow cab sat behind her truck with Shannon just climbing out. "Hey, kiddo," she shouted and waved as she handed over the fare. "A little help would be appreciated." She reached in the backseat and pulled out two large suitcases.

"Hey, I invited you to supper. I didn't expect you to move in," Tara teased.

"Coco was in the middle of some type of nervous breakdown. She threw the telephone at me and told me to get the hell out," Shannon said handing over one of the cases to Tara. "I hope you don't mind if I stay the night?"

"No problem. I'll pull out the air mattress. It will be like old times. What's up with her anyway?" Tara asked. Coco and Shannon were her dearest friends and Coco's behavior at lunch had bothered her. Coco was always a *prima donna*; this time was different, though, and Tara couldn't quite put her finger on why.

"I don't know. But I think it's time to find a place of my own. Living with Coco never was easy but it's gotten to be impossible since you moved out." Shannon followed Tara up the driveway and onto the porch. "This is a great house."

"She'll be gorgeous once the remodel is complete not to mention the painting. I can't wait. I never thought I could own one of these old beauties. I bought this one for a song. And the work I want to do is going to be less than I thought, too." Tara said the pride in her voice hard to hide. After growing up in a tiny house in West Mobile where money was tight, Tara just never expected to achieve her dream. Falling into modeling all those years ago had been a God send. But instead of blowing the sometimes incredible money she made she had chosen to live cheaply. Always sharing a tiny rent controlled apartment with two or more roommates and eating cereal and salads instead of steak and chicken. Most of her clothes were perks from her jobs. And last but not least, she had a very good investment banker working for her. All these things combined had left her with a nice nest egg on which to retire. A nest egg that was now half-gone, she reminded herself. And if she were to use the rest to go to college and pay Brent, she would have to get a job that would cover basic living expenses. Like insurance and utilities. "Come on in and I'll give you the grand tour."

Later after guiding Shannon through the mostly empty house and ordering pizza for supper, the two settled down to gossip about what had happened in New York after Tara had left. Naturally, the subject came back to Coco. "About three weeks ago, Coco locked herself in the bedroom for two days. If she came out at all, I wasn't there to see it," Shannon said. "Then she started doing stupid stuff, very un-Coco like things. It's hard to describe... She's always been a little wild and very man-hungry but it's almost as if she is living like a woman condemned. I don't know how else to explain it."

"Poor Coco, she's a bit younger than we are. Maybe she's feeling her age creep up on her. Lord knows that I don't relish turning thirty next year but I can't stop it. Do you think that's it, that Coco is trying to stop time...stay twenty-five forever?" Tara suggested as she sat on her bed brushing her hair.

"Maybe. Coco was always vain, which is natural for every model...every model except you that is." Shannon shrugged. She was tired of talking about Coco, tired of thinking about Coco, tired of the world revolving around Coco. Coco got all the best jobs, Coco got all the best men, but mostly Coco got on her nerves more than anyone else ever had. The doorbell chiming interrupted Shannon's thoughts.

"Who could that be at this time of night?" Tara set her hairbrush down and looked around for something big to use as a weapon. Her tennis racket lay on the floor of the closet where she'd thrown it Monday night after unpacking the box it was in so she grabbed it and motioned Shannon to follow her downstairs. There was safety in numbers, wasn't there? The bell began to chime almost frantically.

Whoever it was out there was in an awful hurry to get inside, Tara thought as fear clenched her insides. She had yet to have a security system installed. Tara shifted the racket into her right hand as she neared the door, flipped on the porch light and peered out the peephole. She sighed and set the racket beside the door. "It's Coco."

"Speak of the devil," Shannon uttered as Tara opened the door and let the woman in. "Coco, what a surprise. I thought you weren't speaking to me anymore. What brings you out in the middle of the night?"

Tears stood in Coco's blue eyes and her hands shook as she set her overnight bag on the floor. A major breakdown was imminent and Shannon groaned.

"Come on Coco. Let me get you something to drink." Tara gave Shannon a stern warning look. "I don't have anything potent in the house right now but I can make some coffee or tea or there's colas and juice."

"Coffee sounds good," Coco said her lips trembling as she tried to hold herself together.

"Okay then, come on out to the kitchen and we'll have some coffee and talk like we used to do." Tara grabbed her arm and hauled her to the kitchen. The doorbell rang again and Tara whirled around, this time expecting it to be the cabby that had dropped Coco off. She never dreamed she would open the door to find Brent standing there.

Seems he was going to see her in her bunny slippers after all, she thought, feeling the blush start just under the collar of her T-shirt.

"Uh, hi Tara." He stood there, his hands shoved deep in his pockets. And here she was in her pajamas and old tattered slippers. What could be worse? Her glasses, she suddenly remembered, her hands going automatically to push the small gold-rimmed frames securely on her nose daring him to say something. "Sorry to bother you when you have company but I thought you'd like to know that the permits came through today. I can start whenever you're ready."

"Oh and Tara, about this afternoon..." Brent started to edge toward the steps when she didn't say anything and Tara saw the hint of nervousness he tried to hide. She felt small and petty after the argument that afternoon. Very small and very petty.

"I'm sorry. I—"

"You don't have to apologize for anything. It's me who should be apologizing. I should never have... Sorry, Brent. When can you start on the kitchen?" she stumbled through her apology feeling like a fool.

"Tomorrow night and before I forget, you'll need to move your truck. That dumpster I told you about will be delivered in the morning. If you want I'll do it for you since you're not dressed."

"That's okay. I'm driving Shannon to the airport early in the morning unless you expect it to get here before six."

"No that'll be fine. I'll see you tomorrow night," Brent backed down the steps and started for his yard.

"Brent, wait," Tara called and Brent spun around, the look on his face odd, almost eager. "We haven't settled on the plans for the kitchen remodel yet. Can I see what you've got before you start ripping things out?"

"Sure, stop by the office in the morning and we'll draw up the final plans and decide on materials. See ya then," he smiled, waved and hurried home.

Tara stepped back inside and closed the door. "Wow," Shannon said giving her a wicked smile. "If I didn't know better, I'd say Tara was in love."

"What?" Tara gasped.

Coco burst into tears.

Chapter Ten

&

"Cancer!" Tara held her friend while she cried. "Are you sure?"

"Not yet. I have a biopsy scheduled for this weekend. I'll know then," Coco said between sobs. "How can this happen to me? Breast cancer is for old women. I'm only twenty-five. I'm too young. What will happen if they have to remove my breast? What will I do then? I don't know how to be anything else."

"Oh, Coco." Shannon sat next to her friends on Tara's bed and she felt miserable now for all the horrible things she'd said about Coco these past few days. She should have known something was really wrong and not just Coco being Coco. "It'll work out you'll see and I'll be there with you and your mother." Coco sobbed harder. "You have told her, haven't you?"

"I don't know how. I haven't told anyone until tonight. I just thought if I ignored it, it would all go away. I don't want to lose my breasts. I don't. I couldn't live without them. I want to get married, have children. How am I supposed to do that with no breasts?" Coco wailed hysterically.

"Just think of it as the perfect excuse to get a set of watermelon-sized implants. You always wanted bigger ones, didn't you?" Tara said calmly.

Shannon gasped, stifling a giggle as she waited for Coco to have a fit.

"Really? You think watermelon-sized is big enough?" Coco said, her voice still teary.

"Bigger would just be tacky, don't you think?" Tara said, her eyes sparkling with tears she would not shed for Coco's sake.

"What kind of watermelon? Those little round ones or those big honking oval melons?" Coco emitted a sound that sounded like a half-giggle, half-sob.

"Those big honking oval ones are so heavy you'd need a cart to push 'em around in," Tara said matter-of-factly as the image invaded her head.

"Well then, I guess that would do just fine. Men sure go crazy over-big boobed women. Just look at that Pamela Anderson." Coco sat up and wiped her eyes. "Thanks Tara."

"What are friends for?"

"You know this is morbid? We shouldn't be joking about it like this," Shannon said wiping away her own tears.

"Spoilsport," Tara hissed.

"It's okay. It still hurts but maybe not so much." Coco said her eyes dry now. "Will you guys stay with me while I call my mama? She's gonna break down and I don't think I can handle that alone."

"You know we will Coco. We'll be right here." Shannon said as she clutched Coco's hand.

"And Tara, I'm sorry about lunch. I should have seen that you and Bliss have something going on. I wouldn't have made such a fool of myself if I had. Can you forgive me?"

"We don't. I'm not in love with him... We just met, for Pete's sake."

"Uh-huh," Shannon gave Coco a conspiratorial look.

"We hear the words but after what we saw downstairs we don't believe 'em," Coco agreed.

"Just make your phone call." Tara wanted to shrink away from the notion. Brent had come to matter too much in such a short time; what if they were right, what if she had fallen in love with him? No. Impossible. She'd promised herself never to go that far over a man again.

* * * * *

"Somebody get the door," Tara shouted from the balcony, her wet hair dripping onto her robe. They were running late and she'd forgotten what it was like to share one bathroom with two mirror hogs. "Coco, for Pete's sake, will you get the door? It's probably Brent wondering why I haven't moved my truck yet."

"Yes boss, and since you have no interest in him can I play with him while we wait?" Coco said it just to see Tara's face pinch with jealousy. Oh the girl was gaga, Coco decided wondering why she hadn't seen it the day before.

"Whatever. Just give him my keys. They're hanging on the letter holder in the kitchen."

Coco didn't need to hear an actual verbal warning to know she had just been warned if Tara's growl meant anything. "Okay, okay, keep your robe on."

Tara snorted at her friend's overly happy teasing after the too little sleep she'd had due to worrying about that self-same friend and went to her room to dry her hair.

Coco smirked at the balcony for a second longer then went to the door, throwing it open without checking to see who was on the other side…a fatal mistake.

"Hello, ah…this is the Jenkins house isn't it?" Hutch checked the address on the door with the one on his paperwork. He was sure Brent had said it was the big Victorian. But the dark-skinned beauty standing in the entryway wasn't Tara Jenkins by a long shot. This woman was a touch younger, a touch taller and a touch slimmer. Hutch gulped, his all-too-obvious inadequacies practically screaming out. He sucked in his stomach, standing to his full height of six-foot-two.

"Yes it is. I'm a friend of Tara's. Who may I ask is calling?" Coco didn't miss the subtle actions of a man trying to hide the onset of middle age. Pathetic, she thought initially, spitefully, yet there was something about him that was…cute. He was taller than she was by an inch or so and he was blond and blue-eyed. His face wasn't sculpted like Bliss' but it was cute. Even his receding hairline was cute. And cute bothered Coco this morning as she felt a need to twine her fingers in the curls that brushed his collar.

"Oh, I'm...I'm Hutch. James Hutchinson. I work for the construction firm doing the remodel on Miss Jenkins' house. I have the dumpster and I need to put it in her driveway but her truck is there." Hutch stumbled over his words with a wince for looking oafish in front of the beauty. But that was nothing new, he sighed after the rush of words. Feeling like a fool, he wanted nothing more than to get the delivery over with and head out to the office. Frankly, he had no idea why he was out on this delivery when one of the crew could have taken care of it. But the flu was hitting the crew hard and they were undermanned as it was. He could at least pitch in and drive a truck when needed. Especially with Brent next door to help him offload the bin. Brent, who was just now rounding the corner of his house dressed in nothing but a pair of sweatpants.

Hutch sighed again. He thought he'd stopped envying Brent for being in better shape in college but now he'd give anything to have his old friend's flat stomach and full head of hair.

"Sorry. We're running a bit late but I can get the keys and move the truck in a jiffy." A jiffy, where had that word come from? Coco wondered as she caught sight of the luscious Bliss jogging up the walk and felt...nothing.

"That would be great Miss...?" Hutch said noticing the way the woman eyed his partner and again envy slapped him upside the head. But what did he expect? Women like her never looked twice at men like him. Then she did, smiling a wide beautiful smile that had Hutch's heart thudding in his chest like a fish flapping on dry land.

"I'm Charlotte Jackson but my friends call me Coco." Coco watched the way his blue eyes darkened and his lips stretched into a smile as he held out his hand to grasp hers. What was wrong with her? Her palms were clammy, her pulse racing ninety to nothing.

"Nice to meet you Charlotte." Hutch said, grateful that his voice was normal and not the scared whine he imagined.

"Coco," she whispered back as she let her hand linger in his.

"Coco." Hutch felt his face grow hot. He cursed under his breath for blushing, knowing it would send her into peals of laughter over the fat guy later.

"Hey man, what are you doing hauling that bin out here? Where's Mac?" Brent joined them on the porch and Coco snatched her hand away as if she'd been bitten. Hutch sighed. Well for a moment, at least his fantasy woman had been within reach but now that was over. Time to move on.

"Down with the flu, which by the way makes eight." He couldn't help wishing Brent had taken a few more minutes before he made it over.

"Shit, if this keeps up we'll fall behind on everything. I guess I'll be putting in a few late hours wherever I'm needed the most." Brent ran agitated fingers through his rumpled hair. "Good morning, Coco, didn't see you there. Is Tara up?"

"She's upstairs but I warn you she's not in a good mood." Coco replied. Brent's fast dismissal of her hurt far less than she would have imagined, as she realized he hadn't noticed her because his mind was on Tara. Coco smiled then. Tara deserved someone like Bliss here. She deserved to be happy and she deserved to be loved.

"I'll just have to chance it then, won't I?" Brent pushed past Coco. Coco let him even though she could have gotten the keys to move the truck. He was eager to see Tara so who was she to stand in the way of true love or at least true lust? She turned a conspiratorial grin on Hutch, who blushed so cutely again and she forgot all about her upcoming surgery as she gazed into his eyes. The butterflies in the pit of her stomach took center stage away from her possible cancer...butterflies she'd never experienced before with any man. Butterflies that scared her more than facing the knife ever could. He was cute. She was insane.

She stepped off the threshold and reached for his hand.

"So Jamie, tell me more about yourself. I think we have plenty of time before Bliss or Tara come down." Coco purred as she pulled him over to the old swing that hung on the side of the porch.

Hutch never knew what hit him once Coco made up her mind to make him hers.

* * * * *

The whirring sound of a hair dryer caught Brent's attention as he climbed the stairs to find Tara. Her friend Shannon had said she was in her room, when he'd come across her in the hall. Naturally, Brent had assumed she was up and about but now he wasn't so sure. Her bedroom door stood wide open and Brent put his doubts to rest. She was just drying her hair. People did that at all hours of the day, right? Most did it after they were dressed, right?

Wrong. Brent stepped into Tara's room and every testosterone-filled cell in his body sprang to life. Tara stood with her back to him, dressed in nothing but a pair of white cotton panties and a white satin bra. A white satin bra that did wonderful things to those luscious breasts he saw reflected in the mirror. He gulped as his body responded to all that exposed golden flesh. His gaze lingering on those gently rounded curves, before moving on to those gloriously long legs and finally stopping on those beautiful green eyes. Green eyes that were flashing angrily in the mirror as she stared back at him.

"Sorry," he shouted over the dryer and turned around to give her the privacy she needed to hide all those delectable sights from his greedy eyes. "I didn't know… Your door was open… Your friends could have warned me," he stammered out once the dryer was silent. But he wasn't sorry he realized as he heard her walking around behind him. Not one little bit was he sorry to get a glimpse of that glorious body she hid beneath her clothes. Her tiny waist and round hips would keep him up nights, making him wonder what it felt like to hold her nice round bottom in his hands.

He heard her pull on a pair of jeans, heard the zipper. Heard her sharp intake of breath as she buttoned them and he closed his eyes but that was no good when all he could see there was him unfastening those jeans and sliding the zipper back down.

"You can turn around now," Tara her voice was strained with anger but the image of his hands gently sliding beneath those white cotton briefs obliterated it instantly.

"I'm really sorry, Tara. I never would have come in if I'd thought…" He cleared his throat; right now he wasn't sure at all what he would have done if he'd known. In his present frame of mind, there was just no telling. "Well…sorry."

"It's okay. I should have closed the door. Was there something you needed?" She stared holes through him, her voice still icy.

Needed! Yes hell, there *was* something he needed, all right. He needed her more and more with every meeting. He needed to touch her, to taste her, to explore those dangerous curves of hers. More than that he needed her to touch him, to taste him and to explore him. He needed a cold shower and to see a shrink.

"Ah, yeah, your truck is in the drive still and… Give me your keys and I'll move it for you and then I'll get out of your hair." Don't even think about her hair or you'll spontaneously combust on the spot.

"Didn't Coco get them for you?"

"Was she supposed to?"

"Yes, she was. I'll kill her. That's what I'll do. She let you in here on purpose. She knew I was naked. She's trying…" Tara erupted and Brent could only stand and radiate in all the glorious passion that couldn't be contained anymore.

"Trying to do what?" he asked when she stopped.

"Nothing. The keys are down in the kitchen hanging on the mail holder by the back door. You can't miss them. I'll be down in a minute. Oh and Brent I'm sorry you had to come in here and see me like this. I would have had the truck moved already if we weren't running behind." She turned her back on him in dismissal to search for the mate to her running shoe.

Brent quietly ducked out of the room to retrieve her keys but halfway down the stairs he was brought up short by the realization that Tara had apologized for torturing him with her nudity. She might be a model, he thought, but Tara Jenkins had no idea how desirable she really was. He started to go back upstairs but he couldn't. He wanted to confront her with her own stupidity but he couldn't do that either. To do so he would have to admit how much he wanted her and that was something he was not ready to do. Not yet, anyway.

Chapter Eleven

🕉

Shannon and Coco missed their flight, despite Tara's attempts to hurry them along. Luckily, there was another flight to Atlanta. From there, another to New York, but the wait was long. And at one in the afternoon Tara was tired and hungry and more than a little irritable.

Her day still wasn't over though. She had to stop at Brent's office to sign off on the plans he had drawn up. She needed to stop by and see her mother and she needed to go to the grocery store to stock up. However, since she wasn't sure where her refrigerator would be tomorrow, stocking up didn't make the slightest sense. So she would just have to settle for daily trips for whatever she was in the mood for, which sucked 'cause there were no grocery stores in the downtown area now that Delchamps had gone out of business.

On her way to Brent's office, Tara sighed. She needed to go to the Super Wally-World for a few things and since she could buy food there too, there was no sense in going anywhere else. Nor was there any sense in driving halfway across town to see her mother then coming back to shop. She would skip visiting her mother today and that was all there was to it. Nevertheless, the guilt ate at her all through the meeting with Hutch.

"Brent is out at one of the sites. I paged him the moment you drove up as he requested so he should be in soon. He's only up on North Schillinger, five minutes tops." Tara noticed the dreamy expression on Hutch's face. It was the same dreamy expression Coco was wearing that morning, when she had interrupted their cozy conversation on her front porch.

What a time for Coco to fall in love with Mr. Right, Tara thought enviously. Hutch was a good man. He was financially stable, he had a good job and he was nice-looking to boot. All that Tara had ever hoped for in a man, so why hadn't she been the one to fall for Hutch instead of... No, she squelched that thought. She hadn't fallen for anyone, especially not a man so incredibly gorgeous he had women practically drooling over him.

She heard the outside door whoosh open and the back of her neck began to tingle; she didn't need to turn around to know who was in the lobby. *Speak of the devil*, she thought echoing Shannon's words from the night before. Her body hummed with anticipation or dread. She couldn't tell which. She wished that Hutch could have handled the last details without Brent.

"Hey, you made it," Brent said as he popped the top on a can of soda. Tara turned at the sound and took in the sweat-covered male who took up the entire door. Her heart pitter-pattered in her chest and the task of breathing becoming difficult. His shirt was unbuttoned showing off his tanned chest and Tara noticed that the scrape he'd gotten under her house the other day was scabbed over. And remembered the almost-kiss they'd shared after he'd gotten it and stifled a moan. No. She was not attracted to him in the slightest.

"I just left the airport. They missed their flight." Tara heard Hutch swivel in his chair behind her. She knew if he'd known, he would have been there to see Coco off. She had never believed in love at first sight but the way those two were acting, she decided there might be something to it. "So I'm running late."

"It's all right. I know you probably have things to do, so let's go into my office and get the paperwork done. Is everything ready, Hutch?"

"I put the contract on your desk and the blueprint of her kitchen remodel is on top of your filing cabinet where you left it. So run along, I can entertain myself."

Inside, Brent closed the door and went through the ritual of cleaning off a space for Tara to sit, the photo of Kelly gone now, she noticed, probably still hidden away in a drawer somewhere. There was no satisfaction in the discovery, only sadness.

The discovery left her numb and she couldn't concentrate as well as she should when Brent walked her through the plans he'd drawn up.

But she did catch the basics. Large sections of the wall leading into the dining room were gone leaving the two rooms gloriously open. The old pantry along with the space beneath the stairs would be torn out and replaced with the half bath she wanted downstairs. Perfect, all so perfect, even the southwestern feel in the material samples Brent showed her were exactly what she wanted. All she had left to do was decide on the new appliances so that exact measurements could be made but she could do that tomorrow, he assured her.

"Tara." Setting the rolled blueprint aside, Brent fixed a concerned gaze on her. "What's the matter? If you don't like something I can change it."

"No," Tara blinked away her preoccupation and gave him her full attention. "No don't change anything. It's everything I wanted."

"Then what is it? You're not completely here. Is the company not to your liking? I know I'm dirty but…"

"Dirt doesn't bother me." Lord no, a little dirt and sweat on the man was not a bother at all.

"Then what is it? I've never seen you so withdrawn before. I know we hardly know each other but…"

"Coco has a lump in her breast and she's four years younger than me. Plus I think she just fell in love with your partner. What if it's cancer, Brent? What if it's too late for her? How can she fall in love now how can she…?" She stopped as a sob escaped. "How can I let that man sit in there spinning fantasies of a life with a woman who might be dying? How can I face this new life I want so much when I should go to New York to be with Coco? How can this happen to her? She's so young?"

The tears she couldn't let go the night before fell freely now. "It's not fair, it's not fair."

"Shh, honey." Brent came around his desk and knelt on the floor in front of her. He grasped her hands and pulled her to him where Tara gave in to her grief and dissolved into a puddle. "Life isn't fair Tara, you know that. Coco's young and healthy. She'll pull through this. Women twice her age do it all the time, you'll see. And you know the saying about what doesn't kill us makes us strong. She'll be a better person for it. But you have to make your own decisions about your life. Will it be here in Mobile? Or is it in New York? Only you can decide that Tara. What do you want to do?"

"I want to go to school. I want to be a schoolteacher and I want to teach kindergarten." She grasped the edges of his open shirt in her fist tugging to make her point. "How dare she do this to me when I was about to begin that dream!"

"See I knew you were kindergarten teacher material," he chuckled, ignoring her selfish proclamation. Tara wasn't selfish, that he could see, but her loyalties were being tested. Anyone would feel the same. He felt her sigh, her breath warm against his neck. He fought back the desire that plagued him constantly lately. She needed comforting not molesting. "When do you start school?"

"Winter term in January."

"When will Coco have her surgery?" he asked remembering his aunt's bout with the cancer.

"Next week, more than likely."

"Now see there, she will be completely healed by the time school starts. Tara you don't have to choose. You fly to New York once or twice when she needs you most and then you get on with your new life."

"But I feel so selfish. I feel so useless. she needs all the support she can get and I'm not there."

"Tara, what is important is what matters to you more and if Coco doesn't understand that then that makes her the selfish one, not you. Your willingness to give up what's important to run back to be with her proves that. But you shouldn't. She will have more family and friends around just getting in the way. So go when you're needed most."

"I know you're right. Anyway, I can't pick up and leave right now. My mother needs me more. My brother needs me here now too. I can't run off and leave them."

"What's wrong with your mother?" Brent asked startled. It was the first he'd heard of her having family here.

"Alzheimer's," Tara whispered, silent tears slipping down to mingle with the others in Brent's shirt. "She doesn't know who I am anymore. If only I'd never gone to New York all those years ago. I spent the last good years of her life running around the world, and for what? To sell fat chick clothes."

"You're feeling sorry for yourself Tara. I bet your mom was so proud of you. You made something of yourself. So you weren't a brain surgeon or anything like that but you didn't get pregnant when you were eighteen and end up working at Mickey D's like so many women down here do. Like my wife did," Brent said feeling her self-pity transfer to him.

"You had to get married then?" Tara asked feeling her own misery fade away as he nodded. "At least you married her. You took responsibility and so many men don't anymore."

"I guess but sometimes I wish I hadn't…" Brent said, gently pushing her away before he revealed more than he should about his failure as a husband.

"Why? You had a beautiful baby girl." Tara stopped when she saw him wince.

"She was the second. Kelly lost the first baby while I was away with the baseball team. Auburn won the regional title that year while my wife miscarried our child. I was eighteen and she was seventeen. We had no business having a baby but I never thought we wouldn't. Betsy came along a few years later. I think it was Kelly's way of trying to hold our marriage together. Betsy did for a while. Lord I miss that little girl. She was the best thing I ever created."

"Now who's feeling sorry for themselves." Tara stood from the chair. Two steps had her standing behind Brent, her hand on his shoulder as she came up beside him to rest her cheek against her hand. "We're a pair, aren't we? We've got everything we ever wanted but can't stop the 'if only' from breaking us down."

"I guess, but you aren't responsible for your mother's or Coco's conditions." Brent said, all the misery he'd tried so hard to suppress these last few months settled so thick in his chest he couldn't breathe.

"Neither are you responsible for the loss of… I mean, sorry, forget I said that." She turned to leave, guilt eating at her for bringing him down to her level. She should have never broken down like that. "Thanks for the shoulder, Brent," she said when he turned to look at her, the misery in his eyes killing her. "I'm sorry for burdening you. I'll see you later, okay." She waved as she ducked out of the office missing the wave he gave her in return.

He turned back to the window to think about what she'd said. Maybe just maybe, she was right. Maybe he wasn't to blame for the tragedies in his life. But it sure felt like it from his end.

* * * * *

Tara went to bed that night with a heavy heart. She couldn't shake the sadness that had settled over her that day. Guilt that couldn't be shaken compounded the sadness after visiting with her mother late that evening and going out with Tommy and his wife. Randi, Tommy's second wife announced her pregnancy. She was younger than Tara. Tommy deserved to be happy she reminded herself. After all, he'd been here all those years dealing with their mother's failing health while his first bitch of a wife drove him crazy. He was forty-two and expecting his first child. Tara should be happy for him and she would have been if they hadn't talked funeral arrangements for their mother too.

It was late when she'd gotten home to find her kitchen completely missing. All that was left were the four walls, the ripped vinyl on the floor and the stove and fridge. She'd left Brent a key with the painters, one he'd made good use of. She pulled a bottle of water from the fridge and trudged up the stairs. There was too much upheaval in her life but at least this would soon pass.

* * * * *

Two white lacquered coffins sat at the front of the church, one of them so very tiny it made her heart hurt. Tara gulped back a sob as her gaze rested on the familiar dark head in the front row. He sat straight and slightly apart from those next to him as he listened to the words meant to comfort. Tara knew immediately the agony he was in and she could feel it all the way in the back of the church where she sat.

The church was far from full but it was a large sanctuary and the man sat apart from the others in his row. All four heads were the same shade of brown as his. His family, she realized. She knew him well enough now to recognize the stiffness in his posture. And realized in that instant that he didn't want his family's support or sympathy instead, he seemed more inclined to hold his grief inside even then.

"This is my last visit to you, Tara. Have you a decision for me?" the woman asked and Tara looked over to see a black veil where once there had been a white one. "I've given you plenty of time to decide. So what is it to be? Will you let him go on like this for the rest of his life? He will. He's just that bull-headed."

"I know," Tara, returned her attention to the front row, where he was shaking away the comforting hand of the woman next to him, shaking away his mother's comfort. "I can't let him go on like this, I can't. I'll do anything you ask. Just tell me what you did that was so wrong, so I can end his misery."

"In time, Tara Jenkins, that will be revealed to you," she said and Tara turned to meet her eyes, the veil keeping her from determining the color before the woman faded away right before Tara's eyes. The church began to fade and Tara found herself floating above the room as the odor of rotten magnolia blooms assailed her and she fell through the black void left after the church was gone.

Chapter Twelve

ॐ

It was morning, Tara noticed. Not that she could help it what with the pink tint of dawn peeking through her curtains and all. And strangely enough, the scent of magnolias dying on the tree hung in the air. She'd dreamed again but what she had dreamed was just as elusive as the last time. Though for the life of her, she couldn't shake the thought that somehow this dream was important. But try as she might, she couldn't remember.

The air in the room was cold so she reached for her robe, tying the belt tight against her body. She had to get going. There were things to do and she was wasting daylight. Tara stopped halfway to the bathroom. She couldn't think of a single thing that she had to do that day. Except do the grocery shopping she'd put off the day before and she shuddered tugging the robe tighter around her body to ward off the fear that crawled over her skin.

* * * * *

Another two crewmen called in with the flu that morning. Fortunately though, the first two to succumb were healthy and coming back to work. But that still left them with eight men out. Brent stood on his front porch drinking the last of his coffee. He was tired of feeling as if he were being pulled in a million directions at once. Was it just last week he'd been moaning about the lack of work? He wondered as he set the cup inside, then closed and locked the door on his way out to work.

He had wanted to spend that entire day stripping Tara's kitchen but he couldn't. Now he would spend the day at the Millers' trying to keep that small job on schedule. This evening he could break away early as he'd done the day before, when he'd been able to strip all the cabinets out of Tara's kitchen with little problem. It helped that she hadn't been there to distract him. As it was, this constant lusting after her was getting old, fast.

He had to stop by on his way to work to let Tara know his plans. Of course, he had promised her the use of his kitchen while hers was unusable, which he could find no other way to do than to give her the key to his house. But he couldn't quite force his feet to take him across the hedge to her front door; he didn't want to see her in those fuzzy pink slippers with the bunny ears poking up. He didn't want to think about what she might be wearing under that faded gray robe. He didn't want to see himself reflected in her glasses or, the worst of all tortures, itch to run his fingers through her sleep-tousled hair.

He heard a muffled curse coming from the direction of Tara's house and he walked to the end of his porch to see if the painters had arrived yet. They were making good progress he admitted and the slate blue paint Tara had chosen for the main color suited the old house. But it wasn't the painters that were cussing next door he discovered much to his delight and dismay.

Tara knelt on the ground at the side of the house, her curvy backside swaying from side to side as she dug in the wet earth. Brent moaned. It was more than his lust-besieged mind could stand and he was seriously going to have to do something about it soon if he ever expected to function normally again.

"Tara!" He cut off that train of thought before he found himself sinking into his favorite fantasy. The one where she came to him dressed in nothing but bunny slippers and gray robe. Tara jumped and cursed again this time loud enough for him to hear. Still chuckling at the obscenity that puckered her lips, he vaulted the railing.

"Yeah." She dropped the garden shovel into the dirt of a long neglected flowerbed and tugged off her garden gloves, dropping them beside the spade. Brent thought he detected a bit of irritation in her voice but it wasn't echoed in her welcoming smile.

"Meet me by the back gate," he called as he walked through the wet grass, pulling the back door key off his key ring as he went.

At the gate Brent waited for her to hop the hedge and join him before he went in. "I promised you my kitchen remember? I thought you'd like the key so you can use it whenever you need to." He led her up to his back porch and the back door that opened into his kitchen.

"You don't have to do this, Brent. I can eat takeout for awhile," Tara argued but Brent ignored her as he placed the key in her palm and showed her how to shut off the alarm. "This really is not necessary. Oh for Pete's sake. I could be a serial killer for all you know!"

"So could I. Remember, I have your house key, too. And besides, I have ulterior motives." He fought the urge to reach out and capture a lock of her hair. She was so close and she smelled of soap and sunshine and wet earth. She stood in front of him leaning against the kitchen door her eyes held fast to his and he wanted to stay that way for eternity if he could.

"How ulterior?" she asked, her smile wide and teasing as she leaned a bit toward him. Leaned enough that her lips were close enough to capture with little trouble. Lips that were bare and pink and maybe a little pouty, he thought as he shifted his gaze back to her eyes.

"Make enough for me," he whispered as if it were a great secret.

"Oh, okay sure," she said leaning back against the wall. She seemed disappointed as if she had expected something else, which left Brent feeling as if he'd stepped over the finely drawn line of male-female jobs again.

"I'm sorry. That was out of line. I could get my own meals." He backed away too wondering why he was trying so hard to stay in her good graces.

"No, it's fine, I don't mind. It's been a long time since I cooked for more than just myself. I wonder if I still remember how?" Tara stepped out onto the porch, his key clutched tight in her hand. Her face blushed a rosy red and Brent felt desire tingle to his fingertips. He felt his own blush start then as he fought down the urge to grab her and lick away her embarrassment, starting at her pretty cheeks and ending where the color stopped beneath her shirt. "What do you like?"

Brent stifled a moan. His mind, in a sexual heat, had turned the innocent question into something carnal. "Anything, I'm not picky."

"I'll leave you something in the oven for when you get home." She stepped off the porch into the wet grass and hurried to the gate. "Bye and thanks."

Brent lifted his hand in a wave and she waved back just before disappearing from sight. He leaned against the door for a moment longer cursing himself for the fool that he was. He wanted her too damned much. So much that he couldn't stop when he knew he was making a fool of himself. He shook off the sticky remains of idiocy and locked the house. He had to get to work. Had to pound his frustrations out on something solid before he found himself giving into his baser urges and pounding those frustrations out on his neighbor.

* * * * *

"Idiot, idiot, idiot!" Tara leaned against her own back door her heart beating a war dance in her chest. What did you think he meant? That he was going to ask you out, maybe declare a crazy desire to kiss you. "Idiot! Men like him aren't interested in women like you. He likes them slim and petite. Amazons need not apply." Her heart stopped racing as she sabotaged her self-esteem and felt the tears prickle in her eyes. When had she let what one Neanderthal thought of her come to matter so much?

Could she feed him? Yes, she could feed him and it was only fair after monopolizing his kitchen to feed her own ample body. Self-destruction was something at which she had always excelled. Tara went upstairs to wash up. She needed to make that trip to the grocery store she'd been putting off but first she needed to see what Brent might have in his fridge. Which she couldn't do until he left for work and as if on cue she heard his truck engine start. Great, she already had the sound memorized. So much for her vow to never build castles without foundations.

Chapter Thirteen

ເວ

Significant progress was made on the Millers' kitchen remodel that afternoon. Brent, impatient to get the job done, pulled an extra man off the mini-mall job to fill in. Between the two of them and the one new crewmember they were able to get the new bay window installed completely that afternoon, as well as the new cupboards and the island cabinetry.

Tomorrow the electricians would come to do the new wiring and then he and his crew would install the new flooring and appliances. All that remained were the countertops, the new plumbing and finally, the painting. One more day, two tops and it would be complete on schedule, just in time for the Millers' return from their stay at The Grand. A feeling of pride washed over him as he surveyed the almost finished room. This would have been enough to hold him if he hadn't worked through lunch in an effort to stay on schedule.

His stomach growling reminded him of Tara and dinner, and her kitchen. And lust...

Boy what a way to end the day, he sighed as he climbed into his truck to start the trek home. Hopefully by then the grumbling in his stomach would wipe the lust clean from his mind.

Cross-town traffic was a bitch and a half. A wreck on the interstate had traffic backed up for miles. Brent pulled off the main highway to take the longer route home but even that route was slow going. Of course, it being a Friday night would explain a lot and here he was going home just to work some more. Where *had* he misplaced his life?

At home, he breathed deeply. The mouthwatering aroma of barbecue perfumed the air in his little cottage. He dropped his mail and his briefcase on the foyer table and ignored the flashing answering machine as he followed his nose to the kitchen.

Tara stood at the sink slicing yellow summer squash in French fry-like slivers. "Mmm, that smells heavenly," Brent said by way of a greeting as he took in her appearance. Dressed in a pair of cotton khaki pants that stopped mid-calf and a bright emerald green tank top thingy, she looked heavenly. She was barefoot, he noticed because he had tripped over her shoes by the door. And her hair was twisted into a sort of ponytail fastened by one of those large spring-loaded clip things that gave him the willies.

"Hey, you're home..." Tara said breathlessly. She had hoped he would show up before she left but hadn't really expected him to. "Thanks. I hope you don't mind barbecued chicken?"

"Barbecued chicken is without a doubt on my list of top forty favorite edibles right behind burgers but in front of pizza."

"The sauce is from a bottle. I just didn't have time to whip some up from scratch. I was planning on fried squash but I can fix it some other way if you don't like it that way."

"Nope that's fine. My grandma used to fry squash. My mom hated it, so I haven't had any since I was a kid." Small talk about food, it seemed so comfortable, so domestic. Brent backed up suddenly. He didn't like the way this felt. He wanted to run fast in the other direction until she was gone. "I'm gonna go wash up some, okay? Don't wait on me. I might be awhile. I'm wearing enough drywall dust to choke a horse."

"Okay sure," Tara said as she watched him retreat out of the kitchen at a fast clip. She felt his unease this time and realized how cozy and domestic her being here in his kitchen in her bare feet must seem to him. She couldn't help it if the man had a problem with her, couldn't help it at all she told herself as she went back to slicing the squash. The oil was ready and she just needed to lightly salt and flour the vegetable. The unmistakable sound of the shower came from down the hall and Tara stopped tossing the flour-coated slices. He was showering.

He'd warned her but she hadn't thought about him being naked. *Naked* with a few feet of thin drywall being the only thing separating them.

"Get a grip, Tara," she warned herself as she turned on the radio Brent kept on the counter by the fridge and cranked up the volume to drown out the sound of the shower. "That's better." She added a handful of floured squash to the hot oil. After the commercials, Garth Brooks came on the radio with his song about a woman who was waiting in her kitchen for her husband in nothing but her apron. Tara groaned. The image was all too clear. But instead of some obscure-faced woman, Tara saw herself standing there in a red "Kiss the Cook" apron. And Brent standing in the door in a big Garth-style black hat. The image was way too vivid when the man who haunted her fantasies was way too close and oh-so naked.

Yet she didn't change the channel. She liked country music too and she hoped the formula of only one sappy love song in a set still applied. No such luck. The DJ seemed to be on a sappy love song kick that evening.

The hot oil sizzled. The squash began to turn golden brown and the music changed again, this time to a fast-paced love song. Somebody sure liked love songs and Tara's skin tingled. She was listening for him to leave the bathroom wondering, what he would be wearing? Would his hair be wet? Would water droplets cling to his shoulders and back? He would smell all clean and male? He probably used soaps without the perfume. His hair would stick up in spikes. She could picture him strolling so casually from the bathroom with a crisp white towel wrapped around his waist leaving wet footprints on the floor as he went. Those broad tanned shoulders of his, bare and just begging for her touch.

"I think the squash is burning," the subject of her very vivid fantasy whispered He was so close she could feel his breath on her ear. She shivered, embarrassed to be caught daydreaming by him. "Where were you just now?"

"Nowhere. I was just thinking about…stuff. I went job-hunting today. I'm looking for a makeup artist position at the TV stations," she answered hurriedly trying to steer the topic far away from mentally ogling his nude body. If he knew, he would laugh and she would die a thousand deaths right on the spot.

"Do you need money Tara? What about the modeling and school?" Brent asked stealing one of the squash fries she scooped out of the oil before it had a chance to cool.

"Well, yes and no. I have a nice nest egg saved up, which would see me through a few years without having to work. That is if I didn't do any work on the house and if I didn't plan to go to school this winter." Tara answered honestly as she refilled the frying pan with more vegetables. "I bought the house outright and I paid off my truck two years ago, so I'm not in danger of going into bankruptcy any time soon. I'd just like to eat on a daily basis and pay the utilities without touching my savings is all."

"There are always places like Glamour Photos in the mall." Brent opened a cabinet, took out two plates and walked over to the table. "Or private photography places all over town that could probably use a talented makeup woman."

"You think?"

"Tell you what, if you can't find a job painting faces then I'll have to hire you to paint walls." Brent teased as he laid out placemats and flatware on the table.

"Deal." Forgetting her embarrassment, she turned to face him, which was a mistake for he was wearing only a pair of faded jeans, his hair, indeed, wet and spiky. She felt her face flame up all over again. His torso was bare and tanned with a light smattering of dark hair curling on his chest, forming a vee that ran down the center of his flat belly and disappeared behind his jeans. She'd forgotten how devastatingly lethal he could be without his shirt.

Tiny ripples of need swam a marathon through her body and her mouth went dry then wet then dry again. "Um, your chest…looks to be healing nicely." *Stupid, stupid, stupid!* Now he *knows* you were checking his body out! "I see you haven't gotten stuck under any more joists lately."

"Not lately." Brent laughed as he filled glasses with ice and poured sweet tea into them. Tara returned her attention to the stove grateful to have something to keep her busy. Was it hot in here or was it just her?

"There's potato salad in the fridge. If you wouldn't mind getting it out we'll be ready to eat in a couple of minutes."

"No problem," Brent replaced the tea pitcher in the refrigerator and located the sealed bowl of salad. The cold air inside a welcome relief to the heat of the kitchen. Heat that he had never felt before in all the years he'd lived here. Heat that could only be attributed to this runaway case of lust that wouldn't leave him alone.

God, she was making him crazy in that green silky top that clung to her breasts as he imagined water would. He could see the lace of her bra outlined beneath the fabric. He wanted to open the freezer and climb in before he did something foolish like ripping her blouse off and seeing if her bra was white like the last time or something much more…

The oven door slamming jolted him out of that fantasy in the nick of time. "Need any help with that?" he asked in hopes of taking his mind off the dessert he craved in the place of supper.

"No. Everything is fine here." Tara couldn't look his way again, for fear he would see the lust shining in her eyes and laugh at her. "To cut down on dishes afterward, I thought we could serve ourselves from here, without bringing everything over to the table. Everything is ready if you are."

"Oh of course," Brent closed his eyes. God but he was more than ready to explode from just wanting her.

"Ah, crap!" He heard Tara hiss at the same time as something metal hit the stovetop. He unclenched his eyes in time to see her rush for the sink and turn the cold water on.

"What happened?" His heart pounded furiously as he rushed to help.

"Just a little grease splatter, that's all." She held her left thumb under the soothing water. "Nothing to worry about. See? All better." She held up the offending digit with its two very pink splotches.

"Are you sure? Would you like some ice or something?"

"I'm sure. Don't worry about it, happens all the time. But thanks…for worrying, I mean. It's been a long time since anyone worried about me like that." She wanted him to care for her just as he did now, forever. What was that old fairy rhyme, she wondered? *If wishes were horses beggars would ride.* "Let's eat before the food gets cold."

They sat across from one another at the small table in Brent's kitchen. Tara picked at her food while Brent tore into his as if he were starving. "Miss Belle, from across the street, made the potato salad. She told me a lot about you." Ooh great going Tara. Let him think you were pumping the woman for information. Smooth move.

"Really. I thought I recognized the taste. What did she have to tell you? Nothing too embarrassing, I hope." Brent cut into his third piece of chicken.

"Only what a little terror you were as a child but she didn't tell me how she knew you and I didn't ask." Tara busied herself with her own piece of chicken cutting it into tiny slivers.

"I'm the youngest of four kids. I have two older brothers and a sister. My mom was a stay-at-home mommy. You know, devoting her life to all us kids and her husband. I came along just ten months after my next-oldest brother. And, well, two pregnancies that close together had taken a toll on her weight, you know how it is." Brent said with a shrug. It was old news, something he didn't like to talk about but wasn't a deep dark secret and since Tara was asking him and not the neighbors, he would tell her.

"My dad worked for a big law firm in town that had offices in New Orleans and Atlanta as well, where he could be sent at any given moment. Anyway, after I was born he decided that he didn't like having a dowdy little wife and four kids who constantly needed attention and he walked out. This was back before women had much recourse against their deadbeat husbands so she went to work at Delchamps Grocery as a checker. Miss Belle lived next door and, being the wonderful woman that she is, she took care of me and my brother all day while my mom worked and the older two were in school. She did it for nothing, too. Without her, I'm not sure what would have happened to us. So she got to know me pretty well in those years and let's just leave it at that."

"I'm sorry. I didn't mean to pry."

"It's okay, Tara, really. I have no memory of my dad. He never came back to see us. I think he is living in Atlanta but you know I could walk up on him on the street and wouldn't know him from Adam. So when Miss Belle's sons all pitched in and bought her that house five years ago, I did the remodel for the cost of material. I felt like I owed it to her and her family for helping us when we needed it."

"Your dad ought to be shot for leaving like that." Tara forgot her nervousness as anger took its place. "Where's your mom now?"

"She became a successful real estate agent and remarried ten years ago. Now she and my stepfather live in a big RV. I think they are in Arizona right now, next week they could be in Vegas. She calls every day or two to let me know. She's happier than I ever remember. She loves Mike and she's getting to see the world. I can't think of a more deserving woman."

"Good for her. What about your brothers and sister, where are they?"

"Scattered here and there. Caleb my next-up brother is in the Navy, serving on an aircraft carrier somewhere in the Middle East. Darren the oldest of us all is in Seattle working for

Microtech. And Laura is in DC lobbying for better public school funding."

"Boy, talk about a bunch of underprivileged kids!" Tara said to tease him as she finished her supper and started to clear away the dishes, stacking them in the sink. "Your mom must be very proud of what the four of you turned out to be."

"Laura and Darren are enough to make any mama proud don't you think?"

"A computer geek and a political groupie, yeah sure I can see where she would be proud of them. But what about the son defending his country and the one who can take a worn-out old house and turn it into a showplace?" Tara said but Brent only snorted. "You don't think what you've become is worth being proud of, do you?"

"And just what is there to be proud of? I'm a dried-up drunk. My wife and daughter are dead because of my drinking. I nearly lost everything I had. I am part owner of a struggling contracting firm but even now, I struggle just to make enough money to pay my mortgage. Yeah I can work miracles with a saw and a hammer, big deal, so what. We could go under in January then I'd be back to being just another guy who can swing a hammer lined up at the big companies' doors waiting for a job. Where's the respect in that?" Brent said without anger. He sounded tired. Sad… The dishes forgotten, Tara walked over to him and placed her hand on his shoulder. She felt him stiffen at her touch but didn't move her hand. She ignored the smooth hot flesh as she spoke.

"From what I know about you I'd be proud. You realized you had a problem and you did something about it. You're sober, you're working hard to keep a business going, which is more than any of your siblings are doing. A drunk driver killed your wife and daughter. It wasn't your fault. It was just their time to go."

"That's all well and good, miss supermodel. But I know what I am. All I'll ever be is a glorified carpenter. My dreams shelved forever—" Brent stopped. He thought he had overcome his anger at having to give up baseball to become a husband and a father. But the bitterness was still there, festering just beneath the surface making him hate the life he was stuck in. And the wife he'd taken.

"Do you think I wanted to be a model? Do you think my life has been easy? True I have never been married. I have no children living or otherwise. I wanted to go to college but there wasn't enough money for that, so instead of getting a job and working my way through college, what did I do? I took my graduation money and followed a friend off to New York. She was going to be the model, not me. I was just along to make her look good, I guess. But they didn't want her, there were too many beauty queens running around up there. She was too short, too blonde, her breasts were too big and her nose too long. But me, the agent took one look at me and boom! Instant career. My friend came home and has never returned a single call or answered a letter so I stopped writing. My mother was so proud but I felt like a fraud. I was a plus-size model. Plus-size, why didn't they just call us the pretty fat chicks to our faces instead of behind our backs? I made loads of money but it costs loads of money to live in New York. So I lived in the low-rent district with three roommates. I ate cereal for dinner and slept on the sofa, some glamorous life. And in all those years I jet-setted around the world I was wasting the last good years of my mother's life. She doesn't even know my name anymore. And to top it off, I've had exactly two boyfriends in my entire life, two. And both of them made it very plain that they were just out for sex afterwards. How's that for a life? But do you see me wallowing in the muck of my own making? I haven't had a pity party, yet. I moved on. I do what I have to do even if that means putting my mother in a nursing home so that she has constant care. Even if that means working at Wal-Mart to make ends meet while I do what I should have done ten years ago."

She circled the kitchen as she spoke coming back to face him with each point made, finally stopping in front of him, glaring down at him as if he were nothing more than an insignificant ant at her feet. Brent sat there stunned to see her so angry so impassioned that he forgot his own problems. But not his lust for the dynamic wonder of a woman she was turning out to be.

"You have barbecue sauce on your chin."

"What?" After all that, the complete change of mood startled him. He's been expecting her to…what? Run from the room pouting?

"You have sauce on your— Never mind. Hold still," Tara licked the tip of her finger and swiped at the red smear on his chin, her touch so whisper light, so tender, so electric that the air was sucked from his lungs. Her clear green gaze licked over his face to lock with his and he shuddered with desire.

"Kiss me," he said, his voice strained with need.

"What?" It was Tara's turn to be dumbfounded.

"Kiss me, Tara. Please?" He sounded pathetic to his own ears but he needed to taste her so badly. He just couldn't make himself act on the urge. He couldn't bear it if she walked away leaving him feeling like a fool.

"I ca—" Tara wanted to argue and she wanted to run before he made a fool out of her too. But she couldn't. She wanted him so bad she didn't care if he only wanted to kiss her to shut her up. But the pleading she heard in his voice confused her. Her finger lingered on his chin and her mouth inched closer, the word "can't" forming again.

"Please! I need you to kiss me." She leaned over him where he sat at the table still, running her finger up his jawline to his hair where the other fingers joined in to hold him captive.

"Okay," she breathed out as she lowered her mouth, gently touching her lips to his. She whimpered against his lips, her eyes never leaving his and Brent knew he was lost.

"Kiss me," he breathed against her mouth and she again grazed her lips across his.

It wasn't enough. He had to have her lips pressed tight to his. He had to know how she tasted, how she felt in his arms as she trembled with need. "Kiss me."

This time her lips met his, fusing to his would be more accurate, and he allowed himself to touch her. Carefully placing one hand on each hip, he pulled her closer. She straddled his legs and he pulled her closer still until she sat, her body pressed full length against his. His hands held her tight as he closed his eyes and drowned in her kiss forgetting his own name as the fire she ignited in him threatened to melt them both.

"Oh God," Tara breathed. She never knew a kiss could be like this. She had no idea how she had gotten onto his lap but she wasn't about to move away. She had wanted to know the feel of him, the taste of him for so long now that not even an earthquake could shake her from that spot. Her hands roamed along his bare back as if she were trying to memorize the feel of him just in case he came to his senses and sent her away.

Molten waves of need washed through her in a way that frightened her. His hands stroked a path along her back exploring the flesh beneath her blouse. She trembled and burned with every touch, yet at the same time she longed for the clothing barrier to disappear. She needed to feel his skin pressed to hers, needed to feel everything.

She wrapped her arms around his shoulders and pressed herself shamelessly against him to ease the ache in her breasts. Her mouth melded to his feasting as if she were starving. It was too much. It wasn't enough. She wanted to feel that ridge that pressed between her legs without her pants in the way. She wanted to stay this way forever, afraid that anything more would be unbearable. He freed the clasp of her bra yet his hands stayed on her back to stroke the skin he had just uncovered. His teeth caught her bottom lip, drawing it into his mouth to suckle, finally breaking the kiss that had threatened to suffocate her.

"Touch me," she whispered against his mouth. "Touch me here." She guided his hands to her chest allowing him enough room between them to explore. This time it was Brent who whimpered when she placed his hands on her breasts. It was Brent who moaned when she urged him to stroke. She rocked her body along his jeans-covered erection in time with his strokes. Sweat beaded on his brow as he fought to retain some semblance of control or he would take her right here at the kitchen table with the remains of their supper lying around them.

"Hold on," he said breaking the kiss long enough to capture her round bottom and stand. Tara instinctively wrapped her legs around his waist careful not to lose the exquisite feel of him and let him carry her out of the kitchen and down the hall to his room. As long as his mouth was on hers, she didn't care where he carried her.

As he laid her on his bed, the clip holding her hair snapped in two halves but neither Tara nor Brent noticed.

"I want..." Tara started to whisper but she never got the chance. Brent transferred his kisses to her neck robbing her of speech. He trailed hot silken kisses along her arched throat. His busy hands stripped away her blouse and bra, only pausing long enough on his journey south to slide the material over her head.

He explored her newly bared skin with his hands, gently clasping her nipples between his thumb and forefinger and squeezing slightly. She arched her body, tiny delicate moans escaping her lips as she rocked against him. He felt himself grow harder in response to her stroking and answered her moan with one of his own.

He couldn't bear it any longer. He needed everything she had to offer and he needed it now. Latching on to one nipple, he suckled until she arched beneath him.

"Love me Brent," she pleaded, "Love me now."

The button on her pants came undone easily enough and he slid the zipper down and slipped his hand inside her pants, beneath her cotton panties and into her hot wetness. He found that one delicate spot and stroked. She went still beneath him, her arms locked tight around his body holding on for dear life while he took her to paradise.

The sound of glass shattering across the room brought reality crashing down on him and Brent propelled himself off the woman lying in his bed. The large, framed wedding portrait of him and Kelly laid face out on the dresser directly across from him. Glass from it and a lamp spread out across the surface. Brent watched as one large jagged shard fell to the carpet below.

What the hell was he doing? He raked his fingers through his hair. Was he completely insane? He didn't have anything in the form of protection in the house and he doubted very much if Tara had come prepared. Tara!

He looked down at the woman lying on the bed. Her eyes were shaded as she watched him pace the small area. Her body shamelessly uncovered as if she expected him to return, his body still throbbing with need. And for one split second, he considered ignoring the warnings to finish what he had started. But the portrait of Kelly staring out at him made that impossible. She wasn't smiling, as she should have been, it was almost as if she knew he had brought another woman into their bed.

"Brent?" Something had happened to destroy the mood before they could go any further and she wasn't exactly sure what it was.

"I'm so sorry. I shouldn't have… We shouldn't have. Tara, I don't have a condom. I…" Tara felt dizzy at this admission. How could she have been so completely wrapped up in getting out of her clothes that she hadn't stopped to think about protection? Tara crossed her arms over her chest and sat up. She found her top on the floor and pulled it over her head forgetting the lacy bra that Brent had kicked under the bed.

"I… It's okay. No harm done, nothing happened that we would regret later." Tara said unable to shake the feeling that nothing would happen between them ever again. The skin on the back of her neck prickled and she reached up to smooth it down. "I have dishes to do."

"Yeah, um…I'll be next door if you need me." Brent grabbed a T-shirt and work boots and fled the room, escaping to the safe world of work, leaving her alone to straighten out her clothing and this new mess she'd made of her life.

After he left, Tara sat on the bed shaking with unspent emotion. She was confused and maybe a little frightened. It was just sex, she told herself, that's all. But what if it wasn't? What if she had let herself want more than just a convenient roll in the hay every once in a while? What then? She couldn't let this happen again. Couldn't let him close enough to hurt her if it were all just sex to him. And she was sure that was all that it was; after all, sex was sex to every man she'd ever met.

She felt that peculiar prickling sensation at the back of her neck again. A touch of fear raced through her and she studied the room more closely noticing for the first time that the blinds on the window were partially open. Half afraid that someone was outside looking in, she stood and peered out into the inky night but saw nothing. Just her house, where a dull light shone from one of the upstairs bedrooms and Tara tried to remember if she'd left one on. But she couldn't remember even going upstairs that afternoon.

Odd, so very odd. Maybe Brent was moving around up there.

That was it, just Brent looking for the breaker box or something. She rubbed her bare arms and turned to leave the room but the fallen portrait on the dresser caught her attention.

So that was it then. The reason Brent had flown away in a panic. His wife had come between them again. Tara walked out of the room and closed the door behind her. God help the woman who ever does fall for Brent Chambliss. Living with his wife's ghost wasn't the best way to have a happy life.

* * * * *

A shape formed in the window of the second upstairs bedroom in the old Victorian. Dressed in white she looked out across the azalea hedge and into the room that had once been hers and laughed. She was all-powerful even if she couldn't leave her prison. One well-aimed thought had brought an end to her beloved's intentions.

And the woman was just far enough in love with him that she would be willing to do anything that was asked of her. All in the name of healing the wounded soul of the man she was fast falling in love with. She laughed again when the woman spotted her. And though she knew she couldn't be seen, Kelly shimmered once more before fading into the dark. The woman would be very afraid before this was all over. She would make sure of that.

Chapter Fourteen

৪৩

Five days.

Brent pounded his hammer into the old plaster wall hard enough to shake the rafters.

Five days, in which he hadn't seen Tara once. She came and went before he could get home, always leaving a plate of something in the oven for him. And another thing, he couldn't remember when his kitchen had been so clean. She'd even vacuumed for him a couple of times. He didn't like it. Not one bit. It felt too much like a maid service when what he really wanted was...

He stopped pounding the wall, the hammer suspended mid-swing. What he really wanted was... He didn't have a clue. Sex was the easy answer but for some reason, it just didn't seem right. Not after last week's embarrassing episode in his bedroom. Obviously, this was the reason Tara was giving him the silent treatment. He slammed the wall again sending dust raining down on him from above.

A thud from the front of the house snapped him out of his reverie and he shook the dust off. Footsteps pounding on the stairs behind the wall he was working on echoed like thunder inside the closed-in space.

Tara was home.

The three little words echoed through his brain causing him to grow at once cold and hot. Tara was home. After five days she was in the same house as him, within shouting distance and -if he made the effort to crawl out of the old pantry—within touching distance.

Brent had never thought of himself as a coward but the very fact that she was within touching distance scared him spitless. There was no way he was going to follow her up those stairs. No way he was going to get anywhere near that bedroom of hers, just to say hi, when all he wanted to do was finish what he started five nights ago.

Okay, so maybe he did know what he wanted after all and maybe it did begin with an *s* and end with an *x* and have an *e* in the middle. Was that so terribly wrong? Yes, rang out as he made another gash in the pantry wall.

* * * * *

Upstairs, Tara listened to the sound of Brent pounding away at something and for a brief moment, she wished she had a hammer. She felt a powerful need to do some pounding of her own. For five long days, she had stayed away, wanting to give him time to come to terms with what he wanted from her. Sex was the first word that came to mind, sex she was more than willing to give him with no strings attached. But somehow that didn't sit right. She knew there was more to what was between them. It wasn't sex that had come between them that night but something deeper, something more defining, more binding. She knew it just as sure as she knew her own name. That Brent was running scared was obvious. He was without a doubt afraid that anything more than a passing acquaintance between them would change his life irrevocably.

So, not wanting to appear to be pushing him for something he wasn't ready to give, she stayed away. Which wasn't easy in the slightest. Several times these past few days, she had slipped out his back door to avoid him just as he was coming in the front, only to do the reverse when she heard him come in her back door. Especially since what she really wanted to was to stay and talk while he worked. But she couldn't. Not yet anyway. Even now when she had to share her home with him, she couldn't just wander down and say hi as much as she wanted to. In fact, she wouldn't have come home now except she really did want to celebrate Halloween the way she remembered it from childhood. And she had the perfect costume too. So what if there was no one to see it but a bunch of neighborhood kids?

The little trick-or-treaters would love her fairy getup for its whimsy, not to mention those great wings a friend of hers in New York had worked magic on. And maybe just maybe someone else would like it, if he stuck around long enough. She opened her makeup kit and set to work.

The pounding downstairs continued while Tara experimented with the best way to transform her normal peaches and cream complexion into that of a dainty lavender fairy without going overboard with the color. Then there was the problem of making the color last through the evening without leaving it on everything she touched.

After a few false starts she finally found the combination of powder and liquid makeup that would not only hold the color to her skin for more than a few seconds but gave her a faint lavender glow on her face and hands. Satisfied, she painted her lips hot pink. Her eyes she framed with blues and greens to resemble a set of matching peacock feathers. Her eyebrows and lashes she coated with a darker shade of purple and using the blue eye shadow as blusher to highlight her cheekbones, she felt phase one of her transformation was a success.

Turning her attention to her hair, she pulled out a comb and began to tease the shoulder-length mass into a funky bouffant, which she sprayed a bright neon purple, very reminiscent of the former paint job on her house.

Once done, she surveyed the damage in the mirror and was pleased. She certainly wasn't Tara Jenkins anymore but an attractive member of the fae variety but a fairy without wings isn't really a fairy. She needed more than just makeup and colored hairspray for that; she needed a very talented costume designer.

And Kerry Porter another modeling friend in New York had designed her dream costume. On very short notice, too. The purple nylons were the first to emerge from the box that had arrived by special delivery that very afternoon and Tara tugged them on over her underwear. Next came a skirt made of an incredibly wispy material in a lavender blue shade that resembled a Morning Glory just opening its petals to the sun. Tara pulled it on over the tights and rummaged through the tissue for the top.

The blouse, with attached wings, was green at the neckline, she noticed, slipping her arms carefully into the long fitted sleeves, which were the same shade of lavender as the tights. She did up the tiny buttons Kerry had so deftly hidden on the inside facing to give the piece a seamless look. The green at the neck stretched down in jagged points eventually giving way to more of the same lavender blue from the skirt. It fit her snugly at the neck and gradually loosened until it blended with the skirt at her waist so that no one could tell it was two pieces instead one. The skirt flowed on from there to form a scalloped bell mid-thigh, which swayed with her every movement. She glanced in the mirror for the full effect and realized for the first time that the dress really was a Morning Glory.

Next came the accessories, a darling but practical purse made out of silk Bluebells and a hot-pink ribbon studded with Bluebells that could be worn as a choker or in the hair. Last but not least a pair of hot pink slippers to match her lips.

Tara wiggled her shoulders and watched transfixed as the wings to each side of her head fluttered making it look as if she were about to fly around her room. She giggled with pure delight. Never had she had such a great costume. She would be the belle of the ball. If only there were a ball to attend, she sighed reminding herself that she had never cared much for parties before.

One quick peek out her window showed that night was swiftly setting in, The first kids would be along any time now and she needed to get a move on.

* * * * *

Downstairs, Brent pounded away at the ancient plaster, pulverizing it into dust as he beat the frustration out of his system. It was too quiet up there. Just what was she doing that took her so long?

"You know, there are easier ways to do that." He dropped the hammer and bumped his head on the beam he had just exposed. Brent whirled around biting back the foul oath he felt welling up as he rubbed his head only to be caught off guard once again.

"What the hell are you wearing? Are you purple?" he spat out with more ire than he meant to. Tara only laughed, a light tinkling sound that seemed in keeping with her dress. "And I know how to take out a wall, this way is just more—satisfying."

"Not to mention messier. I take it you don't like my costume then?" Tara pivoted on her toes to give him the full effect of Kerry's beautiful creation.

Brent stopped rubbing the knot on his head as he took in the purple vision before him. The flimsy dress looked like an upside down flower and did little to hide her curves. Her legs, which he had only seen once, seemed to mesmerize him making him want to do things that no innocent fairy should be exposed to.

"What's that getup for anyway?" He wanted to deck the guy who had the privilege of taking this particular fair fae out that night.

"For Halloween, what did you think?"

"I know what day it is," he snapped letting the jealousy overtake good sense. "Where are you off to?"

"Nowhere. I haven't spent a Halloween just giving out candy to kids in a very long time." Tara retreated self-consciously out of the kitchen to the hall closet where she had stored the goodies. Brent followed close behind and one quick look at his scowl told her he still didn't like her costume.

"You went to all the trouble to make yourself up like that just to stay home?" He didn't like what he was hearing although he had no reason to doubt her word. "Never mind, it's none of my business. I better get back to work." He walked away in a huff leaving Tara standing there with her mouth agape.

Rude. That's what he was, very rude. Why hadn't she seen it before? The man was rude and infuriating too. Apparently, five days hadn't been enough. Maybe she needed to give him more time without her company if it bothered him so much, a whole lot more time. Say forever.

The doorbell rang distracting her from her silent rant and she hauled the two large tubs of candy and toys over to the front door, opening it on her first set of trick-or-treaters, an adorable little ballerina with blond hair and a rough-looking pirate with matching curls sticking out from beneath his tricorn. Their eyes were round with awe, their mouths slightly open as they stared at her and Tara grinned.

"Happy Halloween!" She caught the eye of the kid's dad wearing the same expression as the children and her smile broadened. Exactly the look she was going for. Exactly.

As the night wore on Tara's spirits were boosted when group after group that came to her door reacted in much the same way every time. Her costume was a hit and she was glad she had worn it despite Mr. Chambliss' disapproval. But as the children became fewer and farther between Tara felt her spirits flagging. She knew it was getting very late and that the kids interested in candy were all heading home to inspect their hoard. But she didn't want the night to be over just yet.

She paced the porch restlessly. The pumpkins she had carved over the course of the last week still gave off a warm cozy glow to light her way. She found herself in front of the swing at the end of the porch. She perched in the center and pushed off with the toe of one soft slipper. Older kids raced along the street, the beams from their flashlights flickering along her porch before they disappeared from sight. Tara sighed. She wanted to follow them to see where they were going in such a hurry. She wanted to play but there was no one to play with.

She was so caught up in feeling sorry for herself that she missed the light tread of someone creeping across her porch.

"What's the story, Morning Glory?" Brent said from the shadows his voice warm and seductive to her ears.

"That is so awful, not to mention almost cliché." Tara sniffed, trying to hang onto her earlier peevishness.

"Yeah, I know. But it's oddly fitting — don't you think? — considering how you're dressed." Brent stepped into the soft glow of the nearest jack-o'-lantern. Tara continued to swing feeling the air flutter the wings back and forth.

"I thought you didn't like my outfit?"

"I never said that."

"No, but your reaction implied as much."

"I like your costume, Tara. You are without a doubt the sexiest fairy I've ever met."

"Really, then what was all that about earlier?"

"I— Damn it. I thought you were getting ready to go out with some guy and I didn't like it. After the last time we were together, I… It was a shock to the system, okay, especially considering what I've been thinking these last few days."

Tara smiled, "And just what would that be… No, don't answer that, I don't really want to know. It's over and done with."

"Yes. Over and done with," Brent agreed as a flash of bare breasts invaded his mind making him wonder if she had painted everything purple. "Listen, Tara, I was wondering if you would like to go to a party. A few of my old college friends have rented a ballroom at the Adam's Mark. I wasn't going to go but if you'd like to…"

"Are you asking me out?"

" Yes. I think I am. Tara Jenkins, would you like to go to a Halloween ball with me? I think you are guaranteed to win the prize for best costume."

"Since you put it so sweetly, I'd love to, Brent Chambliss. Just let me fetch my purse." Tara launched herself out of the moving swing seemingly to flutter in midair only to land lightly on the porch in front of Brent. "Is that what you're going to wear?" She asked taking in the work attire he still wore from the clunky boots to the heavy tool belt that rode low on his hips.

"Have you got a problem with the way I'm dressed?"

"Not if you don't," she said as she breezed past him into the house.

Brent awaited her on her front steps and together they went from pumpkin to pumpkin blowing out the candles before he escorted her to his truck.

In the dim cab light, Tara noticed that he wasn't wearing exactly what he had been before. For one thing, the dust coating his hair was gone. For another, he wore a tight white T-shirt with a pack of something rolled into the sleeve on his right arm and tight jeans that were ripped in several strategic spots. The tool belt was the same but the tools inside were plastic. His hair slicked back from a recent shower was beginning to spike as it dried.

"What are you? A reject from the Village People?" He didn't say a word. Instead he just smiled as he helped her into the truck and shut the door. Tara felt the traitorous heart in her chest begin to palpitate with excitement.

Stop it, she ordered the rogue muscle, *we are supposed to be angry with him, remember.*

Moments later, the driver side door opened and Brent tossed a shiny gold hard hat onto the console between them and climbed in. "Sorry, the damned thing wasn't where I thought it was. I had to dig through the tool chest to find it." He apologized for taking so long.

Tara picked up the hard hat and peered at her reflection in the smooth gold surface. "I take it this isn't your usual safety hat?"

"My brother Caleb sent it to me for Christmas a couple years ago; he always did have an odd sense of humor." Brent said smiling as he buckled his seatbelt and started the truck. "I hung on to it in case he ever comes home and wants to see it, that sort of thing. Never knew I'd actually wear the damned thing."

"You really are a Village People reject then aren't you?" Tara lost the fight, collapsing into a fit of full-scale giggles.

"Keep on laughing fairy woman and I'll pluck your wings," he grinned, delighted by the sound of her laughter, which seemed to caress something deep within him.

"Oh, no. My wings, I forgot," Tara leaned forward in seat. "Are they squashed?"

"They look fine," Brent said stopping at the intersection. "Just don't wiggle around too much and they should be fine. It's a short ride to the hotel, just hold your breath, okay."

Tara sucked in her breath at his suggestion but after a few seconds, she let it go and convulsed into the giggles again. "Sorry, I caught sight of myself in the mirror. I was all purple."

"I think all that makeup has gone to your head." Brent chuckled along with her, glad for the light banter.

"I think it's the purple hairspray. It's left me quite lightheaded." Tara said even as she wondered what had really caused her euphoria. Never in a million years would she guess that she enjoyed Brent's company enough to actually be her self. Usually she had to guard her real self away to avoid ridicule. But somehow Brent was different. Somehow she felt comfortable with him in a way she had never been with other men. And maybe she decided that was exactly how he felt about her, comfortable.

No wonder he was scared out of his wits.

Chapter Fifteen

ఇ

"Are you nervous?" Tara asked once they stepped onto the elevator. The good-natured teasing they had shared in the truck had suddenly given way to silent tension. "I thought this was a friend of yours?"

"He is, but we were never really of the same mind about life. He went to Auburn to party. His daddy was footing the bill. I went on a baseball scholarship, which I lost my sophomore year."

"How—? Oh…sorry." She remembered what Brent had said days before about the loss of his first child. Kelly's miscarriage had interfered with his scholarship. "Listen Brent, we don't have to go if you'd rather not; I mean, I would understand if you didn't want to show up with me as your date."

"Tara?"

"What?"

"Shut up?"

She was about to tell him where to stick his shut up when the elevator dinged open and he all but pushed her out and down the hallway.

"Hey, Brent man, I thought you weren't going to show?" A tall well-built man dressed as Caesar called out from the center of the crowded room as he jockeyed his way through the people and chairs to get to them.

"Change of plans," Brent answered as he exchanged back slaps and handshakes. "How's it going Taylor? How's the wife?"

"How the hell should I know? She left me two days ago," Taylor said with a huge grin and Tara felt an instant dislike for the man. "Who's the babe?" He looked her up and down, his eyes lingering too long in certain spots. Oh yeah, a really strong dislike.

"Taylor this is Tara. Tara, Jeff Taylor. An old friend."

"How do you do Mr. Taylor," Tara said politely letting him engulf her hand in his soft one.

"Much better now that you're here I'm sure." He eased so close to her that Tara could smell the whiskey on his breath.

"Lay off, Taylor. She's not your type." Brent said and Tara looked up in time to see a streak of something primal flash across his face.

"How do you know what my type is, Chambliss?" Jeff Taylor wanted to know and Tara felt his hand tighten on hers.

"Listen boys, I'm not interested in all this testosterone-driven crap, so for the moment just assume I'm not the right type for either of you." She didn't like feeling like a choice steak bone in front of a room full of strangers. "It was nice meeting you, Mr. Taylor." She extracted her hand from his and walked away to look for the bar.

"So what type is she?" Taylor asked once Tara was out of earshot, his interest in her not diminished in the least.

Brent sighed, "Damned if I know." And he followed her into the crowd.

Jeff Taylor lingered for a moment in the entrance sipping his drink and watching the curvaceous purple beauty walk away. His buddy Brent had always had exquisite taste in women but this time he had outdone himself. Now, how to get the exotic Tara alone later? He had something that his buddy Brent would never have and money made all the difference with women like her.

* * * * *

119

"Hey, thought I'd lost you," Brent said as he closed a protective hand around her right elbow. Tara glanced his way to make sure he was alone before deigning to speak to him.

"No chance in that happening if that fine specimen of manhood is typical of what might be lurking in this pond." She found the bar loaded with bottles of expensive alcohol and Tara knew at once that she was out of her comfort zone and possibly over her head. "What type of colas you got?" she asked the bartender and he held out a nice normal can of Classic Cola, which Tara accepted.

"Make that two." Brent said to the man and after popping the top and pouring it into the glass that followed, he pulled Tara off to the side. "I'm sorry about Jeff. He is a thirty-three year old adolescent. The wife that just left him was his fourth and I think he's hunting for number five. If he bothers you, we can go," he offered, knowing now that it had been a major mistake to bring her here.

"Don't worry about it, Brent. I was a model remember. I've been to bigger more glamorous parties than this, in bigger, more glamorous cities all over the world. Once, this Arabic prince offered me a spot in his harem. I turned him down, of course, so I think I can handle someone like Jeff Taylor."

"Really, a prince wanted you for his harem?"

"Is that so hard to believe? After all not all the countries in this world worship women who are so stick-thin their clothes look better on the hanger."

"No. I didn't mean it that way Tara. I was impressed and relieved that you didn't agree. And maybe a bit jealous." Hearing the hurt in her voice, Brent hastened to explain before she convinced herself he was ashamed to be seen with her.

"Jealous? Now I find that hard to believe."

"Tara, why do you belittle yourself like that?"

"I do not belittle myself. I know what I am. I know what people see when they look at me."

"Do you?"

"Brent, darling, I haven't seen you in forever." A tall slender woman with glossy black hair interrupted just as Tara was about to reply. Holding the glass of expensive champagne out, she air-kissed each of Brent's cheeks and Tara relaxed. Serious girlfriends don't air-kiss.

"Lydia, it has been such a long time. Tara this is Lydia. She has the honor of being the first Mrs. Taylor."

"A very youthful mistake to be sure. I've learned a great deal since then I assure you." Lydia beamed a wide red smile at Tara as she held out her gold encrusted hand. Predictably, Lydia was dressed as Cleopatra in a very expensive silk sarong and loads of gold. The hair, though, was real.

"I can imagine. Nice to meet you Lydia." Tara said smiling sympathetically for the woman's misfortune even if it did look as if she had mended the bridges between them if they could work the same party without killing each other.

"I hate to be a busybody but I couldn't help wondering about how you managed to snag our fair Brent's attention?" Lydia cooed, stepping closer to Tara as if they were the best of friends. Tara didn't back away. She knew the score. Lydia was challenging her claim on Brent. The ritual didn't change and neither did the people, just the venue. "Considering how antisocial he has become these last few years, of course."

"Of course." Tara's smile turned brittle. She knew how to play games, too. "Oh, well, it's no big secret really. I'm a stripper over at Caligula's and this is my stage costume. Brent is one of my regular customers, ya know. Ain't that right, Bliss honey? Hey, Lyds, I've got to pee like a racehorse, mind pointing out the ladies' room in this joint?"

Lydia with mouth agape nodded off to the far back corner of the room. With a saucy smile directed solely at Brent, Tara turned and sauntered in that direction, her nice round hips swinging in time to the song blaring over the speakers.

Embarrassed and tickled all at the same time, Brent watched her go. Lydia's mouth snapped closed as she whirled on him. "You brought a stripper here? Brent, how could you do such a thing? This was supposed to be a quiet little get-together, nothing sordid, just decent hardworking…"

"Can it, Lydia. There is nothing decent about anyone in this bunch including me and we both know it. Tara is without a doubt the most decent person I've ever met in my entire life. If she has the misguided notion that she's helping all the lonely men in this world by hanging bare-naked off a gold pole then I say more power to her." Brent chuckled. Tara was one of a kind. So honest it was like a breath of fresh air.

"What do you think Kelly would think to hear you say that?" Brent felt all the blood drain from his face. He'd forgotten about Kelly, forgotten that Lydia had been her lifelong best friend. Forgotten all because of that same fresh-faced woman who had somehow taken over his very life.

"Um-hum, that's exactly what I thought." Lydia leaned closer to him gloating over his obvious discomfort. "I'm glad to see you're no longer wallowing in grief, Brent darling, but until some nice woman catches your eye, be a gentleman and be discreet." With that said Lydia marched away her back rigid and Brent wondered why he hadn't denied Tara's little joke. Things were bound to get out of hand before they left.

"Hey, man, I thought you said you weren't coming tonight," Hutch said coming up from behind with a glass of champagne in one hand, a beer in the other.

"I wasn't but I thought Tara would like to— I made a mistake, Hutch, a terrible mistake showing up here. I'd forgotten how much I hate my friends." Brent confessed as he took a long swallow of his forgotten soda. "Present company excluded of course."

"Of course. What happened to jog your memory if I may be so bold?" Hutch asked but Brent could tell his heart just wasn't in it as he was busy scanning the crowd for someone.

"Taylor hit on Tara first thing. Who are you looking for?" He couldn't help it. He followed Hutch's gaze around the room.

"My date. So Taylor hit on her. Big deal, she's a beautiful woman and Taylor hits on all the beautiful women; that's why he can't stay married." Hutch smiled then, a huge grin that lit up his whole face and Brent realized he must have found his date. And judging by that look the man was smitten, which was a relief. Brent was afraid there for a while that he was falling in love with the she-cat Coco and was destined for heartbreak.

"Then she told Lydia she was a stripper from Caligula's." That got Hutch's full attention.

"She didn't?" he exhaled in disbelief. "What did Lydia say? Tell me she knew she was kidding; tell me she realizes Caligula's closed down years ago?"

"Apparently not. She about busted a gut lecturing me for bringing my plaything around decent people like her." It was too much for Hutch and he burst out laughing just as a long-legged beauty stepped out of the crowd and hooked her arm into his.

"What's so funny? Did I miss something?" she said curiously and all thoughts flew out of Brent's head. He knew that voice, heard it in his nightmares sometimes. "Hi, Bliss, nice to see you again."

"Nice to see you too, Coco," he replied as Coco turned adoring eyes on his best friend and immediately felt like a cad for all the mean-spirited things he'd thought about the woman over the past week.

"So what is so funny?" she asked again as she accepted the glass of champagne Hutch held in his hand.

"Tara just told one of Brent's old girlfriends that she's a stripper."

"She's not my old girlfriend." Brent vehemently denied the rumor. He and Lydia had never dated, had never even spoke of it.

"Whatever you say." Hutch couldn't resist the dig, as he wondered if Brent really was that oblivious to the fact that the woman made no bones about wanting to be the next Mrs.

Chambliss, going so far as to say she would have been the first if Kelly hadn't caught him first.

"Tara's here?" Coco piped in when the two looked as if they wanted to square off. "Where, I don't see her?" She strained to see over the crowd looking for Tara's golden brown mane.

"She went to the ladies' room. You can't miss her. She's purple." Brent supplied pointing off in the direction of the restrooms with his glass.

"You guys wait here and I'll go see what is keeping her. Besides I need to powder my nose too." Coco gently withdrew her arm from Hutch's and placed a sweet kiss on his cheek before she sauntered away in that same graceful way Tara had about her.

"Why is it all women have to go to the restroom at the same time?" Hutch asked as he watched her walk away his voice wistful with love.

"To gossip about us men," Brent replied, regarding his friend with interest. "So how serious is this thing between you and the she-cat?" Hutch rewarded him with a blush and Brent sighed. Hutch was long gone on the woman. Lord, he hoped he knew what he was doing by getting involved with her.

* * * * *

The remote hallway where the restrooms and telephones were housed in the vast ballroom was blessedly deserted as Tara all but flew to the sanctuary of the ladies' room. She'd let her tongue overrule her common sense with her parting comments to that — that woman.

"Just admit it — you *are* jealous," she said to the image in the mirror as she passed it on her way to the toilet.

Jealous of that over-blown rich society witch. Ha, that would be the day. But she was, she realized. Why else would she have the urge to strangle her with one of her gold necklaces the second she laid claim on Brent? Instead she had retreated to the safety of the restroom hoping Brent had enough sense to make some sort of excuse for her behavior.

Once she returned she would just have to apologize to Brent and the woman, if she were still hanging onto him. What else could she do after embarrassing him?

"Ah, just the woman I was looking for." Fear coursed through Tara's body. The voice was male and she was alone.

She turned in time to see Jeff Taylor emerge from the little vanity area set aside for powdering noses, with a glass full of whiskey in one hand, an empty one in the other. The look in his eyes reminded her of a predator. And she was the prey.

"I brought you a drink," his words were slightly slurred already and Tara knew he was well on his way to needing a liver transplant. "The finest Scottish whiskey, from my own personal supply."

"Sorry, I don't drink." Warning bells were blaring in her head so loud she expected the fire department to arrive at any moment.

"Pity." He knocked the contents back in one swallow. Tara took comfort in the fact the drink wasn't drugged. He had some scruples at least. But her comfort was short-lived as he advanced on her, placing a hand on each side of her, effectively trapping her against the sink.

Tara met his eye squarely hoping any fear she felt wasn't evident there. "I believe this is the ladies' room."

"Is it? I hadn't noticed." He replied the expensive liquor on his breath just as foul as the cheap variety her high school boyfriend had preferred.

"So nice of you to visit but I'm a big girl. I haven't needed any help since I was potty-trained." His gaze dipped to study her chest and Tara wished she'd kept her smart mouth shut.

"Now *that* I noticed." He leaned closer and she felt his breath rasp over her cheek. "I like your costume, very imaginative. The purple skin is quite lovely. Tell me, how much will it cost to get you to open your petals for me?"

"Let's just say if you have to ask you can't afford it."

"I'm sure I can. I'm rich you know. Unlike my friend Brent out there."

"How nice for you. But the way you seem to be collecting wives I doubt you'll stay that way too much longer."

"What does that matter to a woman in your line of work?"

"I see you've been speaking with the charming Cleopatra. I hate to break it to you but it's my day off so if you wouldn't mind letting me by I'm sure my date is worried."

"How much is he paying you?" He took the arm she used to try to push him away, his grip much stronger than she had given him credit for.

"Let's just say I felt sorry for him and I'm giving him a freebie. I feel nothing for you."

"Come on baby, my buddy Brent will never know," he guided her hand to a certain part of his anatomy she really didn't want to become familiar with. "Just a quickie."

"Does that thing come in adult sizes?" Tara asked calmly, trying to divorce herself from what was happening so she could keep a clear head.

"Ahem. Sorry to interrupt. Tara honey, why didn't you tell me your chlamydia had cleared up? We could have doubled." Tara looked past the man who held her prisoner to see the last person she expected to walk into the restroom.

"Sorry, honey, it hasn't but this bozo won't take a hint." Taylor stepped away quickly swaying a bit, the small bulge in his trousers shrinking quickly under their close scrutiny.

"Ah. Well, if you're done here—" Coco only had to ask once before Tara joined her and they escaped into the deserted hallway leaving Jeff Taylor alone and embarrassed.

"Do I need to ask what was going on in there?" Coco attached herself to Tara's arm and walked quickly back to the party.

"Exactly what it looked like." Tara closed her mind to it before she started to tremble. "How did you know where to find me? Never mind it doesn't matter. By the way, what are you doing here? Why didn't you call me to let me know you were coming?"

"Bliss told me. I came to see Jamie—I didn't want to worry you."

"I'm grateful you're here, Coco, really. Just do me a favor and don't mention this to Brent?"

"I promise." But that didn't mean she wouldn't tell Jamie.

"You're a real friend. So, what about your biopsy? Any news yet?" Tara pasted a broad smile on her face and let the last of the fear drain off her at the sign of Brent's concerned face.

"It was malignant." Coco replied and Tara forgot completely about her own problems.

"Oh no."

"It's awful. They want to go in and see how far it's spread. They may have to remove part of my breast or all of it." Coco choked off the sob that threatened to escape, her eyes locked on Hutch's as she whispered her pain to Tara. "I love Jamie., There I said it. I love him. I had to come. I have to find out if he loves me, too. And if he does, I need to know if he will love me after my surgery. Oh, Tara, why did I have to meet the man of my dreams right now? I don't know if I can bear this pain much longer."

"It will be all right Coco. Hutch, ah, Jamie loves you; I can see it in his eyes right now. That's more than just lust. And from what I see of him, he's a good man not like...not like Brent's other friends. He will be there for you, I'm sure of it." Tara said her heart breaking for the younger woman but James Hutchinson loved her. She really could see it shining in his eyes and Tara felt a stab of envy so sharp she winced.

"Here we are, noses all powdered." Coco beamed the second they reached the guys. "Jamie, honey, I'm starved and there isn't anything decent here to eat." Coco pouted and Tara sighed out loud. When Coco turned her little pouty mouth on a man, he was putty.

"Why don't we leave then? Go get something to eat." Hutch replied turning to putty before their eyes.

"That would be great. How about you two, want to come? It would be like a double date." Coco turned her winning smile on Brent. Tara sighed. Maybe leaving now before something else could happen would be for the best.

"Fine with me, but it really is up to Brent."

Coco rounded on Brent using all the wiles God gave her. Tara was her friend, maybe one of her best, and she didn't want that jerk Taylor trying anything else. "Oh, Bliss, come on. This party is so lame, nothing but rich people comparing portfolios and I haven't seen Tara in so long." She let her lip quiver her large brown eyes wide and pleading.

Gone was the she-cat from a week ago Brent decided, as Coco put her whole being into getting them out of there. So far, he agreed with her about the party but not about the reason. He had just never thought too much about the people he called friends, choosing to ignore what he didn't like about them. Tonight though, his eyes were wide open and he felt slimy by association. "I doubt there is much open this time of night except the Trendy's drive-through and The Pancake House."

"Pancake House," Tara and Coco said in unison and Brent had to smile.

"Okay, I give. We'll go get something to eat, just let me say goodbye to our hosts."

"Hey, don't I get a say in this?" Hutch said a touch of jealousy in his voice. Coco leaned over taking his face in her hands and kissing him gently on the lips. "Okay, everyone, we're going to The Pancake House. Where's Taylor?"

Oh yeah the man was completely putty. Tara stifled a giggle as Coco took her arm and started tugging her toward the doors. "Great, you guys say your good-byes. Tara and I will meet you down in the lobby."

Outside the ballroom, Coco rushed them into the elevator where Tara was finally able to relax. "You know it was probably my own fault. If I had only kept my big mouth shut about that stripper business, he would have forgotten all about me."

"I don't believe you just said that. Tara, he was drunk. I could smell the whiskey the second I walked in; he had pretty much lost control of any sense he was born with. The man was going to have you in that bathroom one way or another, you know that. It wasn't your fault, you didn't bring it on yourself, you weren't asking for it."

"I know. I think it's just delayed reaction. Coco, I couldn't break his grip on my arm." Tara rubbed her arm as she replayed the incident in her mind wondering what would have happened if Coco hadn't walked in when she did.

Coco draped an arm around her shoulders to offer comfort. "It's all over now and you're safe. I'd say you can put it out of your mind."

"As long as you promise not to tell Brent. I don't want him thinking he was responsible."

"I promised, didn't I? I won't breathe a word of it to Bliss. Cross my heart swear to die." Coco swore as the elevator dinged open and they stepped out to wait for the men to join them.

* * * * *

"I had a good time tonight," Tara said on the way home from their early breakfast. Her voice filled the silence that seemed to encompass the truck as they sped down the deserted city streets. "Thanks for inviting me."

"Tara?" Brent said without turning to face her, his voice tight. "Why didn't you tell me Taylor tried to rape you in the ladies' room?"

"Damn that Coco. She promised!" Tara slumped in her seat not caring if she crushed her wings this time.

"So it's true then?"

"I wouldn't go so far as rape but it's true. Your friend wouldn't take no for an answer. I'll wring her neck; she promised not to tell you."

"She didn't. She told Hutch."

"Oh," was all Tara could say since she hadn't thought to make Coco swear not to tell Hutch.

"I'm sorry you had to go through that. I didn't think the man would stoop that low. That's not true, I knew. I just chose not to believe it."

"It's all right, Brent. It's not your fault one of your friends is a slug."

"It is my fault. If I hadn't taken you there, none of this would ever have happened."

"That's your problem, you know that? You think everything that happens to those around you is your fault. Well, Brent Chambliss, I have news for you. The world does not revolve around you; you can't control everything or everyone try as you might. I am a big girl, you know. I've been taking care of myself for a very long time. I would have handled your friend before things got out of control so you needn't beat yourself up over it."

"Actually, I was going to beat Taylor up over it but since you can handle yourself with someone twice your size, I think I'll leave that to you. And since we are pointing out each other's faults, let me tell you a little something, Tara Jenkins. I am not ashamed to be seen with you."

"What are you talking about?"

"I'm talking about your low self-esteem. You'd think a woman as beautiful as you would know it. But not you, you apologized for me seeing you in your underwear last week remember. And tonight you thought I was ashamed to have you for my date. You thought I was worried about being laughed at because I showed up with a fat chick, didn't you? Let me tell you something you should already know. You were stupid to believe what the men in your past said. Men are pigs, Tara. We'll say anything to avoid commitment."

"Oh…"

"And let me tell you something else." Brent wasn't finished she noticed as he swung into his driveway.

"I think you've said enough. I have low self-esteem and I'm stupid. That about sums me up. Goodnight, Mr. Chambliss. I'll see myself home from here." Tara said her pride hurt by his too astute assessment of her. She angrily popped her seatbelt off and flung the door open and stalked to her own yard.

"Damn it, Tara, you didn't let me finish!" Brent slammed his door and shouted after her but Tara didn't stop. She hopped the hedge and began to run for her porch.

She reached her door and almost had the key in the lock when he grabbed her arm and swung her around to face him. "Will you let me finish?" Tara only stared at him as he continued. "You aren't a fat chick Tara. You have the most beautiful body I've ever seen. A woman's body, made for sinning, made for lust. And I've lusted for you since the night we met. Which is something I'm ashamed of because you deserve better. You're beautiful, you know that to a point, I think. But did you know that you are sweet, funny and so totally honest you scare me? I find myself—"

"What? You find yourself what?" Tara forgot her anger, forgot her embarrassment in the face of his sudden confessions.

"I don't know," Brent released his hold on her arm but didn't step away. Instead, he stood toe-to-toe with her, dragging one hand through his hair, causing it to spike, which made him look like a lost little boy. "You're just too comfortable to be around, that's all. And then of course there is the lust. I can't take that kind of torture on a daily basis, it's killing me."

"Me too," Tara whispered closing the distance between them, placing a hand on his chest. The strong and steady heartbeat beneath her hand seemed to pound faster with each second that passed.

"What do you mean, 'you too'?" She felt his voice vibrate in his chest, along with his heartbeat.

"Lusting after you is killing me—and then there is this peculiar comfort factor with you," Tara admitted, though she didn't really want to.

Brent sighed, his chest rising and falling beneath her hand. "So what do we do now?"

"Nothing, for now. Neither of us are ready for anything more than what we have; we both have too many issues that are doomed to get in the way." She returned his sigh and lifted her hand. "Goodnight, Brent Chambliss. Sleep tight." She meant to leave things that way. She meant to unlock the door and close him out but he caught her hand before she could.

For a moment, his eyes lingered on her lips and Tara wanted desperately for him to kiss her despite what she had just said. Kissing Brent was better than chocolate. Better than anything she had ever experienced before and she couldn't imagine stopping once she got started.

"You're right, you know." He wrapped one arm around her waist just grazing the points of her wings as he studied her face in the dim porch light. "But somehow I don't think I have the willpower to resist your siren song too much longer, Tara Jenkins. I'll try though." Her lips puckered into an O as she was about to say something and Brent felt his newly resolved resistance slip.

She never got out what she was about to say, as Brent touched his lips to hers. Lightly at first just tasting, teasing, allowing the desire begin to build deep inside. "Goodnight," he whispered against her mouth just before he took complete possession of it. Lifting her slightly, he pressed her tightly to his body. He gently traced her lips with his tongue urging her one step further. When she did, he moaned as her tongue touched his, teasing it in return.

"Come inside," she whispered, breaking the kiss.

"I can't. I'm afraid if I do, I'll never be able to leave," he breathed the words he never thought to say against her cheek. Honest words he never thought to have the guts to say to any woman and he waited for her to beg him to change his mind. But Tara wasn't like that. She was honest and caring and she would understand things that he didn't quite understand himself.

"I'll wait then until the time is right." She slipped her hand from his, her body following, leaving him feeling cold despite the sultry night air. "Goodnight," she said one last time before the tumblers turned in the lock and she went inside, closing him out of her life.

"For now, but not forever." He turned and walked across her lawn to his house without looking back. If he had, he would have seen two sets of curtains pulled back, one downstairs, one upstairs. He would have seen Tara's delicate purple hand raised in farewell downstairs. He would have looked twice in disbelief upstairs once he noticed the odd glow in the shape of a person. A glow that seemed to pulse with emotion just before it disappeared.

Chapter Sixteen

🔊

A long phone conversation with Coco the next morning did much to clear Tara's mind. Coco admitted to betraying her confidence to Hutch—er—Jamie. She had wanted Tara's honor defended even if Tara hadn't. Given her friend's state of mind, Tara did her best to let the incident go. If Brent and Hutch chose to pursue defending her honor, there was nothing she could do to stop them now. Coco had dropped the cancer bomb on Hutch the night before. She'd scared him, of that Tara had no doubt but Hutch held up under the strain. He vowed his love no matter what and his support. What more could Tara ask for her friend?

It was late when Tara padded downstairs in her fuzzy slippers. She'd slept in after the late night out but the day was wasting away and she had much to do. The job search continued, then she needed to visit her mother and she had promised Tommy she'd drop by that night for dinner. There was always shopping to do since she was living out of someone else's fridge and that long-neglected flowerbed on the west side of the house needed serious tending. Not to mention the gym membership she couldn't seem to find time for lately. Exhausted by the mere thought of how busy she was, Tara dropped into her oversized armchair with a sigh just as the back door slammed shut.

"It's just me!" Brent shouted from the kitchen before Tara had a chance to race for the front door and safety. Her heart on the other hand was doing plenty of racing all by itself.

"You scared me!" she shouted back wondering as she did if her racing heart was from the fright or something else entirely as she remembered the goodnight kiss they'd shared. "What are you doing..." she continued shouting but Brent's sudden appearance in the living room doorway caused her to catch her breath. "...here?" she went on breathlessly, as if her insides hadn't just turned to mush. "I mean it's early for you, isn't it?"

"We're back up to full crews on every site today so I thought I'd put in a full day here for a change." Brent leaned casually against the jamb. His arms crossed over his chest. Tara, on the other hand, tried to gain some semblance of dignity by tying her robe firmly around her body to cover her flying bunny pj's.

"But I thought you promised Hutch only weekends here?"

"That was before our little flu epidemic. Hutch and I talked this morning. He agreed that since we finished the Miller remodel on time and are pretty much on schedule at the other sites, I could be spared a couple of days this week. If that's a problem, I can find something to do across town," Brent said, his eyes traveling along her bare legs to rest on her fuzzy bunny slippers. Tara held still although she wanted to tuck her feet out of sight.

"It's not a problem. Is there anything I could do to help? I know we talked about the possibility of sweat equity on my part but..." There wasn't anything on her to-do list that couldn't be put off 'til tomorrow, with the exception of visiting her mother, of course.

"I'm sure I could find something if you'd like to pitch in. Taking out a wall isn't exactly brain surgery," Brent answered, his face remaining neutral, which gave Tara no clue as to how he really felt about having her underfoot all day.

"Deal." Tara jumped up from the chair, excitement racing through her at the thought of taking out her frustrations on an unsuspecting wall. "Just let me go and slip into something less comfortable." She skipped past him careful not to touch him but even still, she could feel the heat radiating off his body as she passed and the urge to press her flesh to that heat became unbearable.

Ten minutes later, Tara, dressed in jeans, T-shirt and her sturdy sneakers, all but flew down the stairs in case Brent had changed his mind about letting her help, only to find him right where she had left him. Leaning against the arched entryway into the great room, he was staring bemused at the landing.

When he caught her watching him in return he flushed and looked away guiltily. But not for a moment did Tara let her heart believe he'd been watching for her to return. More than likely some interesting architectural detail had caught his attention. Of course that was it, had to be. The alternative was just too dopey to contemplate.

Embarrassed to find himself still standing at the base of the stairs as if he were somehow waiting on pins and needles for her to return, which of course he had been, Brent cleared his throat but his voice somehow managed to catch when he spoke anyway.

"Ready to get to work? I want to have all of the demolition work done before the plumbers get here on Friday." He launched himself away from the doorjamb just as she touched the last stair step. Not to reach for her hand, as was his first inclination, no not that, he only intended to lead the way into the kitchen.

He cleared his throat again this time. Aware that he did so only to distract him from actually taking her hand in his. Thereby making himself out to be some sort of love starved fool, than to hide any embarrassment he might feel from having impure thoughts about his neighbor. "Then, depending on how long it takes to run pipes to your new bathroom, I should be able to start the reconstruction process next week sometime. A bit later than I'd thought but still soon enough, don't you think?"

"You never said anything about plumbers coming on Friday." Tara stopped mid-stride, her voice rife with accusation. Well at least he had successfully distracted her from his puppy love routine before he started slobbering all over her.

"Oh, sorry. Tara, the plumbers are coming on Friday to install new pipes and replace the ones running up to your kitchen sink, which are lead. I don't know how long it will take them and they'll have to turn your water off until they are finished. After that, it's just a matter of days until I get the new stuff installed." *How absolutely deflating it was to be back on familiar territory.*

"How long will my water be off?"

"A day, two tops, no big deal. You can use my shower and there are ways around any other necessary water needs. Don't worry about it." *Do not blush Brent old boy absolutely whatever you do. Do not blush.*

"Oh yeah, easy for you to say. You aren't the one who has to worry about the neighbor walking in on you when you're naked." She griped then immediately caught her breath when she realized she had embarrassed herself in front of him again.

"Don't tease me like that." The tension between them sparked anew and Tara wondered if maybe, just maybe, using his shower wasn't the answer to what ailed her.

* * * * *

Hours later, Tara sat on the floor in what used to be her kitchen. She was covered in plaster dust from head to toe except for where the goggles and that thingy that keeps dust out of your lungs had covered. She was tired, hungry and desperately in need of a bath. But with Brent's patient tutelage, they had managed to take out the first two studs on either side of the dining room doorway, which was as much as they could do without risking structural problems. Even with only that little bit gone, the two rooms seemed to meld into one. Tara immediately realized she'd been worried about how it would look all this time.

"I'm starved," Brent announced as he flopped down beside her.

"Sorry, Charlie, I can't do anything for you," Tara replied, trying not to move too much for fear her arms might fall off after all that work. If she thought her arms ached after a good workout at the gym, that was nothing compared to the constant swinging of a hammer, even one as light as Brent had let her use. "You'll have to either go across the street and see if Miss Belle will take pity on you or call for takeout."

"As much I as I adore Miss Belle, I don't think I am ready for one of her innocent little gossip teas today. So how's about a pizza?"

"Fine by me."

"What do you like on yours? Everything?"

"I can handle that. Just get a soda or something, will ya? I've had all the water I can stand today." Tara attempted to toss the empty water bottle she had just drained across the room to the trash. But her arms ached so bad she couldn't muster the strength and it landed in the middle of the floor way off target.

"Pathetic." Brent picked it up and lobbed it the rest of the way home on his way to place the pizza order.

"It's worse than that. I lettered in basketball in high school. You wouldn't know it to look at me today, would you?" She smiled to take the edge off her words as the lecture from the night before came rushing back. God forbid Brent think she was belittling herself again she decided as she let her head fall back against the wall. A loud metallic thunk rattled through her skull, which Tara had to rub for a couple of seconds before the oddity of the metal sound seeped into her brain. "That's odd," she said as she whirled around on her tush to face the wall. With one outstretched hand, she rapped softly on the area and again was treated to the sound and feel of something metal hiding behind what little wallpaper was left.

"What's odd?" Brent shouted from the hallway his attention more on the phone conversation than on her by the sound of his voice, which at that moment seemed to please her and Tara wondered why she felt the need to keep the metal panel to herself. The hairs at the back of her neck prickled as she ran her hand over the seemingly smooth wall before spinning back around and leaning against it.

Odd. Really odd, the strange tingling continued. Brent chose that moment to walk back into the room smiling happily.

"What did you say was odd?"

"Nothing—just how dead my arms feel after that little bit of work, that's all," Tara lied, although she had no earthly idea why she wanted to keep him from finding out about the panel, at least not until after she had a chance to investigate it thoroughly herself. "My kick-boxing instructor assured me that I was in pretty good shape."

"Swinging a hammer or pushing a saw is completely different exercise from most workouts. Real work usually is," Brent replied from where he leaned against the wall just inside the hallway. "Anyway the pizza will be here in about forty minutes, so I'm gonna run over to the house and take a shower. I think we're about through here today anyway."

Did he sound nervous? Tara wondered as she half-listened to Brent run on. "Yeah sure, me too," she said trying to hide her preoccupation. "See ya in a bit."

"Yeah see ya." Brent said giving her an odd look just before he slipped out the back door.

Tara immediately whirled back around and began pulling at the swatch of paper that covered the wall with her fingernails. She could feel where the metal ended and the plaster began and her curiosity spiraled to a strange sense of excitement. She expected to find an old fuse box of some sort as the area was about the same size as the newer breaker box on the back porch. Or the metal plate could simply be a patch in the wall from an old pipe. Absolutely nothing to go completely bonkers over, a tiny voice of reason said in her head but Tara ignored it. She continued pulling strips of red floral paper off until she had stripped an area the size of a small TV.

The metal panel was hinged but with no visible handle, Tara discovered, her excitement nearly bounding through the roof. She ran her fingers around the seam trying to pry it open but it refused to budge. Frustrated, she glanced around the kitchen for some idea as to what to do next.

Brent's large toolbox sat against the wall by the back door next to a huge shop vacuum. With a great whoop of joy, Tara jumped up nearly skidding across the dusty floor until she reached the box. Inside, she found several tools that looked as if they might do the job, among them, a straight head screwdriver, a flat putty blade, and if those two failed, a crowbar.

Settling herself back in front of the mysterious panel, Tara set to work. The screwdriver didn't work. Glue from the wallpaper had settled into the cracks so Tara used the putty blade, poking it through the seam all the way around until she had unglued the panel from the wall. Then it was just a matter of popping the door open and forcing the stiff hinges to work.

The panel hid a cabinet much like the one behind the mirror in the bathroom. Inside it wasn't very deep, no more than four inches or so from front to back, but it was fairly tall. Much taller than the typical medicine cabinet or any breaker box Tara had ever seen. And she realized she was looking at a secret compartment very much like a safe. There were several metal shelves with a few trinkets laid on them, along with several cigar boxes stored on their sides and a half dozen or so books that looked like ledgers or journals of some type.

The previous owner's secrets, Tara realized. Secrets? What was it about secrets that had that effect on her lately? She stretched out a trembling hand, her fingers just grazing the trinkets as she explored.

A silver jewelry box, a matching brush and comb set too tiny to belong to an adult. Some coins that looked to be English in origin were scattered about the shelves, along with what looked like military medals. Her wandering fingers knocked over one of the cigar boxes and Tara jumped when it landed in her lap.

At first, she had visions of long-lost treasures, possibly from the early occupants of the house. But the items inside were way too new for that and Tara felt her excitement diminish somewhat, but not entirely. After all, this was still treasure, just much more current. The box was no more than ten years old and had only just begun to yellow. Someone had bound it with a rubber band, which Tara stripped off and wrapped around her wrist to keep from losing it. The lid opened easily and inside was a stack of photos, the top one turned over so that she could only see the printer's logo.

Tara sat on the floor in her kitchen, time slipping by fast as she looked through the photos. Almost all of them were of a distinguished older man with a neatly trimmed mustache and goatee, his brown hair liberally sprinkled with gray. In some, he held a large cigar in his mouth, which explained where the boxes came from. The clothes were definitely from the latter part of the twentieth century. Some were of him in military dress, but not of any American uniform she had ever seen. The initials RAF on the collar explained that. The man in the photos was English, which would explain the coins in the cabinet too.

He was somewhere between forty-five and fifty, Tara decided as she came to the bottom of the stack, which had begun when he was much younger. One after another the photos became more recent in time. In the last few a familiar woman began to appear and with trembling hands Tara turned over the last one, dropping it with a gasp as the heartwarming family portrait made her blood run cold. The distinguished English gentleman held a bouncing red-haired toddler girl.

The same pretty little girl she had seen only recently in a portrait on the mantel next door.

Chapter Seventeen

ಬಿ

Tara swept the small trinkets and other items into the open cigar box and grabbed the remaining boxes and books. When she was certain the secret compartment was completely empty, she pushed the door closed and raced upstairs to hide the contents.

Her mind whirled with too many emotions to name as she tried to figure out a plausible explanation for finding Brent's wife and child snuggled up to a man that was not husband or father to them.

One explanation kept leaping into her mind. An explanation she didn't want to consider, an explanation so unfounded that it couldn't possibly be true. Yet, the only other possibility was that the man was Kelly's father but he just didn't seem old enough.

Tara tossed the things into one of her suitcases, which she then buried in the bottom of her closet. She didn't want Brent finding the photos just yet, not until she had a chance to make double damned sure those photos were completely innocent.

No sooner had Tara closed the closet door on the offending items than she hear the back door slam.

"Pizza's here," Brent shouted from downstairs.

"Give me a few minutes, will ya?" she shouted from her doorway. She was trembling and far from ready to face him after making such a vile discovery. Alleged vile discovery, she reminded herself.

"Take your time but be warned that I'm not promising you'll find any pizza left if you take too long."

Tara gathered clean clothes and raced into the bathroom to shower away the filth that covered her. A few minutes later she padded downstairs dressed in a pair of capri leggings and salmon-colored tunic sweater, her feet bare, her wet hair wrapped in a towel. Some of the shock had worn off and she felt she could face Brent now without blurting out things about his wife that might not be true.

The big vacuum hummed from somewhere out back and she followed the sound to the kitchen where Brent was busy cleaning up the last of the dust and debris. She watched him work for a few minutes, her mind drifting over what she knew of his marriage — which was very little.

They weren't happy, Kelly and Brent, she knew that much. The marriage was troubled, she suspected from the beginning, if she put together all the things Brent had said. Brent blamed himself for everything but maybe just maybe he was blameless after all.

"Hey, what's this?" Brent shut off the vacuum and crouched in front of the metal cabinet. A tingling sense of foreboding washed over Tara as he opened the panel but she knew she couldn't pretend she didn't know what it was; after all, it hadn't been there earlier.

"I bumped my head on it just after you left. It seems to be some type of secret cabinet."

"Anything inside?" He picked up the putty knife and popped the door open without waiting for her to answer.

"Just dust." Tara winced as the lie tripped off her tongue. She didn't want to lie to him. It felt so wrong but she didn't want to tell him what she had really found until she had a chance to investigate further. "I scraped most of it out. Have you ever seen anything like it before?"

"No." Brent swung the door back and forth while running his fingers around the seam. "It would have been behind the cabinet, which would be a very hard place to get to."

"Plus it was covered with wallpaper."

"Odd. I wonder how long it's been here? Near as I can tell this part of the house was added on sometime in the forties or fifties, so it was sometime after that."

"You mean the kitchen isn't original to the house?" Tara said forgetting about the box in the face of such an unexpected bombshell. "I thought it was and so did the realtor, I think. So if it isn't, then where was the original kitchen?"

"Out back, probably near the old stables. But when the land was broken down and sold off years ago both buildings were demolished." Brent too forgot about the mystery box and Tara saw his eyes sparkle as he warmed to what was surely one of his favorite topics, old houses. "As near as I can tell this is where the back porch was originally. If you'll take a good look outside you'll notice that both porches are much wider than in front or on the side. The biggest clue though is under the floors. I noticed a difference in the wood types used and other little telltale markings of an add-on."

"Really? I wonder what this old house looked like in the early days. Most of the houses around here wouldn't have been here would they?"

"No, my house dates back to the fifties as do most of these old houses. Miss Belle's house and a couple further down the street would have been the only neighbors back then. But it would be nice to find a photo of the original house. Listen, the university has tons of archive photos. You can always go check them out."

"I'll keep that in mind. In the meantime, I'm starved. Where's that pizza?"

"Out on the porch. I left ya a slice." Brent said a huge grin lighting his face just before he returned to the task of vacuuming up the dust that coated the room.

"Thanks," Tara shouted over the noise before she slipped out the back door expecting to find the pizza box sitting on the floor. Instead, she found a small wrought iron garden table and two chairs perched not far from the door, the pizza and drink cans set on top.

Tara smiled a half smile. She'd seen that table out in Brent's backyard and knew it had to weigh a ton; regardless, he'd brought it over by himself so that she could have somewhere to eat. He was sweet, on top of infuriatingly macho and Tara wondered what other personality surprises the man hid beneath all that tough skin. She flipped open the box and found a whole pie.

Despite the teasing to the contrary, he'd waited for her. Tara felt an odd flutter deep in her being. A flutter she squashed mercilessly. She refused to fall in love with him over such a trivial matter as this. That is if she wasn't already too late to stop the headlong tumble into that forbidden emotion.

Tara looked out across the sky. Dark clouds were rolling in from the north and the breeze had picked up in the last few minutes. She didn't want to dwell on the man. Or for that matter what that little ripple really was, fear maybe, or something more complex. "That looks like it might bring a little cool weather."

Startled, Tara whirled to find him only inches from her and the tiny ripple broadened into a tsunami washing over every inch of her being. She wanted him so very much she could taste him. She also wanted her happily ever after to be with him.

"Hey, what is it?" The look of concern on his face made Tara even more miserable. Happily ever after would never happen with this man and she knew it. He would never let go of his past for someone like her. "Tara?" He reached out and caught a curl that escaped the towel. His thumb brushed her cheek and she shivered with longing.

"I'm a little tired, that's all and hungry. Are you ready to eat before this pizza gets cold?" Tara stepped away from him and flipped the box open again denying what she felt, denying what she'd seen in his eyes just before she turned.

"Yeah sure." He picked up a can of soda and popped the top. If he had any more concerns about her behavior, he didn't let on. "It's early still. You want to maybe catch a movie or something?"

She heard the tremor in his voice, heard the insecurity of a man out of his element and she looked into his dark eyes and melted. "I— I can't. Not tonight. I have to visit my mom," she said with genuine regret but duty came before pleasure. "I'll take a rain check, though, for Friday night if you'd like."

"Friday then, it's a date. I'll pick you up at eight?" Brent took a huge bite of pizza and licked sauce from his bottom lip.

"You bet." Her appetite suddenly gone, Tara nibbled her slice forcing the food to stay down. "It's getting late. I'm going to go finish dressing. I'll see ya tomorrow okay." The words rushed out in a nervous jumble and she jumped up from the table but he caught her hand as she tried to rush by.

Tara wanted to yank free and race for the safety of the house but she didn't. He stood and faced her, her hand still clutched in his. "Tara…I'm sorry for last night."

"Don't Brent. We covered that last night. It's all over and done with."

"No, I don't think it is… Never mind, forget I brought it up. I'll see ya Friday." He cupped her chin in his warm hands and gently touched his lips to hers. His breath tickled her lips but there was no demand in the kiss, just sweetness that made her want to melt. One quick kiss that was all, and he let her go. The next instant he was racing down her back steps and across the yard while Tara simply stood and trembled.

Chapter Eighteen

ಐ

It was late. Brent paced the floor of his small living room watching for the flash of headlights across his front lawn. Rain driven by heavy winds slashed against the windows making it impossible to see. The wind howled outside making him shiver as the temperature plunged.

Midnight ticked by and Tara wasn't tucked safely inside her house. Brent felt his stomach clutch into about a million knots. He was unable to stop his mind traveling back in time to a night when another woman didn't come home. But Tara wasn't Kelly and she wasn't driving around in a blind fury.

She also wasn't his to worry about he reminded himself as he started on another circuit around the candlelit room. Tara was a big girl. She could take care of herself. She'd just decided to wait out the storm with her mother that was all.

Could she do that? Stay at the home where her mother lived after visiting hours?

He really shouldn't be worrying but after the night he'd had, she should be here to appreciate that he'd defended her honor. After all, he had severed ties with his former friends that evening. But damn, coldcocking that son of a bitch Taylor had felt so good.

Lights flashed across the room and he rushed to the window in time to see her truck swing into his driveway. He opened the heavy door and let the wind rip it from his hand. He stepped out onto the porch dressed only in a pair of sweatpants and a thin T-shirt. The hot fury that had settled over him kept him from feeling the cold rain as it slashed against him, soaking him before he stepped off the stairs.

"Where have you been?" He cut across his yard to the drive.

"What?" Tara shouted over the storm, her tired face not registering in his mind.

"Where the hell have you been in this weather? Don't you know you could have been killed?" Fear choked him making him irrational. Tara's narrowed green eyes should have warned him that he had stepped out of bounds but he couldn't stop. Especially now that she was there in front of him unharmed and seemingly unaware of how worried he was.

"You're getting soaked." She pushed past him, umbrella held high.

"Maybe if you had come home at a reasonable time I wouldn't have to stand out here in the rain." Somehow that sounded wrong even to his ears but he was on a roll now and there was no stopping.

"Uh-huh, and what would a reasonable hour be? Or is my curfew negotiable?" She continued across the lawn to her property as if he'd never said a word.

"And didn't you notice the storm? All of the electricity on this side of town is out." He followed her swinging his arm out toward the darkened street.

"I noticed. Before you go any further Mr. Chambliss, may I say something?" she went on without giving him a chance to answer. "I've been in the emergency room most of the night and I'd really like to go to bed. Can we finish this tomorrow please?"

Brent opened his mouth to argue but her words sank in.

"Your mother?" he said feeling shame wash over him for his behavior.

"She had a mild stroke this afternoon." This time he noticed the pain in her eyes.

"I'm sorry Tara, I don't know what got into me... Is there anything I can do?"

"She's resting comfortably for tonight. The nurse on duty promised to call if there is any change. Right now, I just need some sleep."

"I understand. And Tara, I really am sorry—for everything."

"I know." She took a step toward him placing a dry hand on his face. "You're soaking wet. Go home before you catch your death." She leaned forward and kissed him lightly on the cheek, her gaze lingering on his mouth for a few seconds before she turned and unlocked her door. "Oh and Brent, thanks for worrying about me."

"You're welcome." He stood grinning like a fool even after she was safely inside. His anger no longer protected him from the cold and he began to shiver. Served him right, only fools stood around in the pouring rain in the dark yelling at a woman for no reason at all.

Sense returned too late and he went home to a warm shower and bed, hoping this would seem funny in the morning, because right now he was downright pathetic.

Chapter Nineteen

෨

A cold front straight out of Canada settled over the Deep South that first week of November bringing with it dreary skies, biting winds and constant drizzle. But the ugly weather wasn't what awakened Brent that morning. The piercing shrill of the bedside phone did.

"This better be important," he grumbled bringing the phone to his ear.

"It's as serious as a heart attack buddy." Wide awake now, Brent sat up in bed.

"Don't tell me a tornado took out the mini-mall?"

"Not that drastic," Hutch said over the line. "I just received an early morning wake-up call myself from a friend at the bank financing said mini-mall. The bigwigs over there want to do an inspection this morning. To make sure the status is quo."

"I thought the next inspection wasn't until around Thanksgiving." Brent brushed his free hand through his hair wondering if it were merely a coincidence that this surprise inspection was scheduled so soon after the little altercation with Jeff Taylor? Yeah, and he was next in line for the English throne.

"Me too. Listen we're on schedule, there is nothing to worry about. Just get out there before they do. And Brent, wear a tie." After Hutch hung up Brent tossed off the covers and dashed across the cold floor to the closet. Next time he wouldn't just give his buddy Taylor a shiner for his trouble. He would geld the sumbitch.

As per Hutch's orders, Brent dressed for business, complete with a tie. Outside, he took one look at the sky, covered his head with his briefcase and dashed through the cold drizzle to his truck. Tara's truck was already gone he noticed once inside the cold but dry cab.

Somehow, he would apologize for his continued jerky behavior. Maybe sending some flowers to her mother would show her he wasn't quite the ass he seemed to keep making himself out to be. He growled as he turned the key in the ignition. Why was it he never had this peculiar problem before he met Tara Jenkins?

* * * * *

The windshield wipers beat in perfect time with the song on the radio. The station had played a string of sad songs that seemed to complement the weather and Tara's mood, which at that moment was less than spectacular.

Her mother was still in intensive care but improving according to the doctors. She'd spent the day bickering with her brother about petty things until Tommy's wife Randi had arrived and acted as referee. After that, they seemed to get along better but the stress of their mother's failing health weighed heavily on them both. It was just a matter of time before their mother would leave them for a better place and neither really wanted to face that future.

To top off the day, her first job interview hadn't gone the way she wanted. Apparently, there were no openings available for a talented makeup artist anywhere in the city. So until she finished college and got a teaching certificate it was beginning to look as if she would have to find a minimum wage job as a grocery store checkout girl or a hamburger flipper. On the other hand, she *could* go to Marty for anything scheduled in the South.

Tara sat in Brent's driveway for a moment watching the rain outside the warm truck cab. Her future looked bleak but in that instant she decided she would rather eat dirt than go back to modeling at this point in her life.

No use pouting over it now. She had very little time to kill especially if she were going to meet her brother back at the hospital that evening. She grabbed the loops of all seven plastic grocery bags and her purse, pushed open the door and gasped as cold raindrops fell on her knee. Foregoing the umbrella she held her breath and raced through the cold rain to Brent's back door. She had just enough time to fix something to eat and change clothes before Brent was due to come home.

The house was quiet and very cold. Tara shivered while she put away the groceries she'd bought to tide her and Brent over for the next few days. Glancing at the clock on the stove, she cursed the lack of time as she popped the large pan of frozen lasagna into the oven and set the timer. She would really like something homemade but she could settle this one time.

She washed fresh vegetables under warm water and began to prepare a salad. But the cold seemed to penetrate her wet clothing and Tara began to shiver so hard the knife shook in her hand until she feared slicing off a finger.

There was nothing for it, she needed heat to be able to function. In the living room, the fireplace was already set up for the first fire of the season. She checked to make sure the flue was open before she lit the starter log with one of the long matches she found on the mantel next to the portrait of baby Betsy. In seconds, the starter log was giving off enough warmth to tame the worst of her shivers. Soon the other logs would catch and some of the cold in the rest of the room would dissipate.

Changing out of her wet clothes would help tremendously but Tara didn't have time to run home just then. So she would have to settle for shedding her wet nylons and letting the heat of the fire dry her feet and legs. From there, she should be able to cope.

Rain-soaked and miserable Brent stood on his front porch trying hard to put the events of the day into perspective. His company had been fined for scaffolding that was below code. Scaffolding that had previously passed all the other inspections without a batted eyelash. The fine wasn't hefty, merely a nuisance that wouldn't have happened if Taylor had kept his hands off Tara. Otherwise, the inspectors from both the bank and county went away satisfied that the job was proceeding without a hitch. For that alone, he should be grateful but he had a feeling that Taylor had declared war and this mess was far from finished.

He was miserable, more from the events of the day than the weather. He fumbled with the keys, dropping them once before he was able to get the door unlocked. What else would go wrong? So far, the week was off to a grand start.

He set his briefcase on the floor and dropped his keys on the foyer table. But that was as far as he got before all coherent thought escaped him.

It was as if the answers to all his prayers had come true. Tara the object of all his fantasies sat on his fireplace ledge, her skirt hiked up, one stocking rolled halfway down her thigh.

He had died and gone to heaven.

She looked up then, her eyes wide with horror.

"Tara, wait. It's all right." Afraid she was going to bolt, he practically flew across the room and caught her cold hand in his.

"I should go."

"No," he said too sharply. The thought of her leaving just then scared him more than her staying ever had. Her eyes grew even more round and she sucked in an angry breath ready to do battle. "I mean, I don't want to chase you away. I… Here let me help you." Kneeling in front of her, he rubbed the cold from her hands. When she sighed, he dropped his fingers to her thigh to help remove the sodden stocking. He had the best of intentions. Really, he did. But the feel of her soft flesh was intoxicating. His fingers lingered long after the hosiery lay in a silken puddle on the floor.

Tara stopped shivering as heat coursed through her body. She gasped for breath as his hands stroked her legs, soothing away the wet and the cold that lingered there. She gripped his shoulders, her hands frantic to find skin of her own to stroke. "You're soaked," she said, surprised to find his gray dress shirt plastered to his shoulders.

"It's raining outside." How absurd, of course it was raining outside. Why else would she be nearly as sodden as he was?

"Yes, I know," she tugged at his striped tie, pulling it free of the knot. She dropped it to the floor beside her stockings.

"Here, let me get you out of this wet shirt." She slipped the top button free as she spoke.

"Tara," he groaned as her sweet lips nuzzled his neck sending shivers racing through him. His fingers tightened convulsively on her knees, pushing them apart so that he could fit between, thereby closing the distance between them. "Oh God, Tara," he caught her face in his hands forcing her to look at him. He searched her eyes hoping to find denial. Instead he found a hunger to match his own.

He didn't beg her to kiss him this time and he didn't ask for permission either. He simply took what he wanted, what he'd been denying himself these last few days. He was through denying this attraction to her, this need to taste her to hold her, to make her his. And when his lips touched hers, he knew he could never deny her anything ever again.

Tara opened her lips and her tongue met his, not in surrender but as if she were prepared to do battle, which was more than fine by him. He wouldn't mind being conquered. The thought had barely left his brain when her long legs encircled him, holding him captive. And he knew without a doubt he would be the happiest POW ever to walk the planet.

Her hands were less than gentle as she pulled his shirt from his pants. After making quick work of the rest of the buttons, she pushed his shirt from his shoulders, sliding the sleeves down his arms until they caught at his wrists. Muttering a curse against his lips, she fumbled with the buttons on his cuffs, finally freeing his arms, and she dropped the shirt into the growing pile on the floor.

The heat from the fire scalded her back adding to Tara's desire for the man on his knees before her. Eyes the shade of rich dark coffee watched her, gauging her reaction when he slipped beneath her skirt to stroke her thighs. She drew in one ragged breath after another, unable to get enough of his fingers playing over her flesh or the taste and feel of his mouth on her lips. It wasn't enough. She wanted more, so much more. She opened her legs wider, encouraging him to stroke higher. She stroked his bare back, the smoothness of it stoking the fire inside until she thought she would explode.

It was more than she could bear. She found the metal buckle of his belt and, sliding the black leather through the cold steel, Tara let the two ends fall to his sides and fingered the button the belt had attempted to hide from her seeking hands. With a flick of her wrist she popped the button free and worked the zipper down and within seconds she moaned throatily as she finally found the skin that would satisfy her craving.

Warm hands slid beneath his underwear cupping the swell of his backside and Brent gasped, his own busy hands shocked into stillness for a moment. In truth, her questing hands left him weak and unable to focus. Her small soft hands stroked his skin, baring him to the heat of the fire. He released her mouth throwing his head back when her hands settled on the most sensitive part of his body and began to caress him right into madness.

Hot, wet lips found a new place to work their magic on the center of his belly, where Tara licked a path ever lower. Leaning back to aid her in her search, Brent gasped again when her mouth claimed him. Desire hot and painful pooled in that one spot and he wanted nothing more than to give in to her demands. But he couldn't, not this time. He wanted his first orgasm with Tara to happen when he was deep inside her and preferably with her in the throes of an orgasm of her own.

"Not yet," he said lifting her away from him until her mouth was even with his. "Not without you." His smile strengthened then as the tips of his work-roughened hands slipped beneath the cotton barrier that shielded her womanhood.

This time it was her voice echoing in the cold room, her cries of pleasure that drifted through the empty house. Trembling Tara clung to him as he stroked her to madness. Her fingers clutched his bare back harder than she intended when one long finger delved inside her to stroke a little more, his hot mouth nuzzling her neck just below her ear. Tara felt the first tremors begin but she was helpless to fight the onslaught of orgasm.

"Not without you," she whimpered his words back to him as she tried to push him away but it was too late. She shattered beneath those expert fingers, his name the only word to come to mind.

He withdrew his hand immediately and Tara, expecting him to leave her as he had before, felt the pain of rejection wash over her. She looked into his eyes expecting to see anger or fear. Instead, she found flames of desire flickering in those dark pools when he looked at her.

"Tara," was all he said before his mouth once again claimed hers. This time, though, the gentleness was gone. His mouth, hard against hers, sought to punish. But Tara met him with a fury of her own, taking his demands and returning them until she thought she would explode.

He stripped her of her panties, his vision glazed as he plunged inside her. His mind cleared of everything except the shock of being where he had longed to be for so long now.

Her hands gripped him hard, her nails digging in. And for a brief moment, Brent fought to remember why this was wrong. Tara chose that moment to wrap her legs around his hips pulling him deeper inside. The shadows of doubt were replaced by desire rising fast and furious as she forced him to keep pace with the rhythm she set. His eyes wide open, filled with the vision of the wanton woman wrapped around him, Brent allowed all that he knew before to cease to exist as he gave his whole body and soul over to Tara's safekeeping.

Lost in his eyes, Tara held tight to Brent as his body rocked into hers with a need that matched hers. His hands cupped her bottom lifting her slightly and Tara cried out as he slid deeper inside her body drawing her passion to a fever-pitch. The orgasm convulsed through her and Tara clung to him waiting for sanity to return. But the passion burning in Brent's gaze told her that it would be a long time before that would happen.

He scooped her off the brick hearth swiveling his body until he could snag a pillow from the nearby footstool, which he dropped on the carpeted floor in front of the fireplace and laid her upon it.

"You came without me," he whispered, his weight settling over her as he began to move ever so slowly inside her.

"It won't happen again," Tara encircled his neck drawing him to her as she lifted her hips to meet his thrust. Her lips fused to his, her tongue matching the movement of their lower bodies. Their eyes focused on each other as they loved. She saw his orgasm begin in his eyes, felt him stiffen his breathing turning ragged and Tara arched into him stroking him with a fierce need she didn't know she possessed. Only then did she allow her body the release it sought once more. Her cries mingled with his, her arms and legs leaden as she drifted back to earth.

* * * * *

Warm and sated Tara floated somewhere in a daze. She couldn't remember anything ever being so incredible and she never wanted to come down. Brent seemed content to lie atop her allowing her fingers to trace circles on his sweat-covered back.

"Can you get pregnant?" His voice sounded far-off.

"Hmmm?" she sighed, the meaning behind his question not registering in her brain.

"Damn it, Tara, are you on birth control?" He raised his head and Tara gazed groggily into his eyes where she found fear. Almost immediately, the full brunt of what they had just shared hit her with the force of a nuclear explosion.

"No, I... It's been years since I..." She didn't get a chance to finish. Brent scrambled off her. Panic, full-blown and frightening, was clearly etched on his face. And Tara realized for the first time that she was still fully dressed. She had needed him so badly and when he returned that need she had let desire take the place of good sense. She had condoms in her purse. She felt a flutter of panic grip her stomach as the repercussions of what a few moments of unbridled passion could mean to them.

"Oh God," Brent rocked back on his heels and stood up in one graceful, fluent movement dragging his pants up and fastening them as he went.

Dreading what he might say, what he might do, Tara pulled herself into a sitting position squeezing her legs together and resting her forehead on her knees. She felt a rush of something hot and sticky between her legs and tears of shame prickled behind her eyes.

"I'm sorry," she stated lamely. "If it's any comfort it's the wrong time of the month."

"There is no wrong time of the month," he looked at her as if she had somehow lost her mind. "Not when it comes to making babies. Don't you know anything?"

"Yes, I know Brent. I just thought, well, I didn't think but I wasn't the only one. You're as much to blame as I am. You could have stopped and picked up a condom somewhere. You could have pulled out or something." She would not be the bad guy here.

"I did. Bought a box of condoms I mean. They're in the bathroom." He looked as miserable as she felt but it wasn't enough to make her feel better.

"They didn't do us any good in there did they," she said with all the sarcasm that she could muster, hoping the brave front would hide the fact that she was dying inside.

He was just like the others, just like every man she had ever dated. Nothing mattered to him but getting his rocks off. Just once, she wanted to make love with a man who wouldn't start accusing her of something as soon as he was done with her.

Tara swallowed the sob that bubbled up from her chest and stood. No way was she going to let him know just how bad her heart was breaking. Intending to go home and lick her wounds she gathered her things in her hands and stumbled toward the front door. But Brent intercepted her before she could reach the knob. "Where are you going?" His voice was a little shaky and Tara felt the persistent sob grow stronger in her chest.

"Home, to wash up. I'll— I'll be sure to let you know if anything comes of this."

"I'm sure you will." He spun around and paced toward the kitchen, his fingers clenching and unclenching at his sides as he walked.

"What's that supposed to mean?" Tara stood where she was, all the hurt inside her welling into one great ball of anger.

"Nothing, forget I said anything." He spun back to face her and the emotion in his eyes that had once been so easy to read was hidden from her now.

"I can't. You think I set out to trap you don't you? That I seduced you so I could get pregnant. Damn your hide, Brent Chambliss. Just because you had to get married once, does not mean... Oh never mind. Like you said, just forget it. You're not worth the effort." Tara said her voice breaking with the tears she fought to control. She wouldn't cry in front of him, wouldn't give him the satisfaction of knowing how badly she ached."Just try to forget this ever happened. I already have." She turned to leave, her fingertips just grazing the knob when he spoke.

"What about the other consequences? You know. The diseases? Shouldn't we talk about that before you storm out of here?" He seemed so calm now. Way too calm and Tara turned back to face him. His features had gone rigid, his face blank, as if he had dismissed her already, as if she never mattered to him as anything more than an afternoon pick me up after a bad day at work.

"I have been celibate for nearly four years now. I couldn't take the heartache anymore. I had a physical three months ago, before I left for Paris the last time I was clean so you don't have to worry about that." Tara said going for the same indifference he wore like a shield. She opened the door and stepped out onto the porch with what felt like finality ringing in her ears.

"Tara," he called to her. "I haven't been celibate. There have been women since Kelly died."

Tara froze in her tracks, ice water flowing through her veins now, and she just wanted to curl up into a ball and cry. "Were you more careful with them than you were with me?"

"Yes."

"That's something at least. So there's nothing to worry about is there? I'll see ya around sometime." She took a step but he called out to her again and she stopped.

"Tara, they didn't mean anything to me. And I'm clean, I swear, I—"

"And what makes them any different than me?" She couldn't stop the question from jumping out. She didn't really want to know the answer.

Knowing that she didn't mean anything to him would kill her but she waited for a split second hoping against all hope that he would put her fears to rest. That he would tell her she meant something and that she wasn't just another conquest to talk about down on a job site somewhere. But he didn't answer. Tara fled the damning silence. The cold rain outside soaked her to the skin before she made it to the azalea hedge but Tara didn't mind. This way she could pretend the tears she fought so hard to control were not sliding down her face. This way she would catch her death of pneumonia and end her misery before her broken heart could do the job.

Chapter Twenty

శ్రు

A high-pitched beep snapped Brent out of the stupor he had fallen into when Tara raced out on him. He bolted across the room for the door but he was too late. He slammed his fist into the porch railing when he heard her front door slam.

He didn't feel the sting of wood grating his knuckles, nor did he feel the cold as he stood on the porch wondering why he had said the things he'd said. He didn't mean to utter the words that had brought such pain to her face, didn't mean to accuse her of anything, hadn't even thought of accusing her of planning to trap him. He didn't mean to throw his less-than-stellar sexual past in her face either. But he had and for the life of him he didn't know what demon possessed him.

Making love to Tara had been better than anything he had ever experienced before in his life and that alone had scared him. The fact that he had forgotten their safety on top of it had freaked him out. He never forgot protection anymore. But he couldn't remember ever being so driven by desire that he couldn't remember to stop for a condom.

He stepped back inside where the beeping continued. He closed the door and followed the sound to the kitchen where he turned off the timer on the stove and checked the oven.

Tara's pan of lasagna was golden brown and bubbling. His appetite gone, he slammed the door closed and turned off the oven. He swiped the salad makings Tara had left on the cutting board into a bowl, which he shoved into the fridge.

He couldn't face the meal without Tara there to share it. He turned and left the room. In the living room he spotted the pile of clothing on the floor and went to retrieve his shirt and tie. There on the carpet beneath his shirt were the stockings he had stripped from her long legs. He resisted the urge to bury his face in the sheer material. It was then that he realized he hadn't bothered to undress her. He just took without a thought of the consequences. His fault, it was all his fault. He saw that now. He had wanted her so badly for so long he just couldn't resist anymore.

And afterward he'd treated her like a five-dollar whore when he should have made her feel as special as she'd just made him feel. Words, he knew, could hurt worse than a slap and he had slapped her around pretty hard.

"Damn." He carried his clothes to his room and looked around at the reminders of his wife. The hairs on the back of his neck stood on end as if she were watching him, condemning him for the fool he really was. He rushed to his closet, pulled out as many of his clothes as he could carry and backed out of the room without taking his eyes off the open window that faced Tara's house. In the hallway, he pushed open the door to the spare bedroom they had used more for storage than as a guestroom and hung his clothes in the empty closet. The bed was only a double, smaller than the one in the room he'd shared with Kelly. But it was almost new and would do.

Twenty minutes later he had all of his personal belongings transferred to the room across the hall and without another look he closed the door on his wife's memory. But he still couldn't shake the restlessness that consumed him.

He paced the house picking up a knickknack here, a throw pillow there, hiding the objects in the hall closet until the place lost Kelly's decorative stamp. For three years, he'd kept things exactly the same as she'd left them.

It was high time he moved on. Suddenly, he stopped pacing and looked around at the room. Grabbing the pair of stockings from the back of the couch where he'd left them Brent all but staggered to the kitchen where he pulled the key to Tara's house off the hook.

For three years, everything had been fine. He darted out into the rain. Leaving the gate open, he crossed the hedge that separated his house from Tara's.

For three years, he'd been content to live with his guilt. He stepped into the shell of what used to be Tara's kitchen, closed the door quietly behind him and twisted the lock. The house was dark and eerily quiet as he walked through to the stairs. He stood for a moment one hand on the railing, one foot on the bottom step.

For three years, he'd been miserable. A condition he hadn't realized until that day. He climbed the stairs as silently as he could considering the bottom of his shoes were wet and wanted to squeak on the bare wood. The door to her room stood open and he stepped into the darkened room. "Tara," he called softly trying to see through the dark to the bed.

"When I was seventeen years old, I lost my virginity in the backseat of a Buick to a boy I'd had a crush on for two years. It was the week before graduation. He never paid me much attention before but that last week it was almost as if we were the best of friends. He kissed me when we danced at the prom and sought me out at all the graduation parties. One night my best friend and I went to a party, or rather I tagged along with her and her boyfriend but they slipped off a couple hours later. Justin, the crush, offered me a ride home when they didn't come back and I took it." Brent winced when the lamp came on, not from the light shining in his eyes but from the tears he found trickling down her cheeks. She sat on the bed dressed in a pair of faded jeans and a sweatshirt, her feet bare and her hair wet as if she'd just stepped out of the shower. She wouldn't look at him. She just sat there hugging her knees.

"We lived out in the country in West Mobile and there were plenty of places to park if you know what I mean. Anyway, he didn't ask me or say anything, he just drove out to this field. I found out later it was his grandfather's peanut field. He left the radio on and at first we just talked about what we were going to do with our lives after high school. I was scared to death. I knew what he wanted so I let him kiss me. I thought it would end there but it didn't. He said all sorts of things. Words he'd used before so he knew they would work. I forget most of them but the general gist was how he'd never noticed how pretty I was and how he didn't want to let me go now that he'd found me, stuff like that. I fell for it of course. After all I'd had it bad for him since I was fifteen. After it was over, he took me home and told me we'd get together again. Needless to say, we didn't. I waited for him to call me, to ask me out properly. Then the rumors started at school, about how I lured him away from his date and how I'd tried to get him to come to my room. Finally on graduation day, he stood up in front of the whole class and said vile things about me, ending with how he'd never dare fuck a fat chick again. I don't remember how I made it through the ceremony after that. But I did and I've never been back." She wiped her face again before she continued her story.

"A few years later, I met this guy in New York. Oh, he was spectacular to look at, curly blond hair, big blue eyes and a nice rear end. He preyed on models. I found out later that I wasn't the first. Anyway, he wined me and dined me until I decided there was something special there and I went to bed with him. Afterward he made it plain that he was only interested in me because of a bet he made with his buddies. That he did not intend to see me again." She laughed weakly, almost bitterly.

"You see, I've had exactly three intimate relationships in my whole life and every single one ended in disaster." She wiped her face with the palm of her hands still refusing to look his way.

"I'm sorry seems so lame, I know. But I am. Truly." Brent shoved his hands into the pockets of his slacks and stepped one step into the room. "I didn't mean to lash out like that but damn it Tara. I'm afraid." She turned untrusting eyes on him then and he felt more than saw the hurt that she was nursing.

"Afraid of what?" Her voice quivered from the tears that she'd shed and he felt like a heel all over again.

"Of you. Of this need that takes over whenever we're together. I've never wanted a woman so much that I forgot everything else in the world until I met you. Tonight... There's no excuse for it. I messed up and I blamed you and I take full responsibility for the consequences."

"You are a complete lunkhead, you know that?" Tara said. "When will you learn that you are not solely responsible for every person that enters your life?"

"Tara..."

"Don't 'Tara' me, Brent. I stopped at the drugstore with my sister-in-law today and I picked up a box of condoms. It was a spur of the moment decision considering the past couple of times we were together. But that's beside the point. The point is I wasn't thinking either. My purse was on the couch with the condoms inside. It would have taken what...twenty, thirty seconds? But I didn't think about anything but getting inside your pants." She blushed and looked away.

"Listen Tara, if there are any—uh—consequences. I'll, damn it... I don't know what to say. 'I'll do right by you' wants to roll off my tongue but I've already lost two children. I'm not ready to think about another. I want to do the right thing but the thought terrifies me."

"I understand."

"Do you? That's good, 'cause I damn sure don't." Brent ran his hand through his hair and flinched as drops of water bounced off the short spikes onto his face. "Children, my children anyway, have a tendency to..." He left off not wanting to think of the child he'd buried or the one that never had a chance to live. "I'm afraid of bringing another into the world." He dragged in a long ragged breath to ease the knot that had formed in his chest. His eyes stung and he turned swiftly away before the woman on the bed could see the telltale glistening of the tears.

"We're a pair, the two of us." Tara curled into herself on the bed, her knees tucked tight against her as if to ward off the hurt that wanted to grab her chest and squeeze. She wanted to forgive the haunted man with her whole being but a small part of her couldn't summon up the courage. "Two blind fools bumbling through life without a clue how or even who to trust."

"I like to think I'm not quite that pathetic. Tara, about tonight I…"

"Listen, Brent, I've got to get back to the hospital. My mom's been moved to a regular room and she might even get to go home in a day or two." Tara let the pain she held close go for now. There would be time later to worry about the consequences, she reasoned as she slid off the bed and rummaged through a drawer for a pair of warm fluffy socks to help ward off the chill.

"Uh yeah, right. Tara I didn't mean to act like a fool. I didn't mean anything I said. I just want you to know that. I wasn't using you for sex. I-I-I've got this thing for you…you know." Brent stumbled across the words in an attempt to apologize once more for his stupidity.

"I know," Tara stopped digging through her socks. She turned to meet his eye for the first time since he came in. And she smiled a small shy smile that sent razor-sharp pangs of longing through his system. "And Brent, I've got this…thing for you, too."

"Well. Okay then." Brent stepped out of the room more to hide the blush that was rapidly racing up his neck. A bubble of something wanted to explode in his chest. "On that note, I'll let myself out. I'll see you later, Tara, right?"

"Yes, later." she dug her fingernails into the pair of socks she gripped as if that were enough to stop the varying emotions that raced through her body at that moment.

She watched as he turned from her doorway and listened as his footsteps echoed through the house and down the stairs. For now it was enough to know he had a thing for her and whatever that thing turned out to be in the end it was more than she had ever expected. For now it was enough. Later, would be another story.

And there would be time then to decide how that story would end.

Chapter Twenty-One

ஐ

"You did what!" Hutch almost shouted over the noise of the crowded bar.

"You heard me." Brent let his gaze linger on the green beer bottle Hutch swirled before taking a sip. He wanted a beer. He *needed* a beer. Instead, he chugged his soda, holding the sweet liquid in his mouth until the need subsided. "I all but raped her on my living room floor."

Hutch shook his head slowly, letting out a long sigh that had Brent's nerves on end. "I don't know what to say. I've known you a long time and I'd say this is the first time you've lost your head over a woman. Then I think about everything you went through with Kelly and I just have to wonder how big a glutton for punishment you really are."

"I know. But she's not like Kelly. Not really. Kelly was so…" Brent trailed off without finding the word he was searching for.

"Needy. Vain. Possessive. Moody. Pick one or if none of those fit I have plenty more stored up."

"Don't hold back buddy. Tell me how you really feel." Brent half-joked but Hutch's words, whether in jest or not, rankled.

"I didn't like Kelly. I thought she was too clingy, too whiny. Sure, she was beautiful with all that red hair. And those tits, man, she could stop traffic. But her problem was that she knew it. And once she set her sights on you, you were done for. She had no ambitions beyond getting your ring on her finger. I don't want to speak ill of her but Brent she sucked everything good out of you while she was alive. I for one am glad she's gone.

Don't get me wrong, I never wished her dead but you are better off now. You have to admit that."

"Thanks, buddy, I'll remember that," Brent glared across the table wondering how his current predicament had degenerated into this. "Especially coming from a man who just recently went ape-shit over a woman with those same characteristics."

"Coco, you mean. Yes, Coco is vain and possessive but that's where the comparison ends I think. Don't think her beauty has me blinded. I know she's selfish but so does she. And news flash, so am I. But, with what's going on in her life right now, she sees the error of her ways."

"You mean the cancer?"

"You know about that?"

"Tara told me the day Coco and that other one left. Tara was a basket case. I let her cry on my shoulder." Brent shrugged the incident off as trivial but admitting it out loud like that made him uneasy. Tara meant something to him and he couldn't get used to the feeling.

"That just tears it. Coco wouldn't have looked twice at a man like me before her cancer scare. I'm too ordinary. She told me about coming on to you when she knew Tara had her sights on you. The fact that you didn't look twice at her hurt her ego. But I think she sincerely likes me and isn't just using me as a prop for her screwed-up emotions. And I think Tara is the cure for what ails you, if only you'd stop treating her as if she were going to explode. So you say you practically raped her. Just how practically are we talking? Throw her on the floor and force her or tie her up and take what you wanted?"

"You've been reading true crime books again haven't you?" Brent grinned, his mood lighter but he was a long way from making sense of what really happened that night. "Neither of those, I... We... I don't know how it happened we just seem to start pawing at each other whenever we get too close. She saps the logical part of my mind bringing out my inner caveman I guess."

"Did she, even once, push you away or say stop, or no, or any of those other danger words?"

"No, she… Why am I telling you all this? It's really none of your business."

"Because you feel guilty for having sex with a beautiful woman and enjoying it. Brent, man, get a clue. Kelly is gone and won't ever come back. It's all right to feel alive. If Tara is the one you want even if it's only for the moment, let yourself have her and be grateful she chose to look twice at you. If she is what you need to finally purge Kelly then I throw my support behind her. Stop feeling guilty for every little thing you can't control and just enjoy it while it lasts."

"But…"

"But nothing, you're happier than I've seen you in a long time."

"I suppose."

"And she seems to return your, shall we say, happiness, right?"

"Yeah, I guess."

"There you have it. She's hot for you. You're hot for her so stop looking for reasons to be miserable and enjoy the moment."

"Maybe you're right."

"Of course I'm right. I am the only friend you have left after all." Hutch leaned back in his seat and watched the emotions play across his friend's face praying that he could be there when Brent discovered he was in love. That would surely be a sight to see. "Now what are we going to do about the little problem between you and our buddy Taylor? Personal vendettas are bad for business."

Chapter Twenty-Two

සා

That night Tara was disappointed to find Brent's house dark when she pulled into his driveway. She didn't really want to talk but it was comforting just knowing he was nearby.

Her house, when she entered, was warmer than it had been earlier that evening but she still tugged her jacket close around her body while she made the rounds downstairs to check the locks and turn out any stray lights. Her footsteps echoed eerily in the skeleton of her kitchen and she hurried to the stairs.

To say she was uneasy was putting it mildly, being alone in the house as she was. But she brushed off the dread that clutched at her and climbed the stairs to the second floor.

"You're just tired and confused. That's all." She said aloud to help alleviate her fear but she twisted the lock to her bedroom door anyway.

Outside the wind and the rain howled an answer. Tara shivered as she undressed in the small bathroom that opened into both her bedroom and the hallway. She pulled on a pair of warm flannel pj's, removed her contacts and brushed her teeth. And with a check to make sure the hall door into the bathroom was locked as securely as her bedroom door, she bolted across the room and dove into bed, dragging the covers up to her chin as she went. Craving noise she turned on the radio and reached for her books and glasses.

Maybe a murder mystery wasn't the best choice in her current frame of mind but there was absolutely no way she intended to get out of bed to look for something else to read. Besides the book was really good and she wanted to finish it sometime before the next century rolled around.

Cold air drifted around the room making Tara shiver as she tried in vain to get back into the flow of the book. Giving up she returned the book facedown to her bedside table and snuggled deep under the covers.

Normally, she liked the cooler temperature, considering it the perfect climate for sleeping. Just so long as it wasn't so cold that her nose turned icy that is. But tonight she just couldn't seem to get comfortable despite the toasty warmth of her bed. As she lay in bed staring up at the gold ring around the ceiling light fixture her thoughts drifted back to that afternoon and without really trying she could almost feel Brent's hands on her body as he loved her.

He had wonderful hands, all work-worn and strong. And those lips of his, they should be registered as a lethal weapon. Tara stretched and realized she was smiling.

Making love with Brent Chambliss was the pinnacle of pleasure. Too bad he had to go and open his mouth and ruin everything. Maybe it was for the best. After all a relationship based on sex wouldn't stand a chance in hell of surviving once the passion began to wear thin. And let's face it she and Brent were all chemistry, she told herself just as a blast of cold air swooped through the room fluttering the curtains.

Fighting the urge to pull the blankets over her head as she had done as a child whenever she was afraid, Tara huddled under the heavy covers thinking brave thoughts. While outside the rain that had become a steady downpour began to lash against the side of the house with a ferocity that sent Tara diving under the protective shelter of her warm comforter.

"This is ridiculous," Tara said aloud, all the better to convince herself, and relaxed her death grip on the material. "It's just a storm, a little eensy weensy cold front making its way down to the tropics, nothing to worry about. Nothing at all."

Slowly she eased the covers down from her face but clutched them tightly underneath her chin for the minimal protection that provided. "See. Nothing but a little rain and wind." Just then the electricity snapped, crackled and popped, leaving Tara to stare at the dark ceiling. With a yelp Tara dove back beneath the cover and stayed there until the air trapped with her began to grow heavy.

Deciding enough was enough; she flung off the covers and walked over to the window. She wanted to prove to herself that there was nothing to worry about except a leaky window.

She pulled the curtain back and peered out through the sheet of water that rolled down the glass to the house across the hedge. The lights were out there as well but she hadn't really expected to see them. Still she was a bit disappointed that Brent wasn't close by in case...

Bright headlights swept the walls of both houses. Tara angled her head so that she could see out toward the driveway. She could just make out Brent's strong form racing for his porch. And without realizing it, Tara relaxed. Just knowing he was nearby seemed to vanquish all the boogeymen hiding in her closet or underneath her bed.

She waited a few moments more hoping to see his shadow against the blinds that shielded his room from view. But it was too dark in the house and he didn't appear. Giving up Tara returned to her bed and bundled up beneath the blankets.

She shivered with cold once before the warmth seeped back into her body. Fatigue quickly overcame her now that the irrational fear of being alone in the old house had passed and she drifted off to sleep.

* * * * *

"Tara, you have all that you need to discover my secret." She sat on the bed next to Tara her black veiled head glowing as if the red hair shrouded beneath were fire. "Time is running out and you must tell him the truth about me soon."

"I know. But...does he really have to know? He seems to be getting along just fine lately. I mean..." Tara swallowed and hugged her knees close to her chest tugging the blankets close to fight the frigid cold that seemed to have invaded the room since she fell asleep.

The figure beside her seemed to glow brighter. "He can't be allowed to put me out of his mind this way. Sooner or later the guilt will return and later will be too late for me to change things. I can't allow that to happen. You have all the evidence you need. Tell him, Tara. Before it is too late."

"I…" Tara turned to the figure intending to argue her out of this single-minded determination to air her dirty laundry but the space she once occupied on the bed was empty. Still the cold lingered along with the scent of putrid magnolias.

* * * * *

Tara sat up in bed, the light from the bedside lamp blinding her, letting her know that the electricity had come back on. She reached over to turn it off when she found the old magnolia blossom lying on the bed beside her pillow, its petals soft and pearly white at the center, but brown and crisp at the tips.

Every hair on her body stood on end. Just a dream, she tried to tell her overactive imagination. It's a dream that's all. The same dream she'd been having since she moved in…sort of.

Brent could have slipped in after she'd left for the hospital and left the flower there. Couldn't he? But magnolias were long out of season and this one was fresh, well, almost fresh. And why hadn't she seen it before?

Why, indeed?

She picked up the flower and laid it on the bedside table. Tomorrow she would ask Brent about it. She reached for the lamp again and clicked it off. She rolled over onto her side and snuggled deeper into the covers, sheltered there with the covers as her magical shield against strange dreams and even stranger flowers. The odor of a ripe magnolia blossom was pungent, smelling somewhat like a rotten orange, and she found it impossible to go back to sleep.

So she rolled back over and plucked the flower up from the table. She would put it in the bathroom for the night. Tomorrow she would figure out how it got into her room.

But halfway across the room Tara noticed that the flower was ice-cold as if it had just been plucked from a wintry tree and laid in her bed. What few hairs that had a chance to relax were suddenly on alert. She quickened her pace but the flower, waxy white in the moonlit room, seemed to glow in her hand, its light almost brilliant in the dark.

With her heart thudding dangerously in her chest, Tara scurried to her bedroom door and twisted the lock. Opening the panel just wide enough for her arm to fit through, she tossed the flower into the hallway and slammed the door shut to keep it out lest it somehow tried to return.

"You are being completely unreasonable," Tara all but collapsed against the cold wood. Her hands trembled as she twisted the lock. "Completely and utterly idiotic. That flower can be explained with logic and reason. And before you even go there, there is no such thing as ghosts. There I said it. There are no ghosts in this house. No ghosts anywhere."

Calmer now, Tara pushed herself off the door and walked with shaky knees back toward her bed. But just as she passed her closet she stumbled and fell onto the cold hardwood floor. She righted herself and reached for the object that tripped her.

In the dim light from the window she was able to make out one of the cigar boxes she'd found in the kitchen wall and had thrown into her closet. The others lay scattered around her on the floor. The closet door visible in the light was closed just as it had been since early that evening.

Clamping her lips tightly together to hold in the scream she felt building up inside her, she dropped the box and scrambled across the room on her hands and knees to her bed. Climbing in she pulled the covers up over her head and shivered. Pincers of fear raced and clawed at her body as all of the dreams she'd had came rumbling and jumbling back to mind.

There was no doubt about it, logical Tara Jenkins decided from the safety of her magical tent, she was being haunted. And not just by any old ghost, no sir, she was being haunted by none other than Kelly Chambliss.

If that didn't sour a woman on men she had no idea what would.

Chapter Twenty-Three

ॐ

Brent, debating whether or not to ring the bell, stood outside Tara's front door. He could just as easily use his key but after last night, he didn't feel comfortable enough to walk into her house without announcing himself.

He wanted to see her before he went across town. He wanted to make sure she was all right. So he pushed the bell and listened as it chimed clearly throughout the house. No answer so he rang again. A few heart-stopping moments later he was relieved when Tara stuck her head out.

"Hey," was all he could think to say as he took in her tired face and tousled hair, the dark circles that her glasses couldn't hide. "I thought I'd stop by and see how you were before I headed into the office today. And to see if you needed anything."

"I'm fine. I just didn't sleep very well last night." Tara ran a hand through her hair as she squinted into the bright morning sunlight. "It's cold out here. Why don't you come in?"

"No, I have to get to work. We had a couple problems yesterday. And I've got to see about them... Uh, Tara, since we missed our date last night. Ah, would you like to meet me for lunch this afternoon?" Brent stuffed his hands deep into his pockets and scuffed one workboot-encased foot across the boards of her porch. He felt just like a teenager arranging his first date with the homecoming queen.

"I'd like that," she said with a smile.

"You do?"

"Yes, I think I do."

"Uh okay, how about around two."

"Sounds good, I'll see you then." Tara smiled again a tired smile that caused a tidal wave of guilt to wash over him.

"Tara, um, about yesterday…"

"It's in the past, Brent, no harm done." Her smile faded a bit making him feel worse for bringing the subject up again.

"Yeah okay, I'll see you this afternoon." He took a step back toward the stairs.

"Brent," she called just as he hit the walkway, "have you… I mean, do you know of any magnolia trees that might be in bloom this time of year?"

Magnolias were Kelly's favorite flowers. The memory assailed Brent with the force of a fist to the gut. Just the mention of the flower brought the sickly sweet smell back as clearly as if he were standing beneath a tree in full bloom. "No, it's been months since I've seen one in bloom. Why do you ask?"

"Uh, no reason, my mom, um, she likes them. I thought I might bring her one but I couldn't remember when they bloomed." She stumbled over the words, her brows knit together as if in deep concentration and Brent wondered if maybe she were telling him the truth. "Thanks anyway. I'm going to go back to bed for a while now, so I'll see you at two. At the office, right?"

"Right." He hesitated for a moment, the thought of her in bed enough to send his body into fits.

"I'll be there." She curled her hand into a wave and after a second's hesitation closed the door.

Brent heard the locks click into place as he trotted over to the hedge. He looked back to see her standing in the front window, her hands stuffed into the pockets of her old gray robe. And Brent realized he'd never seen anyone look as beautiful as Tara did right then. He waved and went about his day with the image of her sleepy face burned into his memory.

* * * * *

Tara watched as the silver truck backed out of the driveway before she crept upstairs and looked around in the upstairs hall. But didn't see the magnolia anywhere.

"I did not imagine it. I didn't!" She scrambled on her knees looking into every nook and cranny in the vicinity but the white waxy bloom was nowhere to be found.

"Damn." Her skin rippled with gooseflesh. "If you're here watching me I hope you're having a good laugh because I am not going to fall for your tricks again."

She could have sworn she heard laughter as she rose to her feet and rushed into her room. No sense in locking the door. Obviously, the ghost or whatever didn't need the door to come and go. She sidestepped the boxes scattered on the floor and climbed back into bed where she just sat and stared at the mess.

The dreams came back to her in snatches, a wedding, the couple at the park, the funeral. They weren't dreams at all, but key events in the late Mrs. Chambliss' life. And in every one, there had been the veiled figure pleading with Tara for help in straightening out the mess she had made of her life.

"Why me?" she asked waiting for a reply even though she would rather not have a conversation with a ghost that early in the morning. Not that there really was a good time for that. "Why me?"

"Because I make him happy? Is that it? And he doesn't want to let go of his guilt where you are concerned. Is that it?" Tara said as she remembered more and more of the dream conversations. "So, Kelly Chambliss. What did you do that was so terrible? What are the secrets you are hiding? You are going to have to be a little more forthcoming if I'm going to help you."

Tara sat for a while waiting for a sign that the ghost had heard her. Waiting for a sign that she had finally gone over the deep end into insanity was more like it. She glanced to the mess on the floor and remembered what she'd seen two days ago. "The boxes, of course. You were giving me a push all this time and I was too dense to realize it. Thanks, but next time, try not to scare the bejeezus out of me."

Tara leapt off the bed and gathered up the boxes. She stacked them neatly on her bedside table before she climbed back under the covers. The box she had opened that day was the logical place to start. She dumped the contents out on the bed and settled down to piece together Kelly Chambliss' secret.

* * * * *

Hours passed like minutes while Tara sorted through photos of Kelly and baby Betsy some with Brent but most without. Most she discovered were with the same older man. Nearly all of the boxes contained photos and a few keepsakes but Tara had a sneaking suspicion she knew what Kelly's secret was from just these. And there was no way in hell she wanted the job of informing the man she was rapidly falling in love with that the daughter he had grieved for all these long years wasn't his.

No. There was absolutely no way she would ever tell Brent if this was what Kelly wanted him to know. The truth would kill him. She just knew it.

But without some sort of proof other than a boatload of incriminating photos, she likely never would have to anyway. She closed the box she had just picked through and took the last one from the table.

The rubber band snapped when she tried to remove it, catching the back of her hand. Tara dropped the box in response and two hard-covered journals fell out onto the quilt. Tara picked the one that would have been on the bottom of the box and opened the cover.

"Shit," she said as the phone rang, startling her into dropping the book, the words "Personal Journal of Kelly Chambliss" emblazoned on her retinas, possibly for life.

"Hello." She grabbed the receiver from the table expecting it to be news of her mother. Instead, Brent's deep voice buzzed over the line.

"Tara?"

"Yes," she answered sucking a gasp of dismay as she looked at the clock. A big red digital 2:40 flashed accusingly at her. "Oh no, Brent I'm so sorry. Time slipped by me I guess."

"Calm down sweetheart, it's all right, I understand. You needed the extra sleep, considering how tired you looked this morning." His voice was filled with so much understanding that she felt even guiltier for not sleeping all this time as he assumed.

"I can be there in half an hour if you still have time."

"I'm on my way out to a site. We've had a few problems like I told you this morning. But Tara, that's not the point of my call. Getting together can be rescheduled and I do understand. I just got a call from the plumbing company I do business with. They are running a bit behind schedule. They were supposed to be out at your place yesterday. Obviously, they didn't make it. I know this is very short notice but they will be there in the next hour or so."

"Oh no, I need a shower and I haven't brushed my teeth today. This is not a good time."

"I know sweetheart but they are booked solid for the next two weeks if we cancel now you'll be without a kitchen that much longer."

"How long will it take, do you think? Until they can turn my water back on?"

"They are saying Monday, probably late. So it shouldn't be too much of an inconvenience. Just fill the tub with water for flushing the toilet and you can use my shower whenever you need it."

"That's all right I'll make other arrangements. What's the company name so I'll recognize them when they get here?"

"Oh yeah, that would be a good thing to know wouldn't it? It's Gulf Coast Plumbing. Tony Reynolds is the name of the guy who will be doing the work at your place. All he will be doing is running the line for the new bathroom and replacing the old lead pipes in your kitchen. It's not a very big job but while they work the water has to be off. You do understand that right?"

"Yes, of course I do. Besides, I brought this on myself Brent. I could have waited awhile to do this remodel so I am prepared for the inconvenience."

"All right then, I'll stop by there this evening to lend a hand. Right now, I have to deal with another major catastrophe and…well, no rest for the weary. See ya later."

"Yeah later." Tara waited to hear the line go dead before she pushed the power button on the cordless and laid it on the bed. It was nearly three in the afternoon and she wasn't even dressed yet. She'd missed another date with Brent and hadn't been out to the hospital yet.

"Pathetic, just pathetic," she said to her reflection the second she stepped into the bathroom. "You are getting so very lazy in your retirement, you know that? You need to get a job. And when was the last time you saw the inside of a gym? You need to get your ample fanny in gear, ASAP, before you turn into a couch potato."

Tara turned one way then the other to get a look behind her. But the mirror was just to small to accommodate her vanity and she would just have to trust the size of her butt was about the same as ever and be happy. She reached behind the shower curtain and turned on the water to heat up while she brushed her teeth. She had one hour or so before the plumbers would be there to cut off her water and rip out her pipes and she had at least two hours' worth of getting ready to do before she was presentable enough. Lord help her for biting off more than she could chew with this house.

* * * * *

"Damn, that is one fine female," Tony Reynolds breathed when Tara was safely out the back door.

In an effort not to take the man's head off for him, Brent felt every muscle in his body go stiff. "Hey, Brent, what do you think it would cost me to get inside her pants for just one night?"

All sense thundered out of Brent's head at the words and he flew across the room bringing Tony down with a thud onto the bare kitchen floor in a flying tackle his brother would have been proud of. One of the other plumbers stepped behind him and grabbed his arm before he had a chance to bury the fist he held high in Tony's pretty face.

"Jeezus, Brent. I didn't know. Damn it man, will you get off me. You're a heavy bastard." Tony lay on the floor with Brent straddling him, his breath coming in gulps. "I didn't know she was your woman or I'd a kept my big mouth shut. I didn't mean anything by it. I swear. I wasn't going to go after her or anything, it was just talk. You know, you've talked it yourself a time or two."

Brent felt something inside him snap as he glared down into Tony's face. This was a man he'd known for many years, a man he called friend. And although they weren't close, they had indeed talked the talk on the job site about any female that happened into view. It was harmless prattle really, this Brent knew but, damn, that particular woman had him so messed up inside he couldn't think straight.

"Yeah, okay." He shook off the callused hands that held his wrist and stood up offering Tony a hand up. "Sorry man, I didn't mean anything. I'm sorry."

"Hey don't mention it, buddy." Tony rubbed his shoulder, which had apparently taken the brunt of the fall. "Come on we've got work to do if we are to get the lady's water back on some time this millennium."

Brent watched as the three-man crew filed out of the house presumably to the crawl space underneath. Confused by his behavior he ambled into the living room and collapsed into the one chair Tara owned. He didn't know what just happened in there but he did know one thing for sure. Tara had him so tied up in knots that he didn't know which way was up anymore. What's more, he had no idea what he was going to do about it.

All he knew was he had a taste of her but instead of purging her from his system as it should have done, that taste just made him crave more. He was a mess that was for sure and somehow, someway he was going to have to do something about that condition before he took out a city block when he exploded.

He pounded the arm of the over-padded leather chair and watched the sun disappear through the lace curtains of the front windows. Was it just him or were the nights longer than they were ever before? He wondered as he listened to the telltale sounds of men's voices laughing under the house. He sighed. More laughter than work was going on under there and Brent would bet anything he was the butt of the joke.

If there were a more deserving person for ridicule, Brent would really love to meet him right then so that he wouldn't feel so alone. With that thought, he left the crew to their work and took off down the street at a jog to clear his head of the infuriating Tara Jenkins before it was too late.

Chapter Twenty-Four

∽

Tara didn't return that night. Brent paced the living room waiting. Always waiting. At three in the morning he gave up and went to bed, where he tossed and turned until dawn.

He rolled onto his side and pounded his pillows into a pulp before he curled into a ball and drifted into an uneasy sleep. But his dreams left him even more restless. Around midmorning he awoke to the sounds of a car horn outside. When the horn gave way to someone pounding on his front door, he climbed out of bed and staggered to answer the door, thoughts of mayhem running through his head. But when he opened the door, he could only stare in shock at the person he hadn't seen in nearly two years.

"Hey, pinhead. You gonna let me in or what?" His next-up brother Caleb Chambliss, his Navy uniform all pressed and crisp, stood on the front porch. "And look at that hair. It's shorter than mine."

"Caleb! What the hell are you doing here? When did you get in? Why didn't you call?"

"Visiting you. This morning. And didn't have a chance. Now are you going to let me in? Or do I have to stand out here freezing my ass off?"

"Come on in. Want some breakfast?" Brent stepped back to let his brother pass but his attention was snared by the copper-colored truck just turning into his driveway. A whistle behind him pulled him back from the longing that swelled into his brain the second she stepped from the truck.

"Am I interrupting something?" Caleb drawled the admiration in his voice as he stared at Tara's round bottom, irritating Brent more than he wanted to admit.

"No, ah, she's my neighbor. I'm doing the remodel on her house and she's using my driveway until hers isn't occupied by my dumpster." Brent explained fighting down the hot spurt of jealousy that gripped him.

"Damn, I've been on a carrier with exactly four women for the last two months solid. The sight of a red-blooded American woman this early in the morning sure is a sight for these sore old eyes."

"Put those eyes back in your head, Caleb. I think she's headed this way." Brent's heart slammed in his chest at the sight of Tara coming up his walk. The smile on her lips and in her eyes when they met his made him feel as if he'd died and gone to heaven.

"Good morning," Tara said as she stepped onto the porch.

"Morning." He almost forgot the brother who stood just behind him in the doorway. "Ah Tara, this is my brother Caleb. Caleb, my neighbor, Tara Jenkins."

"Brother?" Tara tore her eyes from his as if she hadn't seen Caleb standing back there leering at her. "Oh yeah, the one in the Navy. How do you do? I live next door…"

"So I was informed," Caleb held out a hand tanned dark from the sun and seawater to envelop Tara's smaller creamy one. Aware that he was jealous Brent gnashed his teeth together but didn't say anything. "Nice to meet you, Tara. At the risk of embarrassing my brother here, I just have to say that you might just be the prettiest thing these old eyes have ever seen."

"I bet you say that to all the women you meet." Tara replied, her neck turning pink.

"Only the ones with a pulse."

"Okay, that's enough. You're embarrassing her." Brent had to bite his tongue to keep his temper, especially after Tara had gone all pink and pretty. "You have to forgive him Tara, he left his brain over in the Middle East somewhere."

"It's okay, I'm used to it." Tara let go of Caleb's hand and stepped away. "It looks like you guys have some catching up to do so why don't I say goodbye and let you get to it."

"Nothing doing. *Baby* brother here, was just about to offer me some coffee. I'm sure we can scrounge up enough for three." Caleb caught her hand before she could make good her escape and tucked it into the crook of his elbow. "And while he's fixing it, you can tell me just why you look so familiar."

Tara looked helplessly at Brent as Caleb dragged her into the house. "Brent I…"

"Don't worry about it Tara, there's no accounting for retarded brothers."

"Who you calling a retard, pinhead? I have half a mind to whoop your rear right now."

"Go ahead. I'd pay good money to see you try. And if you succeed, who will make coffee with me lying in a heap on the floor? Unless of course you somehow figured out how to work that coffeemaker Laura gave you for Christmas before you shipped off two years ago." Brent smirked at his culinarily inept brother. He wasn't much better himself but at least he could throw on a passing fair pot of coffee without help.

"I'm sure I could talk the little lady into making me a cup and she probably could make a better brew than that pond sludge you call coffee." He patted Tara's hand and tugged her into the kitchen with him.

"I'm sure Tara has things she needs to do at home, Caleb. Just because she stopped by to say hi doesn't mean she volunteered to babysit you while you're in town."

"That sounds good. I've always had this particular fantasy about… Hey Brent you remember Tiffany Duncan? Ma hired her to try to keep us in line one summer when you were still a kid. I think I was eleven or twelve, she was about sixteen or so and man I think she was my first wet dream."

"Jeezus, Caleb, don't you have any manners?"

"What?" Caleb pulled out a chair for Tara and perched on the edge of the one closest to her, his eyes filled with humor as he gazed from her to Brent. "Tara doesn't mind do you honey? Damn, pinhead, you're turning into an old woman right before my eyes."

"Stop calling me pinhead. We're not kids anymore."

"It was a silly name anyway. I can't imagine how come it's stuck this long. Pinhead."

"I give up." Brent threw his hands up in the air. "You can just make your own coffee while I go get dressed."

"Touchy, touchy, pinhead—ah, Brent."

"Do you have to treat him like that?" Tara stood up from the table and went to the cupboard where Brent stored his coffee and started a pot. Caleb leaned back in his chair watching her like a cat.

"It's what older brothers do. Besides it keeps him from wanting to take my head off." Caleb offered, noticing how familiar the woman was with his brother's kitchen.

"Why would he want to take your head off when he hasn't seen you in—how long?"

"Almost two years, the last time was on Christmas Eve. Damn it's good to see him again." Caleb sighed as the woman pulled out a griddle and a mixing bowl without searching for them.

"You didn't answer my question," she crossed to the fridge for milk, butter and eggs.

"What question was that?" Caleb rubbed his jaw with the back of his hand. Just how cozy were these two?

"Why he wants to take your head off when you've just come home?"

"Oh that question. Because he thinks I'm putting the moves on his property." Caleb bit back a chuckle when the egg she cracked missed the mixing bowl entirely, landing on the floor instead.

"What do you mean by property?"

"I'm going to change out of these duds into something less conspicuous and maybe later I'll treat everyone to lunch at some ridiculously expensive steakhouse. How's that sound?" he stood abruptly slinging his bag over his shoulder and bounced out of the room leaving the flustered woman behind to clean up the mess he'd caused her to make.

He turned the corner into the hallway just in time to see his brother emerge from the room that had once been the guestroom dressed in a pair of jeans and a sweatshirt.

"Where am I sleeping?" he prudently asked but Brent just stared at him for a moment.

"Who said you were staying here?" Brent said finally, his eyes narrowed to slits.

"I did, now stop being prickly and just enjoy seeing me while I'm here or you'll kick yourself when I'm gone."

"You are so full of it."

"Yeah little brother, I am. It's about time you figured that out."

Brent sighed, his eyes going round for a second, as if he realized he really had just figured him out. "In there," Brent nodded toward the master bedroom.

"Thanks, little brother, now go see if your neighbor needs any help whipping up those pancakes." With that Caleb stepped into the bedroom and after grinning wickedly at his brother closed the door in his face.

Brent stared at the door for a second before shrugging his shoulders and heading back to the kitchen to see if Tara was indeed making pancakes.

"You don't have to do that. We can go out," he said when he discovered her whipping a batter with a wire whisk.

"I'm hungry. I left Tommy's without eating. Randi is suffering from morning sickness and I didn't want to do anything that would make it worse." Tara raised the whisk from the bowl and let it drip into the batter a second before dropping it into the sink.

"Randi is your sister-in law right? So that means you're going to be an aunt."

"Yeah, and I think I am excited about it. I'm certainly happy for my brother. After what he went through with his first wife, he deserves a happy ending." Tara flinched and Brent assumed she thought she had somehow offended him. "There's a bag of blueberries in the freezer. If you wouldn't mind getting it I'll drop a few in the batter."

"Really, Tara, we can go out. You don't have to cook for me and Caleb," Brent repeated but he went to the freezer and rummaged for the bag of blueberries anyway, finally locating it beneath a huge roast. "Where did all this food come from?"

"Don't you ever check your freezer?" Tara gave him a questioning look.

"Why should I? There's never anything in it." He shrugged pulling out both the blueberries and the roast. "When were you planning to fix this?"

Tara took the blueberries from his hand and ripped open the bag, the pleading look on his face as he glanced from her to the meat made her laugh. "Put it in the fridge and we'll see what the day brings. But your brother did say something about a steakhouse."

"I'd rather have the pot roast." Brent grumbled but he put the roast into the refrigerator anyway. "I haven't had pot roast for a long time, almost as long as it's been since I've had pancakes now that I think of it."

"Now see what you would be missing by going out to eat." Tara carefully ladled out several circles of batter onto the sizzling griddle and waited for it to start bubbling to drop a few blueberries into the mix.

"Smells heavenly. Is there any syrup?" Brent asked letting his nose lead him closer to her.

"In the cabinet," she nodded to the cupboard above her head her attention focused on flipping the pancakes.

Brent stepped behind her and reached overhead to retrieve the bottle of syrup noting that it was the real thing and not some overpriced substitute. His hand grazed her arm on the way down, the lightweight T-shirt she wore doing little to cover the warmth of her skin. Brent set the bottle on the counter beside the griddle, the need to touch her too much to resist.

"You smell heavenly too," he whispered next to her ear as his hands caressed her from shoulder to elbow. She shivered at his words, he noticed with pleasure that he had the power to do that to her. Her silky hair stirred against his cheek as he breathed in her scent. She shivered again and leaned against him, the contact of her body making it impossible for him to catch his breath.

"Hey something in here smells great."

"Damn," Brent cursed when Tara jumped away from him. Why, oh why, did his idiot brother have to show up now and ruin everything?

Chapter Twenty-Five

🔊

"Just drop me off here," Tara said when Brent pulled into the visitor's parking lot at Providence Hospital.

"You want me to come back for you or anything?" Brent didn't like the idea of leaving her like this.

"That's all right. I'll either get Tommy to take me home or call a cab." Tara stepped out of the truck and leaned back inside to smile at Caleb in the back. "It was nice meeting you."

"Same here sweet-cheeks. Next time I'm in town we should hook up and I'll show you a side of this boring little city you never dreamed existed." Caleb returned her smile with a wolfish grin that had Brent seeing red. But since his brother was leaving first thing in the morning, he didn't dwell on just how nice his brother's scrawny neck would feel in his hands when he wrung it.

"It's a date." Tara slung her purse over her shoulder and started to close the door when she caught the look on Brent's face and remembered what Caleb had said about trespassing on his brother's territory. Maybe leaving the two of them alone wasn't the best idea after all. What was she thinking? There was absolutely no way she was going to hang around and referee their silly squabbles. "Bye guys. Don't get into too much trouble."

"Tara!" Brent shouted out the open window to catch her attention before she ventured too far away. "Ah, you sure about the cab? I could come back later if you'd like?"

"I'll be all right Brent. I lived in New York City remember. I think I can handle myself here if need be. Besides you haven't seen your brother in a long time. Go do whatever it is brothers do."

"You heard the lady. Let's blow this pop stand." Caleb prodded from the backseat but Brent just nodded and waved.

"You positive?" He ignored his brother. It was either that or kill him.

"I am. And Brent, enjoy him while he's here. You might not have another chance," she gently kissed his cheek before stepping back onto the sidewalk, with her hand raised to wave them off.

Stunned, Brent watched her in the rearview mirror as he drove away.

"You know I for one am glad to see you back in the saddle again." Caleb climbing over the seat distracted him and when he looked back, she was gone.

"Only you could come up with something so crude."

"Then you haven't slept with her yet. Damn, Brent, you must be slipping in your old age. I'd give her a night she wouldn't soon forget if she'd look at me just once like she looks at you."

Brent stared straight ahead in silence as he waited for the light to change. Visions of slamming his brother's face against a brick wall played through his imagination.

"So you have slept with her then. Is that it? And you had plans that I messed up. Damn Brent, sorry." Caleb leaned back in the seat watching as his brother tried to strangle the steering wheel.

"You didn't mess up anything. We... There isn't anything to mess up. Tara is a friend and that's about all."

"Umm-humm, and the Easter Bunny lays square eggs. Listen Brent, I like her."

"Damn it, Caleb if you so much as..."

"Will you shut up a minute and let me finish what I was going to say?" Caleb cut him off before he could launch a full-scale assault. "Jeez Louise, man you are so damned touchy you might just explode."

"I'll wait until you finish."

"As I was saying before you went ballistic. I like her. She seems to be just what the doctor ordered for you. So by all means, sleep with her. Damn, marry her for all I care. Just don't let her get away. You'll never forgive yourself if you do. And don't hand me any crap about your late wife. It's high time you stopped hiding behind all that guilt that's eating you up Brent and get on with the life you were meant to lead."

"What do you know about anything Caleb? You go through women like water and I'd thank you to leave Kelly out of this. She has nothing to do with Tara."

"That's where you're wrong on both counts. Kelly has everything to do with Tara. She is standing between you and true happiness and it's time you realized that, little brother."

"Go to hell."

"One day I just might, now hang a left up here. I know this great little place where the beer is cheap and so are the women." Caleb ordered locking away his own woman troubles before his little brother could gather his wits enough to ask.

"I don't drink anymore."

"Good for you. Turn anyway, I'm sure they stock some fancy French water or something to tide you over."

Brent sighed and let the last few minutes slide away. He didn't like arguing with Caleb but they'd been doing it since he could talk and old habits died hard. Behind him, the sun was setting and the long night loomed ahead so he turned. He didn't want to be alone with Tara on his mind so he may as well tag along with Caleb for the entertainment value if nothing else.

"Good man." Caleb said when Brent slid into the turning lane and headed south toward Dauphin Island and his favorite hangout. "I mean it about the drinking, Brent. I'm proud of you man. It takes a big man to do something about his weakness. One day you'll have to tell me how to go about it. But that day isn't today so just drive."

Brent sighed again and did as his brother ordered. There would be enough time later to find out what demons were chasing Caleb. For now he had his own demons to deal with and all of them seemed to be wrapped up in the curvy blonde package he'd just dropped off at the hospital.

"You got it Caleb. Just don't expect me to haul your drunk ass up off the beach after you've puked your guts up." Brent said but Caleb just grunted and turned the radio to the hard rock station they'd listened to when they were kids heading down to raise a little hell at the Painted Pony. The more things changed, Brent thought letting the music bring back the good times he and Caleb had shared, before Kelly had come into the picture and put distance between them.

Suddenly needing to recapture whatever was left of the boy he'd left behind all those years ago, Brent let his foot ease the accelerator toward the floor. And maybe just maybe he might find the man he'd lost along the way.

Chapter Twenty-Six

ಸಿ

The rain started just before lunch the next day. Tara drove across town to the job interview she had arranged early that morning. But things had not worked out as she had planned. Instead of spending the rest of the day training for her new job, she spent the morning at the hospital, followed up with a trip to the gym to work off a little stress.

The storm came up suddenly, which wasn't uncommon for this time of year in the South. Tara heartily wished it had held off for another hour or so, at the very least until she was safely inside her house. As it was it was black as pitch when she raced across the yard to her house only to find her dreams of a hot shower shattered. The rain had kept the plumbers from finishing that day as scheduled.

"Damn," she tossed her gym bag across the room and paced the length of the hall, her sodden shoes making squishing sounds on the floor. "Double damn."

She crossed over to the living room window and stared out at Brent's drive where only her truck was parked. So far, she had managed to avoid the offer of his shower by staying with her brother. Hoping to take a nice long soak in her own tub, she had skipped the shower at the gym. And she really did need a shower. But did she need one so badly that she should drive all the way across town in the pouring rain?

She glanced at the clock on the mantel. "Damn," she said again when she read the time. Nearly six, he could be in at any moment. Then again, he could have gone out. Either way she wasn't about to stand around dripping a moment longer. With that decided she raced upstairs to gather her favorite bath items and dry clothing.

A few minutes later she stood on her back porch with another gym bag packed with everything she needed to shower. She locked the door and raced across her yard to his.

The house was dark and cold when she entered through the back door. So she turned on the kitchen light and then a lamp in the living room as she headed down the hall to the small bathroom. The door was closed but not locked. She turned the knob and let the door swing open while she reached down and pulled off one of her sodden shoes.

Light and heat spilled out of the little room and a surprised Tara looked up at a very naked man, his face half covered in shaving cream. His dark eyes fixed on hers, *his* surprise fading quickly as she watched. She looked away as Brent grabbed a towel and wrapped it around his waist.

"You're letting out all my heat." He kept his eyes on the mirror pretending to shave.

"S-s-sorry." Tara stammered and turned her head to give him a bit of privacy until she could gather up her wits and get the heck out of there. "I didn't think you were home yet. I-I'll go."

"Get in here," Brent reached out of the warm room, grabbed her by her soaking wet shirtsleeve and dragged her into the bathroom closing the door behind her. "You're wet and cold and I'm just about through."

"No. I'll wait in the kitchen until you're done." She felt the ragged edges of panic swelling up in her chest. After what happened the last time they were together, Tara couldn't bring herself to think of being near him this way again without destroying what was left of her pride.

"Tara." She heard the sigh in his voice. "I'm not going to maul you. Just let me finish shaving and the bathroom is yours."

"I'm sorry, Brent." She said again this time with confidence as the knot of panic receded. "I didn't mean to... What I mean to say... I trust you."

"You do?" He stopped shaving the razor paused mid-stroke the look in his eyes incredulous but when he smiled, a softness she'd never seen before took over.

"I trust you with my very life. I don't know why. Don't know if should but I do." Tara whispered. She watched his eyes, reflected in the mirror, shine with some inner fire that drew her to him. Not that she had far to go in the narrow bathroom.

The urge to touch him was stronger than the last time they were alone together. Tara reached out a trembling hand, placing it lightly on his right shoulder. The razor held in that hand seemed to sag as her hand warmed against his skin.

"Here, let me finish that." She took the razor from him with her right hand and for a moment, they stood that way, her hand on his shoulder their eyes locked in the mirror. "Turn around."

Brent felt the whispered words caress his body as gently as the hand on his shoulder. With all of his senses on high alert he turned to face her, slowly in case she thought to remove her hand and leave him cold and somehow abandoned there in the steamy warm bathroom. "You're too tall. I can't reach," she whispered after one swipe of the razor. So he dropped to his knees in front of her and gazed up into her eyes.

"That's not what I had in mind but it works. Now hold still." She ran her hand along his shoulder to his neck where she left it while she made quick work of his two-day beard. "Where's your truck?"

"Over at Pete's body shop. The last time I saw it, it was a crumpled heap covered in red mud." Brent said with a shrug as if it didn't matter.

"You were in an accident? Are you okay? Where's your brother? What happened?" Tara felt the now familiar panic start to creep back into her chest and she raced to get all of her questions out.

"Slow down, I can only answer on question at a time. I'm okay. Though, I might have a bruise or two in the morning. And Caleb's safely on a plane to Vegas to see our Mom. Basically, what happened was this, too much rain and too little dirt road for two cars. I moved over so the other guy could pass. And with the road being nothing but red clay slime I slid down into a steep ditch and sideswiped a couple of trees. Nothing major."

"Nothing major!" Tara felt the bands of panic tighten at the thought of him lying there in the mud and rain with a tree branch pinning him down. "Nothing major! You could have been killed. You could still be lying out there in the mud pinned under the truck. Oh God!"

"Don't, Tara." Brent took the razor from her shaking hands and laid it on the sink. He wiped his face on a hand towel next to the sink and stood. Taking her hands in his he pulled her to him and wrapped his arms around her wet body. "Don't think of what could have been. I'm okay I promise and I'm going to stay okay. Nobody was hurt and the driver of the other car braved the mud to make sure I was unhurt."

"It's just that I...I don't want to lose you. Not like that. I have enough tragedy in my life right now. I don't think I could handle something happening to you too." Tara let the words rush out without thought to what she was saying. Her deepest fears and feelings were there for him to hear, for him to laugh at.

She stood trembling in his arms fighting to control the emotion that was running through her when she felt the sharp intake of breath. And she knew that he had just realized what she had said without really saying those three little words.

"I'm sorry. I didn't mean that the way it sounded." She tried to step away before the censure she expected could come. But he wouldn't let go. If anything, he held her closer.

"You didn't? And here I was hoping you did." Brent said hoping Tara hadn't heard the break in his voice. She didn't want to lose him. Well that was something wasn't it, especially when he didn't want to be lost.

"You do?" Tara said pulling away just far enough to angle her head to take in his face when he answered.

"Yes." The honest truth in his eyes was scarier than if he had mocked her love. "Are you cold?"

"I'm soaking wet," she said but she knew it wasn't cold making her shiver.

"That can be remedied you know?"

"Yes."

"Yes?"

Tara nodded. She couldn't think of anything else to say. Her body and soul were his for the asking and that he asked made her want him all the more.

Yes, she said yes. Blood raced through Brent's body infecting all the parts of him that had desperately wanted her to say yes. He gazed down into her eyes looking for the truth. What he found was desire hot and burning for him. Yes, oh yes that was exactly the kind of truth he wanted from this woman.

He lowered his head and touched his lips to hers. At the same time he pulled and tugged on her wet clothing until he had every last piece of it on the floor and her cold wet body pressed to his warmth.

Her hands, once they were free, found his bare back and slowly ever so slowly explored every inch of him, just as her soft lips sought to delve deeper inside his soul than any other woman he had ever known.

Taking a cue from her, he let his hands explore relishing every in-drawn breath and every shiver as he found sensitive places. Places he wanted more time to savor but for now, just seeing her bare body pressed against his was enough to send him over the edge. He wanted, no needed, to be with her then. He could explore later.

Tara gasped when she felt her feet come off the floor but she trusted him and besides she didn't want to let go of his delicious mouth long enough to protest. Brent Chambliss was without a doubt the best tasting man she'd ever encountered. She gasped again when her back came up against something cold. And again when insistent fingers slipped between her body and his and found her shamelessly ready for whatever he wanted to do.

She lifted her legs and wrapped them around his waist, her mouth still fastened to his as if she would perish if that connection were ever severed.

His callused fingers stroked her deep inside, his tongue keeping time with the rhythm he set until Tara's whole body began to thrum with a primitive force. In desperation, she ran her hands down his back, in search of more skin to knead as he pushed her to her limits. Instead of skin she found cloth and began to tug at the towel with a ferocity that frightened her. When the material fell free, Tara sighed letting her hands roam free now that she had all that delicious skin to explore.

Body to body, flesh to flesh, she arched into him telling him what she wanted without saying a word. When he withdrew his fingers she felt bereft and waited for him to push her away as he'd done that first time.

He pulled away breaking the kiss and Tara cried out at the loss. She cried out again when he entered her pushing her high against the cold wall as he slowly eased himself deep inside.

When she once again rested against his body, now one with him he lowered his mouth to hers. And she sighed with pleasure, feeling as if she had finally come home. The muscles beneath her hands bunched, warning her that there was more to come as he withdrew ever so slightly.

"Stop." Tara opened her eyes only to catch sight of them in the mirror. "Oh stop please."

"What?" Brent said his voice ragged with desire and confusion.

"I'm sweaty and I stink and…" she said horrified that he could possibly want her after coming in straight from the gym as she had.

"Is that all?" he said, burying his face in her neck as he chuckled. "Well then I don't have to worry about getting you all sweaty later."

"But…" She gasped as his mouth settled on her breast teasing her nipple with his teeth before he pulled it into his mouth to suckle. "Ohhh."

Brent smiled to himself at the sound of her moan. He'd wanted to taste her like this, wanted to have her naked and pressed against him for so long now that he didn't think he could stop. What was a little sweat? In a few seconds, they would both be hot and sweaty so nothing mattered but the sweet taste of her in his mouth. Or the exquisite feel of her inner muscles as she wriggled beneath his suckling.

"Please," she whispered when he switched nipples her voice a mere purr next to his ear. "Oh please Brent, more."

She moaned his name again her hands grasping his shoulders as if she could force him to comply. "Easy, love," he whispered letting go of her breast and returning his mouth to hers. "Wait for me."

Tara whimpered when he rocked into her and wrapped her arms tight around his shoulders. Her body, pushed to the limits of desire, rocked back on its own accord until she felt the familiar pleasure begin to tingle all the way to her very toes. She set the rhythm with her tongue forcing him to move his lower body to match until at last the tingling became unbearable and she shattered in wave after trembling wave there against the wall in the tiny little bathroom.

"Your turn," she whispered when she could find her voice aware that she lay limp in his arms.

"Soon," he said withdrawing from her and setting her on her feet in the tub. "Next time when we've remembered protection."

"Oh," Tara gasped when he turned the water on and stepped in behind her.

"Next time," he said stepping into the tub with her and closing the door. "Right now we need to do something about that shower you wanted."

"Oh," was all Tara could think to say as the spray from the shower hit her sensitive skin. And they set about steaming up the bathroom all over again.

.

Chapter Twenty-Seven

ॐ

The clock on the bedside table blinked midnight when Tara was finally able to focus. The evening had passed by in a blur of passion that left her feeling sated and sleepy. A heavy arm lay draped over her hip. Its warmth was comforting and she snuggled closer to the source of that heat.

"Um," he murmured into her hair and she felt his warm breath on her neck.

"I didn't mean to wake you," she whispered.

"You didn't," he replied, his voice gruff with sleep. "I was just thinking."

"About what?" Tara rolled to face him.

"About this," he pressed closer to her, his body aroused as his mouth fastened onto hers. He stroked her already warm body until it burned with fire from deep inside.

"You spend way too much time thinking and not enough time doing."

"I can remedy that right now if you'd like." He pulled her on top of him for yet one more new experience in a night full of new sensations, his voice catching as he slid deep inside her.

Later she lay sprawled on his body her breathing slowing to normal but still matching his as if they were one person.

"It's late Brent. Maybe I should go." Her heart caught in her throat at the thought of leaving him. But this much this soon couldn't be good for them. Could it?

"Stay with me Tara," he said rolling her beneath him and gazed into her eyes. The fear and longing she saw there in the half-light from outside had her heart beating faster. "Stay tonight. Tomorrow is soon enough to have doubts. Say you'll stay."

"I'll stay for now." *I'll stay forever*, she thought wishing she had the courage to say the words aloud. For now, it was enough that he wanted her with him. Tomorrow would be soon enough to think of leaving.

"Thank you," he said his body already moving in hers as he spoke. "I need you so much I don't think I ever want to see the sun come up again."

"Brent, I…"

"Don't say anything you'll regret later Tara. Just let me love you. Tomorrow will come soon enough."

His lips covered hers cutting off the words she wanted to say. Tomorrow would indeed come soon enough. For now, it was enough to know he needed her. For now, but what would tomorrow bring? Would he love her when the passion of that night gave way to dawn?

She gave herself to him with no more thoughts of tomorrow. Tomorrow hurt too much to think on just then. Tomorrow was ages away, she decided as she floated into that place only Brent could send her. And just then, she too hoped tomorrow would never come if it meant she could float in that place forever.

* * * * *

Morning, like everything else, was out of Brent's control and he rolled over when the muted light from another gray dawn invaded the darkness of sleep.

Odors that were foreign to him pushed through the sleep clouding his mind and he dreamed of fresh coffee and bacon.

Eventually sounds invaded his dreams pulling him completely into reality. Reluctantly, he flung off the covers bracing against the frigid air that normally permeated the house in the mornings. But the chill he expected wasn't there. Instead, heat circulated the room and he heard the furnace shut off.

The sounds coming from somewhere in the house grew louder. The smell of bacon in the air made his stomach growl painfully when he realized he wasn't dreaming.

He lunged from the bed to make sure he really wasn't dreaming. He stopped before he reached the hall and grabbed a pair of sweatpants from the hamper by the door. They still smelled clean at least so he pulled them on and went in search of the breakfast angel he was sure had come to pay him a visit.

She stood in front of the stove in his kitchen, her hair wrapped in a large towel, her body in his robe while the tantalizing smells of breakfast floated around her. Right then, Brent decided he'd never seen anything as beautiful as the woman who filled his dreams, his stomach and his heart.

He faltered, the heart in question skipping a few important beats at the thought that Tara Jenkins could possibly fill the void that resided there. And somehow it seemed as if his heart had known it all along. His head just hadn't caught up. But wasn't that always the way of things.

Filled with new and frightening emotions, Brent stepped into the room. "Good morning," he said drawing her into his arms and nuzzling her neck.

"Um, morning," she yawned as she leaned into him allowing him to raise gooseflesh on her neck that he was sure ran beneath the heavy flannel robe that hid her body from him.

"Something smells delicious."

"Thank you. How do you like your eggs?"

"I was talking about you. But just the same, scrambled, if you don't mind."

"Oh, in that case." She turned in his arms and let him unwrap the robe and run his hands over her bare skin. "Um, don't start that or there will be no eggs."

"A fate worse than death. I don't know which I love more, your body or your cooking. Maybe if I had both at the same time I might figure it out."

"Brent!" Tara laughed and pushed his hands away, her heart trembling in her chest as she retied the belt to the robe she'd borrowed after her shower. He'd said the word love. He loved her body and he loved her cooking. It was too much to hope for and too little. She didn't dare hope for more lest she jinx the love he gave freely.

"What? Can't I have what my heart desires?"

"No."

"You are a cruel woman Tara Jenkins do you know that?" Brent laughed in return as he snagged a piece of bacon from the plate on the counter. "Well if I can't have you with my breakfast I'll have to settle for breakfast. Do you know how long it's been since I had homemade bacon?"

"There are biscuits in the oven," Tara said as she cracked eggs into a bowl.

"Don't tease me like that. I don't think I can stand it... Damn." The telephone ringing in the living room brought him up short. "Let it ring., The machine will get it."

"Damn it, Brent. Pick up!" Came Hutch's frenzied voice over the speaker and Brent cursed again.

"I'm sorry Tara I've got to answer this."

"Go ahead, food will be ready in a few minutes." She waved a fork at him giving him what she imagined to be her most loving smile. But she hadn't missed the look on Brent's face at the sound of his partner's voice.

She poured the eggs into the skillet, listening quietly as she stirred. His voice held a note of anger but she couldn't make out his words. Something was wrong at one of the job sites. She flipped the eggs until the moisture cooked out and neatly halved the fluffy yellow mass onto two plates. The biscuits came out of the oven hot and golden brown and she added them to the plate with the bacon and set everything on the table.

She was pouring coffee into two mugs when he walked into the room rubbing his hand through his hair. "Trouble?" she asked setting the cup in front of him just as he pulled out the chair and sat down.

"The bank wants to see our books."

"Can they do that?"

"They can do whatever they want."

"So what are you going to do?"

"Open the books. We've got nothing to hide. Then I'm going to go hunt Taylor down and whip his ass like I should have done last week."

"Isn't that the guy from the Halloween party?"

"Yeah, that's him. The sorry son of a bitch."

"What does he have to do with the bank wanting to audit you?"

"His daddy is the president of the bank financing the strip mall and last week they pulled a surprise inspection. Didn't find anything worth mentioning and now this…"

"This has to do with what happened in the bathroom that night doesn't it?" Tara couldn't eat. She held her fork in her lap waiting for him to deny that she was the cause of all this. He nodded and looked at his plate guiltily. She laid her fork down to rub her eyes where a headache wanted to start. "I thought I handled him that night. Brent I'm sorry."

"Not your fault. I kinda gave him a shiner the next day."

"Brent." She dragged his name out.

"Tara. He had no business laying a hand on you. And I'll do it again if he dares to mess with what's mine."

"Oh," Tara didn't know how to respond to that declaration. On the one hand, she was offended that he felt the need to play the he-man and rescue her maiden honor. On the other, the warmth that spread through her body when he declared her his property couldn't be denied. And though she considered herself a thoroughly modern woman a part of her shamelessly thrilled at the knowledge that he had marked her as his.

Brent seemed to sense her disquiet and bent his head to wolf down the breakfast on his plate. Tara, after watching him for a moment, wondered if he actually tasted the food she'd worked so hard to make just right.

Once he polished off the eggs and most of his bacon, he lifted his head to look her squarely in the eye. "I'm sorry. I know I should have left it alone but there is just something about being a man. We want to protect everyone we care about. And Tara I'd do it again in a heartbeat. Besides he had it coming since college."

"You're incorrigible aren't you?" Tara smiled at the look on his face.

"Yes ma'am, I sure am."

"When are you leaving?" Tara felt the force of that smile all the way to her toes.

"As soon as Hutch sends someone out to get me."

"Take my truck. I'm not going anywhere today except back to bed."

"Don't tempt me like that."

"What tempting, buster? I'm exhausted. You go play with your buddies while I get some sleep."

"You'll be here when I get home?" he said his face going very still as if he were holding his breath while waiting for her to reply.

Tara simply looked at him for a moment wondering what it was he wanted. She had intended to dress and go home and climb into her own bed for a few hours. But oh, how easy it would be to just slip back into his warm bed and curl up around his pillow and sleep the day away. "I thought I should go home."

Did his face fall or did she just imagine it?

"No matter, I'll find you when I get in. Oh and I'll call Tony and get him off his lazy butt for you." Brent threw his napkin on the table and carried his dishes over to the sink so that she wouldn't see the disappointment on his face. "Are you sure you don't need the truck today? I'd hate to leave you stranded."

"I'm sure. I'm going to clean up here and get some sleep. Okay."

"Okay."

"Good, now that that's settled maybe you should take a shower. You don't smell all that good this morning," she said as lightheartedly as she could when she came up beside him and scraped her uneaten breakfast down the disposal.

"Yes ma'am." He leaned over and kissed her cheek before he took off toward the back of the house.

"I'll leave the keys on the table for you," she called out after him but he already had the water running and couldn't hear her.

Twenty minutes later Brent returned to the kitchen just as Tara finished loading the dishwasher. He grabbed her from behind and twirled her to face him.

"Is this better?" he rubbed his smooth face across her forehead.

"Umm, you smell good enough to eat." Tara sniffed his neck his damp hair just grazing her nose. "Mind if I take a bite?"

"Go ahead," Brent bared his neck to her and gasped when she nipped him. "You know what I want more than anything else right now?"

"No, what?" Tara said thinking she'd like to drag him back into the bedroom to do some serious tasting of her own before she lost her nerve.

"I'd like to forget about Hutch and his damned phone call and take you back to bed. I'd like to watch the rosy red glow climb over your breasts when I enter you. God, Tara, I could spend the rest of my life in bed with you, the rest of the world be damned."

"I'll be here when you get home." Tara said before she could stop herself. "For now there is other business to tend to."

"Will you be wearing this little ensemble?" He tugged at the belt.

"I was thinking something a little less elaborate."

"God Tara," he moaned against her cheek. "I'm not ever going to get out of here if you keep talking like that."

"Sorry." She turned her face to catch his lips for a goodbye kiss that tingled through her body making her moan this time. "I'll remember to keep my smutty mouth closed next time."

"I like your smutty mouth. Especially when it's pressed up against mine."

"Get out of here." She pressed the keys to her truck into his hands and pushed him toward the door. "You need to beat those nosy bankers to the office."

"I'll be home early."

"I'll be here. Now go."

Tara stood in the kitchen doorway and waved as he slipped out the front door. Her body burned with frustrated desire for the man, her mind filled with very large second thoughts.

Second thoughts that had burned a hole through her ego and left her with doubts. He loved her body and he loved her cooking but did he love her? And she knew that no matter how much she wanted to stay it would just be all that much harder to leave when it was time.

She sighed long and loud the sound echoing in the empty house, the dishwasher and the furnace the only sounds that answered.

Restlessly she prowled the living room, straightening here, wiping dust away there. She wandered toward the back of the house past the two closed doors to the bedroom they had shared the night before when it dawned on her that Brent had moved from the room he'd shared with his wife.

Out of curiosity she opened that door and glanced around the room. The portrait that had fallen that night still leaned against the wall. The bed was made but was littered with objects that she remembered seeing in other parts of the house. The blinds were open letting in the gray light of day and Tara glimpsed the side of her house through the slats. A prickling feeling at the back of her neck assailed her. Tara remembered the last time she'd been in the room and wondered if maybe Kelly was able to see into the room she had once shared with Brent.

But that was silly. There were no such things as ghosts, she thought bravely now that time had dulled the memory of that night when the magnolia had mysteriously appeared. And certainly if there were such a thing it wouldn't peek into other people's houses. Would it? Tara rubbed her neck to sooth away the feeling and closed the door.

Across the hall the other closed door beckoned her. She'd never seen inside, never felt the slightest curiosity especially since she could only guess the room had belonged to the darling baby Betsy. But now the closed door practically screamed her name.

Tara took a step toward the door, her hand extended while inside her conscience, a war waged. She didn't need to see the room, she argued with her curiosity but in the end, her argument was weak.

The knob turned easily and she pushed the door open and stepped back as a blast of cold air rushed into the warm hall. The drapes were pulled and the room was dark and shadowy. Tara felt along the wall until she found the switch and light poured into the tiny room with its pink and yellow wallpaper. The floor was covered with a pretty pink rug, the drapes a sunny yellow gingham. Toys lined the shelves over the window and a large brown teddy bear lay on the pretty pink and yellow gingham canopy bed as if its mistress would be home any moment to give it a squeeze.

Tara felt her heart tighten and the prickle of tears sting her eyes. How Brent must miss the sweet little bundle and she wished with all her might she could turn back the clock for him, snag the baby from her mother's arms on that fateful night but that wasn't possible. All she could do for the man was hope her love was enough to keep the pain at bay.

With her heart hurting, Tara stepped out of the room and closed the door. But she couldn't stop thinking of the lost child and the father who still mourned her.

Brent was a father who mourned needlessly, if she were to believe her dreams, a father who needed to know the truth. She rubbed her neck. The truth, she laughed, that was rich when all she had to go on were a box of photos and a suspicion.

Of course, there are those journals, she told herself as she pulled on the clothes she'd packed the night before. The journals, she'd forgotten. And they were right next door and if she hurried home, she would be that much closer to finding out the truth that would set Brent free. The tingling at the back of her neck became unbearable and Tara forgot all about the wet clothes in her haste to get home and into those journals.

Chapter Twenty-Eight

✷

Brent pulled into the gravel driveway in front of his office and parked next to a gray Mercedes sedan. Careful to remember to bring in his briefcase and jacket, he tugged at his tie with impatience and stepped out of the truck.

Inside he followed the muted voices to Hutch's office where he wasn't surprised to find several people including Taylor and his daddy Jefferson Taylor Sr. going over Hutch's meticulously kept books.

"Good morning, Mr. Taylor, gentlemen." He nodded to the other men ignoring his good buddy Taylor altogether.

"Mr. Chambliss," the elder Taylor said and Brent groaned inwardly. The man had called him by his first name for many years. Now he knew he was in big trouble.

"What seems to be the problem?" Brent proceeded to the desk and dropped his briefcase on the cluttered surface.

"It seems there are allegations of misappropriation of funds loaned by my bank to construct a strip mall on property owned by Gonzales Property Management."

"Uh-huh. And just what funds are we talking about?"

"Funds trusted to the contracting firm of Hutchinson Chambliss to purchase and install materials in said strip mall." All this came from one of the two men sitting on the business end of Hutch's desk.

"And who made these allegations?"

"The party wished to remain anonymous."

"So, on the word of some anonymous character you've all decided to ride over here and hassle me and my partner." Brent shook his head when Hutch hissed at him to keep quiet. "And you Mr. Taylor, what brings the president of Azalea City Bank out to my humble little business on a morning such as this?"

"Well, Brent, my boy, I vouched for you when the Gonzales people wanted to go with another firm. I just want to make sure everyone involved gets a fair shake."

"More like you want to make sure the bank can't be implicated in anything since it *was* you who vouched for me."

"Now see here Brent buddy there's no call to talk to my father that way." Jr. chimed in coming to his father's defense.

"Hey, Jeff, didn't see you there. How's the eye?" Brent said taking pleasure in his former friend's discomfort. "So just what are we alleged to have misappropriated again?"

"Basically Brent, there is some doubt as to the quality of materials you've purchased," the elder Taylor said though his attention seemed to be directed at his son as if he was seeing him for the first time in years.

"They're saying we bought below code materials and pocketed the difference." Hutch said from his chair against the wall.

"I gathered as much. Gentlemen let me assure you that my partner James Hutchinson keeps meticulous records. We have receipts of every purchase made as well as records for the amount of manpower we have employed on all our sites. And may I point out that the site in question was inspected by both the bank and the county this past Friday with no problems cited."

"Is that true?" Mr. Taylor said in a booming voice. "Why wasn't I informed of this yesterday when these allegations were brought to me?"

"Ah Father, I didn't know myself." Taylor said taking a step back and Brent could swear he heard the gears in the man's head turning as he tried to explain the double assault Brent was sure Taylor had fabricated against him.

"Mr. Taylor, are you aware that Tuesday night of last week your son tried to force himself on a woman who accompanied me to his Halloween party? He followed her to the ladies' room and suggested an association of a lewd nature and when she refused, he used force to change her mind. That if a friend of hers hadn't walked in when she did, things may very well have gone too far. And did you also know that the black eye your son sports was given to him Wednesday night by me?"

"She's a damn stripper Brent. She has no honor to protect."

"What she is, is a very lovely woman who wouldn't give you the time of day. And quite frankly, I thought you would grow out of the need to dominate every female you meet. Guess I was wrong."

"Junior," Taylor Sr. barked, making the accountants jump, "Am I to understand that these accusations are based on a disagreement over a woman?"

"No Father, I didn't. What I mean to say is that my source is very reliable. There is every reason to believe Mr. Chambliss here is using substandard materials and possibly padding his employee records for his own gain."

"What source? And who authorized an inspection? I certainly didn't."

"I thought it in the bank's best interest. Given the circumstances."

"And there were county inspectors there as well you say?" Sr. turned to Brent for answers now.

"Yes sir. They went over every inch of the site and only found fault with my scaffolding."

"We've heard enough." One of the accountants from the Gonzales Corporation stood up and began packing his set of records into his briefcase. "We apologize for disrupting your day Mr. Chambliss. Mr. Hutchinson. This matter is settled, as far as we are concerned, though we would like to request a walk-through at the site later in the week."

"That can be arranged."

"Good day then, to you Mr. Hutchinson and Mr. Chambliss. Mr. Taylor." Both accountants walked past, purposely ignoring the younger Taylor on their way out.

"I don't know where I went wrong with you son. You are a wastrel. A womanizing wastrel! How could you seek to defame a person in such a potentially harmful way? And he's one of your friends at that. What were you thinking? Never mind. I don't want to know. From now on, Junior, you are cut off. I will not bankroll you or your ex-wives another second. You have a degree in business that cost me a fortune so henceforth you will make use of it to not only support yourself but all three, or is it four, ex-wives, I forget." Taylor Sr. lit into his son the very second the door had closed behind the accountants.

"And as for you young man." He turned to Brent his hand held up to stop the flow of denial from his son's mouth. "Please accept my deepest apologies for this embarrassing incident and extend those apologies to your young woman. My son will not cause you any further trouble."

"Yes sir." Brent said trying to contain the smug smile he felt tugging at the corners of his mouth.

"And if it isn't too much trouble I'd like to join you on that walk-through. I'd like to see for myself the quality of your work. In reference to future business with my bank of course."

"Of course, you'd be more than welcome Mr. Taylor. We'll let you know when a time is settled."

"Good, good. Well then, if you will excuse us we'll leave you to your work. Come along Junior." It would have been poetic justice if the Sr. Taylor had grabbed his errant son by the ear and dragged him out of the building. But it was enough that Taylor simply followed with his eyes downcast and his shoulders slumped. And just as soon as the two were sealed into the airtight piece of German engineering they called a car Hutch let out a whoop.

"You did it. I don't believe you did it. I thought we were screwed for sure. I thought that once the shadow of doubt had crept over us it would take an act of God to clear our name."

"Why wouldn't I do it? We didn't do anything wrong. All our materials are well above code and most are the best that can be bought. Taylor started this and I finished it, no big deal."

"Do you think Taylor will cause trouble for us again?"

"If he has any sense he won't but since I've never attributed that particular ailment to him we can only wait and see."

"Well, what do we do now?"

"Get back to business as usual. But first I have a couple of phone calls to make." Brent said leaving Hutch to his own devices to make the calls from his office. He wanted to call Tara to let her know that things weren't as dire as Hutch had anticipated. And to ask her to come out for a celebratory lunch, completely forgetting that he had her truck.

After three tries at his home number he gave up and called Tony at the plumbing shop verifying that they would finish up out at Tara's that day, rain or no rain. After he hung up he debated calling her at home but decided against it. He didn't want to wake her if that was where she was and what she was doing. Tony wouldn't have to go inside to finish up so it was best to let her sleep while she could.

"So she didn't answer then?"

"Who? Ah, Tara. No she wasn't home."

"Um-hum," Hutch said using the same tone as Brent had used in his arguments just minutes before. "And whose truck is that parked out front?"

"Oh, Tara's. So you caught me, so what. She isn't at my home and I don't want to bother her at her house. There are you happy you old busybody?"

"You could have said she was just loaning you her truck, you know. I didn't need to know any more than that." But the cagey smile he displayed told Brent that Hutch had gotten exactly the information he'd been after.

"And just exactly what do you know? The woman was simply having breakfast at my house, seeing as how her kitchen is nonexistent at this time."

"I give up. Don't shoot." Hutch held up his hands Wild West style. "Why don't you take the rest of the day off? We aren't going to get much done until this rain ends anyway. I'm sure there is something left for breakfast."

"Naw, there's always something that needs doing. I think I'll take the company truck out to the sites and see how things look. You want to come along?"

"Are you kidding? I have to straighten up this office and I should go over those books to make sure those hired number crunchers didn't change anything."

"You are so paranoid," Brent laughed but all the same, he felt grateful to have a friend like Hutch watching his back especially in this business.

"Don't I know it! Now get lost. You bother me."

"Yeah, yeah." Brent said and moseyed back to his office to change into the spare jeans and T-shirt he kept hidden in a file drawer and the work boots that were in the bathroom.

Chapter Twenty-Nine

🔊

His name was Cromwell Thornton. In his youth he had red hair and served in Her Majesty's Royal Air Force. He moved to America when he was forty-five in search of more than just a British military pension to fall back on in his old age, which he feared to be imminent. Kelly Chambliss felt an instant attraction to the gray-haired older man and as she found she couldn't hold her husband's attention for very long turned to Crom for the adoration she craved.

For three years, they carried on a platonic friendship until Kelly began to despair of losing her husband and then in a moment of weakness, she presented herself to Crom as a mistress. He was noble when he declined but the seed was planted and they became lovers soon after.

Kelly became pregnant within the year. She desperately hoped that the child was her husband's. The bitter fact remained that after six years together Brent had yet to fill her womb with a child.

Had yet to fill her womb with a child? Tara squeezed her eyes shut. Oh Brent, she felt her heart break for him. She unclenched her eyes and continued to read her heart pounding at the injustice.

Kelly, it seemed, allowed each man to believe he was the baby's father. Cromwell Thornton was the only one aware that the possibility existed that he wasn't. Brent on the other hand was unaware of his wife's infidelity as far as Kelly knew. Even Kelly was in doubt but because of her and Brent's track record she favored Crom over her own husband and played on the man's need to be the daddy. And for three years Kelly's ploy worked to the point that she began to believe her life was perfect. But then Cromwell began to push her to leave Brent, to marry him and make their daughter one hundred percent his. Still obsessed with her husband Kelly balked. She continued to think that if she could snare his interest he would fall in love with her. That's when Kelly's life fell apart.

Cromwell issued her an ultimatum. Marry him or he would leave. For his heart couldn't stand another moment of loving her and watching her follow a star that was out of her reach. Cromwell failed and after a week of waiting for her to change her mind he packed up and moved away leaving behind the daughter of his heart and the woman he loved.

But Kelly didn't care. She could now concentrate on making Brent love her by giving him the perfect family. She never suspected he would fall in love with the baby and lavish her with the attention she craved. Kelly began to despise the girl.

Again, Tara had to stop reading. She didn't want to know any of this. She didn't want to know that Brent's wife was a disturbed woman who would sell her daughter for a kernel of attention from a distant husband.

She yawned and pulled the blanket tight around her shoulders the journal sagging in her hands as she thought over what she had discovered in the two volumes. She couldn't wrap her mind around the deception Kelly Chambliss was capable of. Faking a pregnancy to keep her high school boyfriend from losing interest once he was off to college. A forged doctor's report stating she'd miscarried. And when he gave up his baseball scholarship to be with her she grew angry and distant, her dreams of him being a major league player shot in an instant.

Tara didn't understand how someone who professed to love a person could be so selfish. If it were her, she'd be thrilled that her husband selflessly gave up his dream in the face of tragedy. If it were her though she never would have set out to trap a husband. If it were her...

"Now you understand my shame Tara Jenkins. Now you know why I can't pass on to the next world. I am not proud of the things I did and I can't justify them."

"Did you love him?"

"I was seventeen. I saw a shining star and wanted to catch a piece of it before it shot out of my grasp."

"But did you love him?"

"I wasn't meant for him Tara. You should know that better than anyone by now. I was never meant to be anything to him. And I let what I was meant for pass through my hands without a moment's hesitation."

"I see. And Betsy?"

"Cromwell Thornton's daughter. Brent wasn't meant to father a child with me. Now you see why I must make amends. My child is waiting for me and I must pass on, so that I may make amends to her as well."

"He'll hate me for telling him. Any good I've done him will be washed down the drain."

"Maybe at first Tara Jenkins but you are his destiny and he will forgive you."

"Just one question, though. Why did you hide all this in my house? Why aren't you haunting your house?"

"Isn't it obvious? This house is the scene of my crime. This house should have been mine. Not the little bungalow or the man inside it."

* * * * *

"Wake up sweetheart. Damn, it's colder in here than it is outside."

Tara jumped in her seat when the warm hand grazed her cheek. The book she was holding slipping unnoticed between the cushion and the arm of the chair. "Hi there, sleepyhead."

Brent's dark eyes met hers. Her sleep fuzzy mind took a moment to recognize him. When she did her heart slammed in her chest so hard, she couldn't breathe. She reached out a hand and cupped his cheek, seeking warmth and reassurance for what she was about to do.

Taking courage from his smile she sucked in a breath and clamped her eyes closed. "I'm so sorry."

"Don't sweat it. I know where you live."

"What?" she said wondering what she had missed.

"You promised to stay put at my house remember. I know where you live and I have a key so don't apologize for going back to where you feel comfortable."

"Oh, no I wasn't. I mean I'd forgotten about that. Sorry."

"If you weren't apologizing for not being naked in my bed when I came home then what are you sorry for?" he asked his smile fading only a little and Tara sucked in another breath. He was playing with her. He was happy and she didn't want to ruin that. Not after all these weeks of his mercurial mood swings. But she had to tell him. She just had to if either he or his wife were to find true happiness.

"I found Kelly's journals. I know I should have given them to you when I discovered what they were. But she's been bugging me to find out her secrets and when I found them and the boxes of pictures in that little wall safe in the kitchen I knew they were the answer."

"I'm lost. Must have mortar in my ear or something 'cause I thought you said Kelly's been bugging you. How does a woman who's been dead for three years bug you? Besides she didn't keep a journal and even if she did why would it be in your house?" Brent said rocking back on his feet his smile now gone, his eyes puzzled as he tried to make sense of what she said.

"That's because she was having an affair with Mr. Thornton. Brent she was lonely and he was here when you weren't. I'm sorry. I never wanted you to be hurt."

"How do you know this is my Kelly?"

"There are boxes of photos with her and him and Betsy, upstairs in my closet."

"Betsy? My Betsy? Why would old man Thornton be anywhere near my daughter?"

"He thought she was his daughter. Oh Brent I'm so sorry."

"Let me get this straight. You're telling me my wife who never kept a journal had an affair with a man old enough to be her father maybe even her grandfather and that he believed my daughter to be his?"

"Yes. And that's not all." In for a penny, in for a pound, Tara thought. Tara rushed on to get everything out before she lost her nerve.

"She claims in her journal that she never carried your child."

"Oh and I suppose the Easter Bunny was the first baby's father then?"

"There never was one Brent. Don't you see, she tricked you into marrying her. She wanted to be the wife of this huge baseball star she'd built you up to be and she thought that once you went away to school you'd forget about her."

"I see." Brent stood and it was only then that Tara realized how low to the floor he was. "And just where is this journal now, so that I can read all about my wife's sins for myself."

"Right here," Tara fumbled in the blanket for the book she'd had not that long ago and couldn't find it anywhere. "Maybe it fell on the floor."

"Not unless it somehow turned invisible." Brent said surveying the bare floor surrounding Tara's chair his mood turning blacker by the second.

"It was here, I swear. I had it just before you came in. I'll find it just give me a second." She fished in the seat lifting the blanket up to search aware that for some reason this wasn't going the way she thought it would.

"Don't bother Tara."

"What? No I have to find it I have to prove to you…"

"I don't want any proof. If Kelly was having an affair then it was over and done with years ago. And no matter what you say, Betsy was my daughter... I can't believe you could do something like this. But I should have known."

"Should have known what? I didn't do anything to you, Brent. I never wanted to hurt you... I love you."

"You love me?" He seemed stunned but not as stunned as Tara felt when the words slipped out, words that now sounded petty and jealous instead of coming from the heart. "Oh that's funny. You love me so much that you wanted to slander my memory of my wife and my daughter. Did you think it would make me set them aside altogether. Tara you can't wipe away a person's past simply because you want to."

"I know. I wasn't trying to do that. She said you needed the truth to set you free."

"Free from what? I've been free for three years. And then you waltz in here with your high-class model's body and stir things up. Damn it, what is it with women, why do they have to decimate the competition at any cost. And here I thought you were different. I thought you were... I thought I could..."

"Thought you could what Brent? Love me?"

"No Tara, I can't love you. I won't love you. You're jealous of a dead woman. I don't need that in my life. I don't need the past coming back to bite me. I don't need... I don't need you. I'm sorry if I led you on Tara. I hope you have a nice life. But I won't be in it." He shoved his fists in his pockets as if he didn't trust himself right that second and then after one last angry look he turned on his heel and slammed out the front door.

"Brent, wait," Tara threw off the covers and raced to the door. "Wait let me explain."

"You've done enough explaining Tara."

"But I didn't mean... She said you'd be angry. Please Brent give us a chance."

"Who said I'd be angry? Who Tara, who put you up to destroying what little hope I have left in my life?"

"Kelly," she said, the look on his face going totally white with disbelief. "She is trapped in this house. She said she couldn't pass on until you knew the truth and forgave her."

"You mean to stand there and tell me that my wife's ghost is haunting you. Making you tell such lies?"

"Yes."

"You are nuts, you know that? Completely out of your mind, nuts."

"Brent?"

"No, Tara, I don't want to hear it. My wife is not a ghost. In fact, there are no such things as ghosts. And she sure as hell wouldn't be haunting you. As if you matter in the scheme of my life."

Tara felt the first tears slip from her eyes but didn't bother to stop the flow as she stood on her front porch watching the man she loved walk out of her life forever. She wouldn't stop them because it was her own pathetic fault that he was going. The truth, she remembered belatedly, will not set you free. It only condemns the speaker to a life of loneliness and regret.

"Goodbye Tara. I'll send you a bill for the remodel and a recommendation for another contractor to finish up the kitchen."

"Brent, please don't go. Not like this," she cried out after him but he just shook his head and kept on walking, past the hedge, past his yard and his driveway, past his house. He kept going until she could no longer see him. Tara drew in a ragged breath just as the street lamps came on and the last of the sun disappeared from view. She stood there willing him to turn around, willing him to come back so that she could beg his forgiveness. But she knew he wouldn't. In a way, she'd done him worse than Kelly ever had. She, after all, had told him the truth of something he didn't need to know.

Finally when the cold biting into her fingers and toes could no longer be ignored Tara stepped back into her house and closed the door.

"You lied to me," she whispered sinking to the floor in front of the door. "You lied to me. You wanted to hurt him even more didn't you. You wanted to destroy any happiness he might have found with me."

Laughter rumbled like thunder through the house and Tara felt her skin crawl with fear as she sat there her hands over her ears to drown out the sound. No answer came to her accusation. No more pleas for help from the trapped soul with whom she shared her home. Nothing but laughter and the strange emptiness of her own shortcomings rattled around in the empty house with her, and then, finally, nothing.

"I'm glad you're gone. But you know what, I hope you never are allowed to pass on. I hope you *are* trapped here for eternity for what you've done. I hope you never see your daughter again. Maybe one day you will learn compassion and look back on this day. You could have saved your soul but you didn't and I'm glad."

No. I am nuts. I'm sitting here in the dark talking to a figment of my imagination. Tara laughed a painful bitter laugh and leaned her head against the door. "Get up Tara, get up."

Just then the telephone rang and she jumped to her feet hoping it was Brent calling from a pay phone now that he'd had time to think about things. But even as she reached for the receiver, she knew it wasn't him. She knew deep in her soul that Brent was lost to her, just as she knew she would mourn the loss the rest of her life.

"Hello," she answered unable to hide the tears in her voice.

"Tara, darling. I have great news." The nasal voice of her agent came on the line and Tara leaned against the wall, her eyes shut, to listen to what Marty had to say. When she hung up she squared her shoulders very much like her mother's favorite heroine and marched up the stairs to pack for a trip to New York. For Scarlett's advice was sound and tomorrow *was* another day.

Chapter Thirty

ଛ

"I thought I might find you here," Hutch said in the smoke-filled haze. Brent just shrugged and took a long drag on the bottle in front of him. "How much have you had?"

"Not enough to do any damage."

"Brent…" Hutch sighed and shook his head. It wouldn't do any good to lecture so he signaled the bartender for a matching longneck and took a swig. "Tara stopped by the office just as I was closing up."

"So."

"So…" So that was it, Hutch shook his head again and forged ahead. "She handed me a check for the amount you quoted her. Said to let her know if it wasn't enough."

"Did she ask for the names of other contractors?"

"No. She said she would be out of town for about three weeks for a shoot now that her mother is in stable condition for a change. That should give you sufficient time to finish the job you started."

"I see." Brent took another swallow.

"You see what? I'm confused here. What happened between the two of you today?"

"She turned into a woman. I'd forgotten about that with her. I'd forgotten how women are when they want something."

"I see. She made some petty demand for your attention that reminded you of Kelly and you turned tail and ran."

"If only it were that simple. No she…she had the audacity to tell me that my wife had been deceiving me all these years.

That Betsy wasn't mine but old man Thornton's, from next door."

"So what's the problem? You suspected yourself that Kelly was having an affair around that time."

"No. I-I didn't pay what she did too much mind," Brent said and for the first time, he wondered why it was that he hadn't cared enough to know what his wife did with her days. Was he that insensitive?

"Then you were the only one." Hutch didn't turn to look at his friend when he spoke. He didn't want to be the one to tell him, especially now that Kelly was gone.

"What's that supposed to mean?" Brent slammed the bottle down on the bar and whirled on the stool, the tingling in his gut making him feel as if he were going to puke. But maybe he was mistaking guilt for the two beers he'd had after years of being on the wagon.

"Brent, nobody liked your wife, except maybe her high school friends. The rest of us, your family included, simply tolerated her tantrums. She wanted money, hell, she wanted the moon but she wanted you to be constantly with her going someplace doing something. Then there was that year she suddenly seemed content. Made me start to wonder ya know."

"No, I didn't know. I thought she had just grown up some."

"Did you love her, Brent? Did you ever for one second love Kelly? And I'm not talking about the harridan she became after the miscarriage but before when you and she were young and well going about making that first baby."

"You know that's another thing. Tara said that there never was a miscarriage," Brent laughed bitterly.

"There always is that possibility you know."

"If there is, then I was a first class chump wouldn't you say."

"I'd say you were a good guy trying to do what was right. But you were also what nineteen or twenty at the time and preoccupied with school and baseball. But you didn't answer the question. Did you love her?"

"No." Brent shrugged feeling the vise tighten in his chest. "I didn't. And as time passed, I grew to hate her. I couldn't help it Hutch she drained me. But I did love Betsy. She was my baby. Mine. And I'd give the world to have her back."

"Even if it meant having Kelly back as well?"

"I never wished her dead. I might not have loved her but I never wanted her dead. I wanted her to be happy and no matter what I did I couldn't make her happy."

"So you've been carrying a load of guilt around all these years for a woman you didn't love. Brent, man, I won't say I understand, 'cause I don't. It's just that it seems to me that these last few weeks that boy I remember from college had somehow found his way back. And here you are letting Kelly come between you and a woman I think you *have* fallen in love with." Brent snorted but Hutch squared his shoulders and went on. "Look Brent, it's immaterial now if Kelly had an affair. It's immaterial now whose child Betsy was. They are both gone. But you are still here. It's time to stop living in the past and look to the future before it's too late and Tara is gone."

"You don't know what you're talking about."

"Maybe I don't." Hutch drained his beer. "But I know when I've had enough, how about you?"

"Mind your own business."

Hutch sighed and signaled the bartender. "This man's an alcoholic and he's had enough. If you know what's good for you, you won't sell him anything stronger than a soda." Hutch then left a silent and brooding Brent to deal with that cheap shot on his own as well as the tab.

"Is that true, buddy?" the bartender asked, giving him a mildly disapproving look.

"Yeah, I guess it is." Brent sighed and fished in his pocket for the few bills he had on him and paid for his folly. Leaving the change as a tip, he wandered out into the parking lot and just stood there breathing in the cold damp air as if his life depended on the very next breath he took.

He roamed the downtown streets looking for another bar crowded with people to lose himself in. But he'd lost the taste for that life he realized as he stared into a darkened store without really seeing the merchandise on display.

Tara was leaving. The thought flitted into his mind. She was running, he thought briefly deciding he didn't care where or how far she ran as long as she stayed there. Still he couldn't help wondering where she was heading and what would happen when she returned and they got on with the business of being neighbors.

"Damn, Tara why'd you have to go and meddle in my past?" he called out to the night not caring what passersby thought of him.

The contents of the store finally caught his eye. And he found himself staring at a larger-than-life-size poster of himself dressed in the tuxedo currently on display. In his arms, he held the woman who was slowly becoming a cancerous growth on his heart. With one last look at the embarrassing photo, he walked on, his mind in even more turmoil than before he'd left the bar.

* * * * *

A week passed before Brent had the courage to return to the house next door. Inside the absolute silence struck him with a jolt, his own breathing echoing in the eerie quiet. He missed the sound of her cheerful laughter and her musical voice, the sound of which always made his heart quicken in his chest. He listened for footsteps upstairs, none came, but then he hadn't really expected her to coming running to greet him, had he?

He walked through the downstairs rooms looking for signs of her. The scarf she'd left hanging on the back of her chair was the only indication she had ever been there. His fingers grazed the soft material itching to pick it up when the doorbell rang.

He shouldn't answer her door, he knew, but he couldn't shake the hope that it might be her standing on the other side.

"Miss Belle," he said in surprise when he flung the door open and found the little old woman from across the street standing there looking like a bulldog with a bone.

"Hello buster, it's been a long time since you've come to see me." Maybelle Lewis thumped her cane on the wooden porch floor indicating her agitation.

"I'm sorry Miss Belle. I've been busy." Brent said as he stepped past her and locked the house up. Taking her arm, he led her across the street where he gently deposited her into her favorite rocker.

"What you've been is bullheaded, boy. Your poor mama won't be happy."

"Aww, Miss Belle you're not still calling my mother, are you?"

"Once a week, she worries about you so."

"Yes I know. I don't want to cause her any more grief."

"Brent, honey, you are a wonderful son. Any mama would be proud to have you but it's yourself you should be thinking of. Haven't you caused yourself enough grief to last three lifetimes?"

"I don't know what you're talking about." Brent took a seat on the step at her feet so that he didn't have to meet her shrewd old eyes with lies on his lips.

"Your wife was no good, boy. It's high time you knew the truth."

"Yes I know and she had an affair with old man Thornton. I already know all that."

"You don't know the half of it. Now shut up and listen."

"Miss Belle, if it's all the same to you I don't think I want to hear any more."

"Tough titty." Miss Belle smiled at his shocked expression before going on. "Yes she had an affair and if you ask me she was better off with the old gentleman. He had time for her and he doted on her in a way that she craved. And I think she even may have loved him. It *was* you she was no good for. You brought out the worst in her to be sure."

"I know all that too," Brent sighed and rubbed the bridge of his nose to hold off the headache he felt coming on.

"Again, shut up, boy. You were a shiny toy to her. We all saw it, your mama, me. Even her own poor mama, but she was too weak to stand up to her daughter. She was spoiled rotten getting everything she wanted and when she made up her mind to want you she meant to get you no matter the cost."

"Was there a baby?" Brent found himself interrupting.

"So you've heard that have you? Well, I'll tell you honest boy. I don't know." She held up her hand to stop him from commenting just yet. "But I suspect there wasn't. That weekend she called your mother crying hysterically that she was bleeding. When your mother wanted to rush over there and see about her, her mother came on the line with reassurances that they were on their way to the hospital. Your mama never found out what hospital. It was all so very convenient, if you ask me."

"That doesn't make it true any more than Betsy being Thornton's is true." Brent said all the bitterness he possessed in his voice.

"Again, no proof but I suspected as much. If you'd ever seen the man with her, you'd have had suspicions too. He was putty in her little hands."

"This is all just speculation Miss Belle. What good is speculation when Kelly isn't alive to defend herself?"

"You could ask her mother."

"Humph," Brent snorted shaking his head. "My mother-in-law made it clear that this was all my fault three years ago. She threatened to sue me for wrongful death. I doubt seriously that she would give me the time of day much less the truth."

"True, even if she knew the truth. Brent honey the point is you need to let her go and get on with your life. Nothing can change what happened but if you let it bog you down you'll be miserable the rest of your life."

"Betsy was my daughter. I won't hear anything otherwise."

"That is a fine attitude boy. Just remember that much and move on."

"Miss Belle, is this little talk absolutely necessary? I mean I love you like a second mother but you have no hard proof that she deceived me."

"I have proof that she made you miserable. I have proof that you made her miserable when you didn't live up to her expectations. Now, that pretty girl over there is different. She has no expectations of anyone but herself. If you ask me you should bury Kelly and open your heart."

"I don't think Tara is the cure for what ails me Miss Belle but I'll try to climb out of the mire if it will make you happy."

"Seeing you happy again, would make me happy."

"Then I'll see what I can do. Right now I have to get back to work."

"You'll come to supper tomorrow night then?"

"I'll try Miss Belle. I'll try. Now if you'll excuse me I have to go."

Belle nodded dismissal though she wasn't happy about it. She'd made a mess of things that was for sure but then it wasn't entirely her fault that he was a brick wall now was it? Maybe Brent's mother would have better luck than she had in setting their boy straight.

* * * * *

Brent passed the next week finishing the work on Tara's kitchen and new bathroom. He ignored the numbness in body and soul as he ignored his friends and family when they sought to lecture him on his wonderful life choices. And since no one could prove their Kelly-bashing gossip he chose to believe as he always had. That he'd done the right thing by marrying his pregnant girlfriend. He gave up his dream to care for her after the loss of the child thinking she needed him at home. Betsy had saved them from divorce but Betsy wasn't enough to save them from themselves in the long run and they argued. Argued badly about trivial matters. And then they had died. It was all cut and dried. Wasn't it?

The kitchen looked great with the new tile and the new cabinets. The columns made a dramatic statement but it tied the kitchen and dining room together nicely. The new bathroom fixtures were in place and working just wonderfully. All that was left was to grout the tile in there, a job that would take most of the night if he worked through.

Up to his elbows in grout Brent felt sweat trickle from his forehead onto the slope of his nose and brushed it away with his shoulder. One more section of tile remained to grout and he would call it a night. But as he worked to clean the last of the grout away the house closed in around him. Even with the radio on full blast to keep his mind off foolish thoughts he still felt as if he were being watched, which wasn't a pleasant feeling to say the least.

Finally, with the last major task complete he stood up to survey the little room that was once a couple of closets. He was proud of the little room if he had to say so himself. When he was satisfied that there was no detail left undone he walked out into the newly remodeled kitchen to wash away the grout that had managed to seep into his gloves and up his arms. When he was finished he turned off the radio and checked his watch. Midnight had ticked by a couple of minutes ago, he noted and froze.

But not because of the late hour.

There was a noise coming from the second floor, followed by the tap, tap, tap of footsteps. Every hair on his body stood on end. Someone was in the house with him and he knew without a doubt that somebody wasn't Tara.

Brent crept over to his open tool chest and searched for something to use as a weapon. For the first time, he wished he had a nail gun handy but the heavy pipe wrench would do. That is, unless the prowler had a gun, of course. Then he figured he would either haul ass or be toast, it didn't much matter.

He made his way up the stairs careful to keep his weight on his toes. But still several of the steps creaked under his weight. And each time he would pause and listen and every time he was rewarded with the muffled sound of someone moving around upstairs.

At the top of the stairs, he sucked in his breath and listened, scanning as he did for any light the prowler might be using to see in the darkened house. Seeing nothing, he moved on. His ears tuned to the busy sounds coming from the far end of the house.

All the doors were open he noticed as he passed by, the pipe wrench held loosely in his right hand should someone walk out to confront him.

A dim light began to glow in one of the far bedrooms as if someone was panning a flashlight around the room and Brent gulped back the fear that tingled his neck.

The smart thing would be to turn tail and call the police from the safety of his own home, he told himself to bolster his courage. But for some reason having someone rattling around in Tara's house made him angry. What if Tara was home right now and this asshole was wandering around? He couldn't bear the thought of losing her in such a cruel manner.

Brent stepped into the doorway the wrench held high like a club ready to strike anyone who came at him and fixed his gaze on the source of the light.

His breath came in spasms as the light glowed brighter and began to take on human form. Cold air whooshed past him, making him shiver as the room became as bright as day. He stood there frozen to the spot, the wrench dangling loosely at his side.

She stepped closer, her body and hair swathed in white, her face covered by the fine veil. Long tendrils of red hair lay against white shoulders. Her wedding dress, he remembered as if it were yesterday. A simple, cotton dress that tied behind her neck, which, he found out later, was for easy removal.

"Hello, my darling," she said, her voice the same yet somehow different, unearthly the only description he could think of at the moment. "You've come for me at last."

"Kelly?" He didn't trust his eyes, didn't trust that the impossible could happen even after seeing it firsthand.

"Who else is there? I've waited for so long, watched for so long, but you never came. You never heard me call for you."

"Why are you here? I mean you're dead, right?"

"The place of my sin." She shrugged her shoulders, the veil swirling with the motion.

"Your sin? I don't understand."

"Didn't your little friend tell you? She was supposed to pave the way for us to reunite."

"You mean Tara?" Brent took a step back. The tone in her voice wasn't sane. Who was he kidding about sanity? He laughed aloud prompting the...ghost or whatever she was to move closer.

"Little fool had to go and fall in love with you. But she can't have you, my darling. You belong with me forever."

"Kelly? I have no idea what's going on here. You're dead, you know."

"I know. And now that you've come to be with me I can rest easier."

"But I'm alive."

"Buy the house from her, my darling. There is money hidden under the floor in the baby's room beside the heating vent. Enough to buy three houses this size. Thornton gave it to me over the years. Buy the house and come to me. Make me strong again and I'll make you happy for the rest of your life."

"You're trapped here?"

"Yes, my prison for my sins. My own personal hell."

"Because you...ah...sinned with Mr. Thornton in this house?"

"Yes. Oh my darling I'm so sorry. I was so lonely and he seduced me and I... Well I'm ashamed of my behavior. I never meant to hurt you."

"Kelly, our daughter. Was Thornton her father?"

"Why should that matter? She is with the angels now. They had plans for her innocent soul."

"Because it matters. I miss her so much."

"You always loved her too much. You always put her before me."

"Who is her father? Tell me, Kelly. I have a right to know." Brent demanded now that the ghost began to sound like the Kelly he knew.

"I don't honestly know. I'm sorry, that's the best I can do. Stay with me my darling, stay the night. Let me love you like I should have years ago."

"I don't love you Kelly." Brent said, his blood chilled at the suggestion. "We weren't right for each other. You must know that by now."

"I've loved you since I was sixteen years old and when we married we vowed to love and honor for all time. Stay with me now. Buy the house from that woman and stay."

"I can't. Forgive me, Kelly for everything. We should have gotten a divorce after the first child died. I can see that now. There was no love between us. We would have been spared years of pain and misery. I'm sorry. I won't spend the rest of my life trapped with the specter of my greatest mistake."

"Mistake!" she shouted, the dress and veil changing color before his eyes. "We were meant to be, you and I. Don't make me angry Brent. You won't like me when I'm angry."

"I didn't like you when you were angry in life Kelly. I don't think that will change now."

"You will regret spurning me Brent Chambliss. If you walk out that door, you will never find love again as long as you live. I'll see to that. I'll see that she never returns to you. Never."

"What are you talking about?"

"The love of your life. I have a power over her. Her mind is open and so easy to manipulate. She will see you as you really are if you leave."

"You put her up to telling me your secrets. You knew I wouldn't believe her. You knew I would think she set out to deliberately slander your memory and that I would what? Hate her? Is that it?"

"Yes. She isn't your soul mate. I am. You are mine for eternity. Don't you see that?"

"All I see is a bitter woman who wasted her life chasing something that didn't belong to her. Don't waste your afterlife on me Kelly. Make your peace with me so that you can be free. I am sorry for not loving you. I thought I would one day. And I forgive you for seeking comfort from another man. I beg of you to forget this madness and let me go."

"Never. I'll never let you go. You are my destiny not hers."

"Then I pity you." Brent turned his back on the glowing spirit and set off toward the stairs as fast as his feet could carry him.

"I'll haunt you forever Brent Chambliss. Forever, do you hear me?" The sound floated around him as he all but slid down the steps to the ground floor. The light from the kitchen streamed out into the hallway inviting him to seek its safety.

Once there he stopped to catch his breath and survey his surroundings. He didn't see her but he heard her if the sound of all hell breaking loose upstairs was any indication.

"Forever," rumbled through the air like thunder and Brent felt all of the fear drain out of him. His fear immediately replaced by anger, anger for being so blind when she was alive, anger for taking all the blame for their failed marriage, anger for holding onto her for so long. And finally anger for choosing

Kelly over Tara. If Kelly were to be believed, then Tara was his soul mate. His destiny. Somehow, that revelation felt so very right.

The air rumbled around him as her anger encompassed the house. She had power all right. But how much? Then his ring finger began to burn. Well, that answered that.

"Mine forever."

Brent stared at the ring as if he had never seen it before. The ring Kelly had given him on their wedding day. The symbol of her love, of his commitment to her, somehow linked them if she were able to use it against him like this. Of course, he could be hallucinating. None of this could be real. There could have been toxic fumes in the grout mixture.

Yes, that explained it—toxic fumes. He tore at the ring on his finger forcing it over his knuckle, which had grown larger since she had placed it on his finger all those years ago. The burning pain grew stronger and Brent tugged harder until the band slipped past the joint with a pop.

"Forgive me Kelly, as I have forgiven you," he shouted into the air. The ring, clutched in his hand, felt almost alive.

"Never. You belong to me for eternity."

"I was never yours." He tossed the ring into the air and watched it sail the length of the room until it vanished from sight.

The air around him became thinner and he sucked in a ragged breath. Silence echoed through the house now. And Brent wondered if she were gone or if she had simply lost her power over him.

He laughed, sounding slightly hysterical to his own ears and after a moment of stunned silence, he set about clearing his things out. By the time he was packed, he had somehow convinced himself the toxic grout theory was true. That is, except for the bright red welt where his wedding band used to be. Tomorrow he would clean up the tile in the bathroom and find a way to track Tara down. Tomorrow he would apologize and do what he could to convince the woman that he wasn't crazy.

But what if tomorrow never comes, he wondered as he closed and locked the door. He would just have to deal with that tomorrow he decided with a laugh. Surely, the fates weren't so cruel as to deny him his soul mate now that he had finally found her.

But what did he know; he was suffering from toxic shock.

Chapter Thirty-One

🔊

Snow fell softly outside the window. Tara leaned against the glass looking out over the city hoping to catch a glimpse of the sun setting. But the gray sky and surrounding buildings got in the way.

Christmas was drawing near and she'd made more money in the past three weeks than she'd ever dreamed existed but shopping was the furthest thing from her mind.

"Coffee," Shannon Summers called from the cubbyhole that passed as a kitchen in their little apartment. "It's not gourmet but it'll do in a pinch."

"No thanks, I'm not in the mood," Tara said without looking away from the window and the swiftly falling night.

"You're not in the mood for a lot of things lately," Shannon said as the delicious aroma of fresh black coffee wafted to Tara's side of the room. "What gives? You feeling all right?"

"I'm fine. In fact I've never felt better." Tara reluctantly left her window seat perch and joined Shannon on the sofa. "I'm just tired I guess."

"More like homesick?"

"Maybe." Tara shrugged. She was too tired to scrutinize the jumble of emotions swirling around inside her.

"Maybe my foot. You've been moping around here for three weeks. And all you ever say is you're tired. Well, baby cakes I've seen doorstops that do more than you have this week. Why don't you just admit you are homesick and do something about it?" Shannon sipped her coffee while she scrutinized Tara's bland expression knowing that her good advice was once again falling on deaf ears. "Okay. Maybe I'm wrong. Maybe you are ecstatically happy. You've just come off a career-making shoot with two more offers waiting in the wings. What girl wouldn't want to see her face plastered all over a Secret Seduction catalog? You have money enough to fly around the world four times and bring home change. And you're in love. What more could a girl ask for?"

Tara shrugged, picking at the nap on her robe. The same robe that covered the same pajamas she had worn for the last three days straight.

"Okay so he broke your heart. Big fat hairy deal. Go home to Alabama, Tara. Hiding out here isn't going to mend your heart. Go home and tell him you love him and that you're sorry for meddling in his life. If he is still acting like a jerk then you can go about the business of getting over him."

"I know you're right Shannon. I just... I have nowhere to go now that I've sold my house."

"Bullshit. You're making excuses that have an easy solution. Your life is there Tara. Don't you see that? Go home."

"You just want me out so you can have the apartment to yourself again."

"There is that. And getting you out of New York once and for all might be the break I need to be the next supermodel for the real-sized world." Shannon struck her best waif pose by sucking in her cheeks and pursing her lips.

"Cross your eyes and you'll look just like that fish I had for dinner last night." Tara said laughing at the comical expression on her friend's face as she crossed her eyes and made fish lips.

"That's better. It feels good to laugh doesn't it?"

"Yes. Thanks for reminding me."

"Welcome. Now get out of my house."

"I will, I promise. I still plan to go to school next month. Right now I just feel the need to hide out for a little while longer and let time heal my wounds."

"Fine. But I still think you're taking the coward's way out." Shannon said just as Coco bounded through the door with another huge bouquet of flowers in her hands.

"Let me guess. Lover boy just couldn't let a week go by without shelling out big bucks to the flower delivery guy," Shannon said sarcastically though she secretly eyed the flowers with longing.

"Jamie is the sweetest man I've ever known." Coco danced around the room with a dreamy expression on her face. "He makes me feel as if I am the most beautiful woman in the world."

"You are the most beautiful woman in the world," Shannon snipped. "And now that you've stopped rubbing our noses in it, I'll tell you something else Charlotte Jackson. I love you."

"What?" Coco stopped spinning with her flowers and stood stock-still in the middle of the room wearing a shocked expression on her beautiful face. "What brought that on? I-I thought you hated me."

"Maybe I did a little but you didn't help any. You were always so snotty. But you've change over these past few weeks Coco. When I thought you were going to die I realized that you were probably my closest friend. And I'm so happy that you're not going to die. And I'm happy that you found your prince. I just don't know what to do now that you're getting ready to move away. I feel like I'm losing my sister." Tears slipped down Shannon's face as she sobbed out the words Tara had wanted to say but never had the guts, words that had her sobbing along with her two friends.

"You'll just have to move to Mobile with me and Tara and then we'll be together forever." Coco said holding up her left hand and showing off the tiny chunk of ice that graced it.

"Oh my God! When did you get that?" Shannon and Tara howled at the same time.

"Last night. This huge package arrived by Fed Ex and inside was a note from Jamie asking me to wait until he called to open the smaller package."

"You mean he asked you over the phone?" Shannon said though she thought it was extremely romantic.

"Kind of, I didn't wait. I tore into the box and was shouting 'yes' before he could get a word out. I know we haven't known each other that long but he makes me so happy." Now Coco was in tears.

"That is the most romantic thing I've ever heard," Shannon said wiping away her tears long enough to pull Coco onto the sofa between them, grab her hand and pull it close for a better look at the rock. "It's just right if you ask me. Not too flashy."

"I didn't but thanks anyway. I like it and that's all that counts."

"You go girl."

"God, I hate that phrase," Coco said as her tears turned to laughter.

"Me too. Don't know why I said it."

"Because you're nuts," Coco said leaning onto Tara to avoid the punch Shannon aimed at her arm and noticed the tears streaming down her face. "Hey you've been quiet about this. Aren't you happy for me?"

"Ecstatic," Tara said wiping uselessly at the tears dripping from her eyes. "I'm relieved that you're cancer-free now and overjoyed that you and Hutch are getting married. He is a really good man and he'll make you happy Coco, he really will."

"So then why are you crying? Don't tell me you've decided to give up on your dream. Give up on Bliss. And stay here where you've been miserable for the last decade."

"Nothing as simple as that," Tara replied feeling a fresh wave of tears coming on.

"Then what is it Tara? You can tell us anything." Coco said sitting up straight and setting aside her need for the spotlight for the first time in her life.

"I think I'm pregnant." Tara acknowledged her secret fear for the first time since she missed her period.

Both Coco and Shannon sat stunned for a moment while they processed the information. Finally, both women burst out with more questions than Tara could answer. There were no answers at that point, only questions. Questions Tara never wanted to have to face alone.

"Does Bliss know?" Coco asked finally bringing Tara's misery to a head.

"No. And he never will. Do you hear me Coco, he is not to find out. And neither is Hutch, is that clear?"

"He has a right to know."

"Because he will think I set out to trap him. I didn't and I don't want him to feel obligated to me in any way."

"But Tara—"

"No, Coco. If he knows he'll marry me for the sake of the baby. I won't have him that way. I won't stand back and watch him grow to hate me. I won't. And you won't so much as breathe a word of this to Hutch, do you hear me?"

"I promise I won't tell Jamie."

"Or Brent?"

"Or Brent. But Tara…" Coco argued her heart breaking for her friend. But a promise was a promise she wouldn't go behind her back and tell. She just wished she knew how to fix it so Tara and Bliss would be together as they should be and live happily ever after.

"Thank you. Now if you two will excuse me I think I'm going to turn in."

Tara raced from the room to the safety of the tiny bedroom she shared with Shannon where she fell across the twin bed she'd occupied for several years and sobbed until she had no tears left.

She was alone, afraid and homesick, just as Shannon had said. Her heart was broken as well and she faced a possible pregnancy now when her life should be coming together instead of falling apart.

Unable to bear the humiliation of facing Brent after the way they had parted she'd called her realtor and put her house back on the market. Never once did she imagine how fast it would sell. So fast, she didn't have a chance to see the finished kitchen she had wanted so much.

Damned kitchen. If she hadn't been in such an all-fired hurry to remodel none of this would have ever happened. She and Brent would only be "hey neighbors" instead of failed lovers, if only, if only, if only. She sat up and wiped her eyes with the back of her sleeve.

Tomorrow she would go home she decided. Mobile was a big enough city that she would likely never run across him again. Unless she went looking that is. But tomorrow was a million years away and right now, there was that big swimsuit shoot Marty wanted her to do. Maybe a week in Hawaii with all the beautiful people would cure her of what ailed her. Maybe…but then, she would never know if she could go home again.

The telephone ringing in the other room distracted her from her pity party, taking the subject of going home again beyond her control.

Chapter Thirty-Two

෨

With two weeks until Christmas, the people on the Gulf Coast were suffering from a heat wave that did little to put them in the Christmas spirit. Brent Chambliss had less cheer than any one.

In one week, his last major project for the year would be finished if the weather held and there were at least three to take its place. Business was booming and the little company was booming along with it. He should be happy he knew but there wasn't much to be happy about.

In fact, he was so miserable he moved out of his house into his mother's small house on the west side of town. He'd packed up the day the For Sale sign went up in front of Tara's house. And moved out the day the sold sign followed. And just like that, his bubble of happiness burst. Tara wasn't coming home. And he could never make amends for his behavior the last time they were together.

He lay in bed listening to the drone of the air conditioner thinking there was something entirely wrong with running the thing in December. In a couple of hours he had to get up and go to work but sleep wasn't something that came easy to him lately. Regardless, he still jumped when the phone on the bedside table rang. And cursing he grabbed it before the machine could kick in.

"This better be good," he growled into the receiver.

"Tara's mother had a stroke late last night and they don't think she's going to make it." Hutch's voice came on the line.

"So what do you want me to do about it? I'm a contractor not a doctor."

"Tara will be on the six o'clock flight from New York. Coco said she didn't have time to let her family know when to expect her. So, there will be no one there to meet her. Do I need to hit your head with a hammer, man? She's going to need a shoulder to cry on so get up and go meet her." With that he hung up and Brent slowly laid the phone back in its cradle.

The clock next to it read five-twenty-five. He flung the covers off and lunged from the bed grabbing a pair of jeans as he went. Less than five minutes later, he was standing in his driveway fiddling with the keys that shook in his hands as he tried to unlock his truck.

Tara, his Tara, was coming home. How would she look after more than a month away? Would she be happy to see him? With too many questions running through his mind, he drove the short distance to the airport grateful that traffic was light.

At the airport, he checked the flight board. The only flight scheduled to land in the next half-hour was on time and Brent could only hope it was the right flight. He raced up the stairs to wait at the security checkpoint to watch for the plane to land. Time seemed to slow down he noticed as he checked his watch for the fourteenth time. Six-oh-one clicked up with no plane in sight, six-oh-two, oh-three, oh-five. He asked the yawning security officer if the flight from New York had come in early. No. So he paced back and forth in the small waiting area, his eyes darting from the wide windows framing the runway to the debarking corridor. Six-ten. He stopped pacing as the huge passenger jet suddenly loomed over the tree line and touched down.

His heart began to beat so fast he thought he would pass out. Terror clutched in the pit of his stomach. What if she took one look at him and walked away? What if he had killed her love and she wouldn't have anything to do with him? What if her plane was landing in Pensacola? So many what ifs raced through his already jumbled mind that he almost missed the first passenger to stumble through the security gates.

It wasn't Tara, but an older woman dressed for winter in a fur coat and boots. Boy was she in for a shock when she stepped outside and found all that warm sunshine pouring down on her.

A young couple followed her, and then a small family. Then he caught sight of a head of honey-colored hair lost in a crowd and his heart beat even faster if that was possible.

Was it her? The crowd separated at the gate, a couple stood back to wait for a straggling friend and several more went in opposite directions once they cleared security, leaving the blonde standing alone in the hallway, her coat draped over her arm. She dug in her purse looking for something, her face turned away from him.

She stepped through security a cloth in her hand for cleaning her glasses. She looked up and Brent forgot to breathe.

Her hair was different, cut in a trendy style with wispy tendrils framing her face. Dark circles smudged her eyes making her look tired and unhappy. She was thinner, her face gaunt and drawn. Her eyes met his but she didn't react. Did she care so little then that the sight of him didn't phase her one bit?

She held up her glasses to the light to check for smears before replacing them on her nose. When she did her eyes widened in recognition and her hand flew to her neck as if in shock.

"Tara," Brent said ordering his feet to move. "I'm so sorry."

"How did you know I would be flying in this morning?" Tara replied her voice shaking to match her hand. He was there waiting as if nothing had ever happened, as if nothing mattered. She had never been so glad to see anyone in her life. Nothing about him had changed, except his hair was longer, but after a month that was to be expected. He was still beautiful, while she was slowly withering away.

"Coco called Hutch. I'm sorry about your mother."

"Oh." She stood taller her shoulders rigid, tucking her hand in her pants pocket to still it. "I see. Thanks."

"Can I give you a ride to the hospital?" How stupid did he sound? He wanted to shout out his love for the entire world to hear but he was too afraid that the Tara that stood before him would throw it back as he had thrown her love back at her on that fateful day.

"That will be fine. Ah...did Coco say anything else to Hutch? About me?" Coco and her big mouth. She couldn't wait even one day to go running to Hutch. Was that why he was here? Did he know about the baby?

"No. Tara, listen. I, ah. Damn it, Tara this isn't going like I'd planned."

"It's all right Brent. I can call a taxi." Tara sighed. At least Coco hadn't tattled but what had she expected, wine and roses?

"This isn't about giving you a ride Tara. I'm trying to tell you that I love you and failing miserably."

"You love me?" Her lip quivered and she caught it between her teeth.

"I do. Oh Tara I'm so sorry, I've been an ass."

"Yes you have." She let go of her lip as she spoke not caring that it continued to tremble.

"Can you forgive me? I don't want to think of life without you."

"You said some pretty harsh things."

"I was afraid of what I was feeling and you blindsided me. I'm sorry. I had no right to throw away your love like that. Would it help if I got down on my knees and begged your forgiveness?"

"Do you really love me?"

"With all my heart." He held up his left hand with its bare ring finger. "She's gone Tara. I've let my past go. I'm giving you my future if you'll have it?"

"I'd like to have children some day."

"I'm a good father." And for the first time since Betsy died Brent knew the truth of those words. He was a good father to

Betsy and would be again if given the chance. "I'm pretty sure there is room in my heart for all the children you wish to give me."

"Do you mean that? Or are you just telling me what you think I want to hear?"

"I mean it Tara. Betsy was my child and she will always hold a place in my heart. But that heart has plenty of room and I'm sure Betsy would approve if she were here."

"Brent, I don't know what to say."

"Say you forgive me, say you love me. Say anything."

"I'm not crazy you know."

"I know. I saw her. I saw her for what she was in life and in death and I let her go."

"I'm sorry Brent."

"Please don't say that. Please give us another chance. I know what I want now. I'm not afraid anymore."

"No. I mean I'm not sorry about that. I'm sorry for meddling in your life. I'm sorry for the things I said. I'm sorry for the way I left. I'm sorry for letting you go when I want to hold on tight to you and never let go." Tara choked back a sob and covered her mouth with her fingers but that couldn't stop the tears from flowing.

"Does that mean you still love me?"

"Yes, oh yes I love you. I love you so much. Look at me. I'm a wreck without you.

I can't eat. I can't sleep. I miss you so much." She dropped her bag to the floor and stepped closer to him. "Look at me. I'm shaking."

He took her trembling hands in his and pulled her closer until he held her tight in his arms. "Say you'll love me until tomorrow."

"Why tomorrow? Why not forever?"

"Because tomorrow never comes and forever is far too long."

"If tomorrow never comes then how are we supposed to have a future together?"

"You've got me there. I suppose I can ask you to love me 'til the cows come home."

"But you're not a farmer."

"Exactly."

"Brent?"

"Yes?"

"Shut up and kiss me."

"Yes ma'am." And he did, right there for the entire world to see.

Epilogue

Christmas morning sunlight filtered through the blinds. The air was icy outside the covers, but hot and steamy within.

"Good morning Mrs. Chambliss. How do you feel?" he asked his hand tenderly cupping her naked belly as he nibbled her neck.

"Well-loved." She turned in his arms until they lay face-to-face, body-to-body, her hand drawing lazy circles on his side.

"No morning sickness."

"Not yet. Maybe it will pass us by," she said not wanting to think of the unpleasant part of making a new life. "Are you hungry?"

"Only for you." His mouth dipped lower searching for more to nibble than just her neck.

"Will you ever get enough?" she laughed when he tickled a sensitive spot and sucked in her breath when he found another.

"It's our wedding night. Give me more credit than that."

"I hate to break it to you but it isn't night any more."

"No? Well, then happy anniversary, Mrs. Chambliss. After one day you still take my breath away." He flung the covers over her head and dragged her under for some serious nibbling.

"Stop." Tara froze hearing a thud in the front of the small house. "Did you hear that?"

"I don't hear anything except my heart beating just for you."

"Brent I'm serious. There it is again, a door closing. There's someone in the house." Footsteps sounded on the hardwood floor and Tara reached for her robe dragging it under the covers. "Do you hear?"

A tiny giggle from somewhere down the hall made Brent sit up and listen. Tara wasn't kidding. There was someone in the house, someone with a laugh that reminded him of Betsy.

"Stay here," he whispered pulling on his own robe and climbing out of bed but he never made it to the door before it burst open.

"Aha, busted." Brent's double stood just outside the door looking smug.

"Caleb!" Brent thundered when his brother walked into the room. "What the hell are you doing here? You nearly scared Tara to death."

"Thought I'd come home for Christmas. Thanks for the welcome."

"Sorry man, it's just you were home on leave last month. I didn't expect you."

"I had some things to take care of so I took emergency leave." He opened the door wider to reveal a tiny little urchin hiding just behind his legs. "Meet your niece."

"Niece? What? When? How did that happen?" He looked at the girl closely and found his and Caleb's eyes staring back out of Betsy's face and his heart started to race. "She looks just like Betsy."

"But with our eyes, I know."

"Bree honey this is your Uncle Brent. And the pretty lady is Tara." Caleb dropped to one knee drawing the little girl into his arms.

"She's Aunt Tara."

"What? When?" It was Caleb's turn to be surprised.

"Yesterday." Tara held up her left hand to show him the silver band Brent had placed there not even twenty-four hours before.

"Why didn't you tell anyone?"

"Why didn't you?" Brent countered. "Where is her mother?"

"No one knows. She ran off a year ago. Bree's granny has been taking care of her but she... Hell, I didn't know she existed until a week ago when this lawyer flies out with papers saying I have a kid. Granny didn't want to be burdened anymore. So that leaves me. She's mine all right. You can look at her and tell."

"And the mother?"

"A fling, she never told me. Bree's mine now, her granny saw to that."

"You can't take care of a baby on a battleship." Tara climbed from the bed and settled on the floor in front of the little girl. Her voice soft her face gentle so as not scare the child she took Bree's fingers in her hand and blew on them making her laugh.

"It's a carrier and I know."

"So what are you going to do?" Brent said the hairs on the back of his neck prickling when the girl laughed.

"Beg a favor of you and my new sister-in-law. Wait, Brent, before you get bent out of shape. I've thought about it. You are the only one of us with kid experience and you were great with Betsy. I know you'll take good care of her, besides it won't be for long. My enlistment is up in six months. I'll come home then. Permanently."

"Caleb, I don't know about this. We just got married. Tara is going to start school in a couple of weeks. We just signed a contract for two banks and another mini-mall. And on top of that Tara's..."

"We'll be happy to." Tara cut him off.

"Are you sure?" The brothers said in unison.

"Oh yes. She is adorable. My mother will love her. Well, she might mistake her for me when I was a kid but at least she's still alive to do that much." Tara sighed.

"Tara don't you think you have enough to deal with?"

"We can handle it. We'll hire a nanny for while I'm in school and other times. She needs someone and we can't say no."

"What about Mom?" Brent thought aloud looking for another solution to the problem. "No, she deserves her retirement. And neither Darren nor Laura would know which end to feed or which end to diaper."

"Speaking of the three of them I think I hear them coming. You two might want to get dressed. Your honeymoon is about to get a lot more crowded," Caleb said smiling now that he knew Bree would be cared for. "That is unless you want me to go tell Mom you've got a girl in your room."

"Caleb, don't you dare. I wanted to tell them. Caleb!" But it was too late. Caleb had already deserted them leaving behind his daughter.

"Oh let him have his fun. We have other news to break anyway. But not today." Tara said leaning against him with the baby snuggled between them.

"Pwetty," Bree said kissing Tara on the cheek before setting her eyes on Brent. "Bwent."

"Well she knows who we are," he laughed letting her curl up against him. "Are you sure about this?"

"Yes."

"Okay," he sighed but his heart was melting as the little girl patted his cheek and yawned. "Better get dressed. We've got a busy day ahead. Remember we promised your brother we'd meet him at the hospital for dinner with your mom and I'm sure my family will want to fawn over you…"

"Brent be quiet or you'll scare the baby," Tara said, leaning across the tiny body to kiss him on the mouth. "I think she likes you."

"Tara?"

"Yes?"

"Thank you."

"For what?"

"Loving me."

"Only until tomorrow."

"Then I hope today never ends."

"Me too. Oh me too."

Enjoy An Excerpt From:
MEANT TO BE

Copyright © DENISE A. AGNEW, 2006.

All Rights Reserved, Ellora's Cave Publishing, Inc.

"Welcome to the Heart Inn," the man said as he put out his hand to her. "I'm Alan Barns. Physical fitness director for the resort."

She smiled as she shook his hand. "Pleased to meet you, Mr. Barns. I'm Courtney Devons."

"I know. Jack at the front desk told me you'd just arrived. He said you put down on your information card that you'd be interested in an aerobics class while you're here. I teach one every day at 8:00am. Not that *you* need the exercise, of course."

Sharp discomfort niggled Morgan as he watched the man's gaze travel over Courtney's slim figure. The overgrown beach boy looked at her as if she wore nothing at all.

She laughed lightly and disengaged her hand from Alan's grip. "Thank you. I've needed to start an exercise routine for weeks and aerobics will be perfect."

When Alan's gaze assessed her again, as if he imagined her in one of those skin-hugging outfits, Morgan approached.

Plastering on a smile, he held his hand out. "Hi. I'm Courtney's husband."

Courtney started, as if Morgan had announced her hair was on fire. "Oh, yes. Sorry. Alan, this is Morgan Lucas."

Alan's grip was firm and no-nonsense, and his smile seemed genuine enough, but Morgan took an instant dislike to the guy. Maybe it was the way he never stopped smiling, or the way he puffed out his impressive pectorals.

Morgan put his arm around her shoulders and brought her close. He gazed down at her with what he hoped was a sufficiently besotted expression. "We're on our honeymoon."

Stiffening, she smiled back and then looked at Alan. "Too bad I missed your class today. Do you hold classes on Sunday morning, too?"

Alan continued to grin. "Actually, on Sunday I like to sleep in. But I have a class Sunday afternoon, so you won't miss out."

"Great. I'll be there."

The porter had their bags on the cart by this time, so they said goodbye to Alan. *None too soon.* Morgan smiled politely at the aerobics instructor but he honestly felt like braining him with the nearest chair. Startled by the violence of his feelings, Morgan inhaled deeply and regained control.

As they crossed to the elevator, Courtney moved out from under his arm and gave him a frown. When she didn't speak, he figured she was only biding her time until the porter was gone.

Twice in one day he'd made her angry. But Alan reminded him of Stanley Ashford. All smarmy smiles and insincerity.

For months, since she'd started dating that creep Stan, Morgan had wrestled with his feelings. At first he'd thought he didn't mind she'd found someone. Then he'd met the guy and immediately revised his opinion. Three words described the asshole. Cocky, conceited, and condescending. Obviously he thought because he came from a rich family and had a high position in a prestigious architectural firm that others remained beneath him in intelligence and worth. Morgan recalled the day Stan had wandered through the antique store spouting limited knowledge about antiques and sniffing indignantly when Morgan had the gall to correct him. When Courtney came in the next day and gave him a mild dressing down because of the way he'd treated Stan, he knew his relationship with her had taken a rocky downturn. Shocked by the way she'd berated him, Morgan hadn't said a thing.

As time had gone by, and he rarely saw Courtney, he realized how much he missed her. Missed her laugh, her teasing taunts, her…beautiful face.

That's when life got rough. He'd plunged into his work fifteen hours a day until he ached in every bone. Last month he'd contracted a flu so serious he'd been forced to close his shop for a week while he recuperated or risk getting pneumonia. Rachel had wanted to tell Courtney he was sick, but he insisted she keep mum.

During his illness he'd laid in bed, and fever had given him crazy dreams about Courtney. Although the dreams stayed foggy, he distinctly remembered kissing her in one dream. When he started having wild dreams about Courtney, he knew he was two bricks short of a load.

He thought of this vacation as an opportunity to put their friendship back into firm standing. When the Land Rover had hydroplaned, and afterward when he'd turned to Courtney and seen her pale face, the implications of what could have happened hit him like a sucker punch. She'd been as white as ghost, and for a terrifying few seconds he'd thought she was hurt.

He shook his head to clear his thoughts. Of course he'd been concerned about her. He would have worried about anyone.

When the elevator halted at the third floor, and when Morgan unlocked the door and Courtney surveyed the room, she let out a gasp. "Would you look at this place?"

He'd stayed in a few sumptuous suites before, but this one outstripped the others in elegance and size. At one end of the room resided a huge four-poster bed with a canopy.

"Damn," he said. "And here I thought they'd have a heart-shaped bed."

"Morgan!"

He laughed, enjoying the light tinge of color rising in her cheeks as she glanced at the porter. The man didn't seem to notice her embarrassment.

After the porter unloaded their bags and left, Morgan scanned the room. An antique dealer's dream, the room sported a mahogany secretary and a high-boy. A large window with rich emerald damask curtains graced one wall. Next to the window nestled a small Queen Anne table with a pair of matching chairs.

"This is a great place," he said, sitting on the edge of the bed and flopping backward with a sigh.

She sat in a chair by the window. "Was it really necessary to put on such a show downstairs?"

"What show?"

"You know what I'm talking about. You practically pulled me away from Alan Barns. Why?"

He propped himself on his elbows. "He's a Neanderthal. He drooled all over you like an overeager puppy. The man needed a bib."

Instead of coming back at him with both barrels, she laughed. "He wasn't that bad. I'll bet he treats all the women guests like that. Probably kisses old women's hands and pats little girls on the head. It's how he gets people into his aerobics classes. Full classes means he keeps his job."

Morgan grunted. "Maybe. I saw how he looked you over. I don't think he leers at little old ladies in pink tights quite the same way."

She stood and advanced to the bed. "What if he *was* flirting with me? It might be nice to have a vacation romance. I've never tried that before."

Morgan grinned. "You'd commit adultery?"

"Don't be a dolt, Morgan. It's harmless fun. Like I said, I'm sure he flirts with all the ladies."

"Don't do it. It'll blow our cover."

Sighing, she sat down next to him on the bed. "And what are you? James Bond?"

Sitting up, he said, "Not a bad thought. Gorgeous women after my bod—"

"Aha! See? I knew it. You're as bad as Alan. You like to ogle women, too. Remember, I've seen you do it before." She stood again. "Isn't that just like a man? It's okay for you to flirt and have a good time, but not for me. What a double standard."

Puzzled, he watched her closely. "Hey, I don't care what you do. Have a good time. Flirt with men right and left."

She sniffed. "Good. As long as we've got that cleared up."

Enjoy An Excerpt From:
PASSION'S BLOOD

Copyright © CHERIF FORTIN & LYNN SANDERS 1998

All Rights Reserved

~Available in Print Only~

Passion's Blood, a hardcover from Genesis Press, features thirty-four enchanting illustrations. A sensual medieval fairytale that is spellbinding in its lyrical imagery!

They lay together as one, their bodies wet against the damp red silk. Even their hair tangled, completing its own mating ritual.

Finally, Leanna laughed, pushing Emric's wayward locks back from his face. "There you are," she teased. "Now I can see your handsome face."

"I need never make love again." Emric sighed. "This moment was all to perfect, my lady."

Leanna only smiled and held him close, for she knew the depth of his passions. It was good to have him home at Brimhall Castle again, and the words found their way to her lips.

His dark lashes veiled the sensual fire in his eyes. He smiled and stretched like a sleepy cat in the heat of the afternoon sun.

"The date of our betrothal is rapidly approaching, Emric, dear heart," she began as she propped herself up on one elbow. "Methinks many a young lady at court will soon have cause to mourn." She traced a blade of grass over his muscular chest.

He arched a dark eyebrow. His reputation for being a rake was, he thought, quite undeserved. He did not deny the occasional liaison, but his exploits with the opposite sex were greatly exaggerated. If truth be told, since their fathers' announcement of their intention to join the houses of Kaherdin and Clairemonde by marrying their second son and only daughter, had had virtuously remained celibate. Well, he grinned, at least virtuously monogamous.

"I must profess my innocence, my lady." His mouth still curved in a roguish grin. "The idleness at court has made me victim of vicious rumors. If anyone will be in mourning, it will surely be the gallant Sir Bracchus." He traced a single finger down her neck and between her breasts. "If I am not mistaken, he holds the distinction of having been your most ardent suitor."

"Next to you," she chided. "Sir Bracchus is a dear man and it is not his fault you are so much more charming."

"And handsome," he said as his finger continued its journey over her breast.

"And handsome," Leanna agreed, her breath catching at his caress. "And courageous, witty and oh...so much more dreadfully conceited."

She watched him shrug his shoulders noncommittally as he laughed. Since the announcement of the intended betrothal, the last year had been a confusing time. Initially, Leanna had been furious over the helplessness of the arranged marriage, but Emric had astonished her by embracing the prospect wholeheartedly and courting her as though the union had been his own intention.

Indeed she had been flattered at the attentions of the kingdom's most eligible knight. True, his elder brother would inherit the throne, but nothing, not even a kingdom could make life with Prince Bran bearable. Emric, on the contrary, was the substance of every young girl's fantasy, possessed as he was of the most intoxicating charms, an indomitable spirit and a noble heart. She had grown to love him deeply. So why, she asked herself, did she continue to feel discomfort at the notion of a marriage with this man?

Why an electronic book?

We live in the Information Age—an exciting time in the history of human civilization, in which technology rules supreme and continues to progress in leaps and bounds every minute of every day. For a multitude of reasons, more and more avid literary fans are opting to purchase e-books instead of paper books. The question from those not yet initiated into the world of electronic reading is simply: *Why?*

1. ***Price.*** An electronic title at Ellora's Cave Publishing and Cerridwen Press runs anywhere from 40% to 75% less than the cover price of the exact same title in paperback format. Why? Basic mathematics and cost. It is less expensive to publish an e-book (no paper and printing, no warehousing and shipping) than it is to publish a paperback, so the savings are passed along to the consumer.

2. ***Space.*** Running out of room in your house for your books? That is one worry you will never have with electronic books. For a low one-time cost, you can purchase a handheld device specifically designed for e-reading. Many e-readers have large, convenient screens for viewing. Better yet, hundreds of titles can be stored within your new library—on a single microchip. There are a variety of e-readers from different manufacturers. You can also read e-books on your PC or laptop computer. (Please note that Ellora's Cave does not endorse any specific brands. You can check our websites at www.ellorascave.com or

www.cerridwenpress.com for information we make available to new consumers.)

3. *Mobility.* Because your new e-library consists of only a microchip within a small, easily transportable e-reader, your entire cache of books can be taken with you wherever you go.

4. ***Personal Viewing Preferences.*** Are the words you are currently reading too small? Too large? Too... ANNOYING? Paperback books cannot be modified according to personal preferences, but e-books can.

5. ***Instant Gratification.*** Is it the middle of the night and all the bookstores near you are closed? Are you tired of waiting days, sometimes weeks, for bookstores to ship the novels you bought? Ellora's Cave Publishing sells instantaneous downloads twenty-four hours a day, seven days a week, every day of the year. Our webstore is never closed. Our e-book delivery system is 100% automated, meaning your order is filled as soon as you pay for it.

Those are a few of the top reasons why electronic books are replacing paperbacks for many avid readers.

As always, Ellora's Cave and Cerridwen Press welcome your questions and comments. We invite you to email us at Comments@ellorascave.com or write to us directly at Ellora's Cave Publishing Inc., 1056 Home Avenue, Akron, OH 44310-3502.

THE
☥ ELLORA'S CAVE ☥
LIBRARY

Stay up to date with Ellora's Cave Titles in
Print with our Quarterly Catalog.

TO RECIEVE A CATALOG,
SEND AN EMAIL WITH YOUR NAME
AND MAILING ADDRESS TO:

CATALOG@ELLORASCAVE.COM
OR SEND A LETTER OR POSTCARD
WITH YOUR MAILING ADDRESS TO:

CATALOG REQUEST
c/o ELLORA'S CAVE PUBLISHING, INC.
1056 HOME AVENUE
AKRON, OHIO 44310-3502

Please be Advised: Ellora's Cave and Websit contain explicit sexual content and you must be 18.

CERRIDWEN PRESS

Cerridwen, the Celtic goddess of wisdom, was the muse who brought inspiration to storytellers and those in the creative arts.

Cerridwen Press encompasses the best and most innovative stories in all genres of today's fiction.

Visit our website and discover the newest titles by talented authors who still get inspired—much like the ancient storytellers did...

once upon a time.

www.cerridwenpress.com